The India Exhibition

The India Exhibition

A Mystery at the Smithsonian

RICHARD TIMOTHY CONROY

ST. MARTIN'S PRESS   NEW YORK

DESIGN BY GLEN M. EDELSTEIN

Library of Congress Cataloging-in-Publication Data

Conroy, Richard Timothy
        The India Exhibition / Richard Timothy Conroy.
                p.   cm.
        "A Thomas Dunne book."
        ISBN 0-312-07807-2
        I. Title.
    PS3553.O51985S6   1992
    813'.54—dc20   92-4254
                                                                      CIP

10 9 8 7 6 5 4 3 2

For my wife, Sarah

Author's Note

This is a tale of skulduggery in the Smithsonian Institution, a place dedicated to the increase and diffusion of knowledge. The author has supposed, for the purposes of this work of fiction, that an exhibition in one of the Smithsonian's great museums, an exhibition commemorating the life of an Indian philosopher, has been perverted to become a vehicle for greed and murder.

And the author has superimposed upon the Smithsonian a totally fictional cast of characters who are reported as doing completely fictional things. The author hastens to add that while he was familiar with (and for the most part, present during) the most recent two decades of the Smithsonian, he is yet unaware that any murder has ever happened within its confines. Nor is he acquainted with any murderous or other criminal intent on the part of real persons associated with the Smithsonian—save that someone made off with one of his teacups, part of a matched set.

This story is presented as taking place a few years ago. The choice of this time is not intended to associate it with the real people who served the Smithsonian with distinction during those years. To the extent that real persons may wish to assume that they played a part in this story, they have the author's assurance that they are mistaken and that they may take no blame, nor indeed any credit, from this bit of fiction.

The India Exhibition

 One

The statue was small, relatively speaking. The figure was a bare seventy-five inches high, in an exhibition hall eighty feet long and forty feet wide. But the statue dominated the room.

Henry had to admit that much of the credit was rightfully due to Violet. As an exhibits designer, Violet Strauss had showed her genius. That was what made everything else worth the anguish.

From the first, Henry had felt as though with Violet he were holding on to the tail of a comet. It had been frightening, exciting, inspiring, tiring, even exhausting, and at times emotionally devastating. But the resulting exhibition, viewed from the gallery entryway, far exceeded anything he had imagined when the work had begun almost a year earlier.

Henry approached the statue. He tried to close out everything else in the hall and to concentrate just on the artwork before him. It was not altogether possible to do so. The gold of the statue picked up the deep blue of the walls. Blue, and just the right shade of blue, was the only right color for the exhibit hall, he thought. He had seen Vishnu before, represented in his many avatars, Vishnu incarnate. Often this god of mercy and goodness was represented in dark blue, particularly when he appeared as Krishna. The blue of the room did not, however,

1

overwhelm the golden statue, for like glowing embers, a broad band of enormous rubies cut across the waist of the figure.

Vishnu here took the form of Rama-chandra. But he had Vishnu's four hands and he stood on the back of a turtle. Henry intended to look it up when he had time, but it did seem that the sculptor was mixing up the metaphors between earthly and spiritual forms. Well! It didn't particularly matter because it looked perfectly splendid. Anyway, since the statue bore a Western artist's conception of the face of K. V. Chandra, it could make no claim to being a traditional work of art.

Henry had never seen so many rubies nor so much gold all in one piece. Eleven hundred pounds of it, more or less. Even at eighteen karat, it must have been frightfully expensive when it was made, almost a hundred years ago. Now the insured value was $10 million for the gold and gems alone, and the artistic and historical value was impossible to calculate, because it was one of a kind and had never in modern times been sold.

There had been, in the beginning, quite an argument about whether the statue should be fitted with its own alarm. In the museum, small things of great value were always protected that way. But alarms cost money and this exhibition had to be installed on the slenderest of shoestring budgets. So, in the end, it was decided that the ordinary museum security would have to suffice. After all, the exhibition gallery backed up to the guard headquarters, manned twenty-four hours a day. And who could carry more than a half ton of gold past the guards who were always posted just outside the gallery door?

There was a sudden cacophony of tiny drums. Someone, probably his assistant, Somnath, was testing the audio equipment. Henry and Violet had decided to use drums as a sort of percussive cadence between the selections of traditional Indian music taped for the exhibition. Henry had used the little hand-held, two-headed drum with tethered balls to make the abrupt, almost shocking sound.

A *Karnatic raga* was beginning and it took Henry a moment to adjust to the microtonal ornaments. The appoggiaturas, mordents, and pralltrillers in Western music of the seventeenth and eighteenth centuries seemed to Henry to have a certain kinship with this Indian musical ornamentation, though they were more orderly and followed harmonic rules he could understand. Now that Henry thought about it, he had seen many errors in Western music scores where mordents were shown before notes that descended diatonically—the mordent being in a position that could be occupied properly only by a pralltriller. Sloppy!

The Indian music was perfect, he decided. It set a mood. You could almost smell India. Or at least the India he imagined. That reminded him, the exhibits people had said they would be able to circulate incense with the air-conditioning system in time for the exhibition's opening tomorrow. Henry hoped they would forget about it. It had been another one of Violet's ideas, one of the few about which he had reservations. All he needed was an asthma attack when the ribbon was cut.

There was, of course, nothing for him to do during the ceremony and he could leave if it got too bad. Everything he might have wanted to say, he put into the speech notes for Dr. Fat Dog, the American Indian (appropriately enough) director of the museum. Henry hated to make speeches and preferred it that way.

Henry pulled his attention away from the statue and the music and surveyed the rest of the exhibition. It only seemed possible to do this with one's back to Vishnu. Even then, as he looked into the depths of the blue walls, he could imagine that light from the gold subtly altered everything. Henry could see why Hindus might understand the phenomenal world as a maya, an illusion.

The visually limitless gallery was contained by a belt of color. Indian yellow, that almost-orange, almost-brown hue best known in the West as butterscotch pudding, formed a girdle a foot high and two hundred feet long, ringing three sides of the exhibits hall.

Against the yellow, the deep blue seemed more like deep space than a solid wall. The yellow of the band should have been wrong for that sort of blue except that it worked. It balanced warm with cold, finite with infinite.

Stenciled on the yellow band was the story, the biography of K. V. Chandra. It had been painstakingly silk-screened on the yellow strip in letters half an inch high. Henry moved up to it until he could read the print through the top part of his bifocals. The print was just large enough to be legible at the distance he had to stand in order to bring it into focus. He could, of course, move in closer and read through the bottom of his glasses, but the yellow strip was too high for this to be a comfortable position. Henry had wanted to move the strip lower for just this reason, but Violet had insisted that the room had to be squeezed in the middle. Violet wore contacts and to hell with everybody else.

The exhibit hall had sixteen-foot-high walls. Putting the band in the middle would have meant placing it seven and a half feet off the floor. Even Violet admitted that would be too high. After her trip to India, Violet came up with the ideal solution. She had been impressed by the seemingly timeless village life, unchanged from when Chandra walked barefoot from village to village, half a century before Gandhi. Violet had photographed these villages during her trip to India. And these pictures, hugely enlarged, now formed right angles with the walls and the ceiling, effectively dropping the wall height to less than ten feet.

Now, everywhere in the gallery you looked, if you raised your sightline above head level, you saw these scenes of village life, some enlarged in three sections to eight by twelve feet. Henry fancied himself a photographer, but Violet's pictures were far better than he could have made. Violet didn't seem to mind going right up to people she didn't know and poking her lens right in their faces. Very intrusive, Henry thought, but it made wonderful pictures.

You felt you were squatting right there in the dust with untouchables, artisans, merchants, beggars, conjurors. By raising your eyes, you traveled from deep space, from the spirit world, from the world of Vishnu, to another kind of eternity, the humanity of India. One stepped as an avatar into the village where Chandra, the bodhisattva, out of compassion, abandoned his claim to nirvana so that he might help the People of India.

The harmony of these parts of the exhibition was such that it made the other elements seem almost intrusive. Like Violet's

4

lens pointed into a circle of village women as they examined a newborn child. A picture Henry simply could not have taken.

But these other elements of the exhibition had their own particular logic. The strip biography of Chandra was accompanied, above or below the appropriate part of the text, by photographs of places important in Chandra's life. And for his life after 1860, there were copies of an ever-increasing number of photographs actually taken of Chandra. There was, for example, an undated photograph of the elderly, bearded Chandra with the young Gandhi just before Gandhi left India to study law in England. It was the only recorded time that Gandhi and Chandra met, and Chandra was dead by the time Gandhi returned from his years in South Africa. There were also several photographs of Chandra with the young Rabindranath Tagore when that poet was studying philosophy with Chandra. Other than the statue of Vishnu, these photographs were the nearest things to museum artifacts in the exhibition, and they were only copies.

Violet had returned from India with a large number of village textiles. She had bought them with Smithsonian money, so to justify them, they had to be used. Besides, they were pretty. Chandra, like Gandhi years later, believed that the strength of India lay in the domestic industries. So Henry stressed this connection when he wrote the exhibit text and Violet arranged the textiles artfully against the fourth wall, scrapping the planned lap-dissolve slide show that would have illuminated that wall and, Henry felt, would have distracted attention from the rest of the exhibition.

Henry decided he was pleased. He returned to the entryway and turned again for an overall view of the gallery and its centerpiece, the gold Vishnu. The exhibition would draw in the visitors. Once they were in, if they could read at all, they would be captivated by the story of Chandra. Chandra, who was so uniquely Indian that he is almost unknown outside of present-day India and Pakistan. They, the visitors, would leave with another window opened to their imagination.

Henry sensed Violet. Violet was a nosegay of scented hair rinse, mouthwash, perfumed bath soap, and what seemed like a dozen other floral odors. Nothing particularly dominating the way some women dump on one scent until it overpowers. But a bouquet. Like lying in the grass with wildflowers. She sometimes made Henry feel a bit giddy and occasionally he sneezed.

Violet wafted up beside him and slipped her hand into his. He extracted it and put his arm around her and squeezed her close, but gently. He felt he should look around and see whether there was anybody around who might disapprove of public cuddling. But he decided he didn't care. Violet made him sluff off twenty years and that was worth a bit of disapproval. Besides, the exhibit hall was closed to the public until tomorrow.

"You are a success, darling. The blue is exactly right."

"Mmm," she replied. Henry could feel a slight shiver go through her waist when the drums sounded again, signaling another change in the music.

Someone came into the gallery. It was Somnath. Henry let his arm drop from Violet's waist.

"It is wonderful," said Somnath, "you have captured the spirit of India. My uncle will be very pleased."

"Well, we will find out at five o'clock tomorrow. That's—Henry looked at his watch—"a bit over twenty-seven hours. I imagine it will pour down rain and nobody'll come."

"No. It will be fine," Violet said, as though it were a fact, not an opinion. "I almost wish I could be here."

"You almost . . . wish?"

"Yes. Almost."

"But you have to come! We've been working toward this for a year! It would be awful if you weren't here!" Henry turned around to face Violet. She looked quite calm, almost serene.

"Henry, I don't want you to be upset. It will be fine without me. You can take all the bows."

"Why can't you come?" Henry demanded.

"I'm going to kill myself," she said, giving him a happy smile.

* * *

"Shit! Red Rosa! Can't you drive no faster?"

"Get hold of yourself, Tyrone, we got enough time. Can't go no faster in this traffic, anyhow. Would have been there by now if you and Floyd hadn't waited so late."

"The paint had to dry, Rosa. Now, how would it a looked drivin' down the street with 'Capi-tol Hill Hospi-tality' runnin' down the sides of the fuckin' truck? You tell me that!"

Red Rosa didn't have an answer for Tyrone's question. She concentrated on her driving. She hunched her small body over the big steering wheel of the van and peered out through her thick round glasses and the rain-streaked windshield into the late November afternoon gloom. Her little feet worked the heavy pedals with the tips of her hiking-boot toes. The Thursday afternoon traffic on Independence Avenue as it descended from Capitol Hill was typically slow, but made worse by the weather. A long line of red brake lights heading west, headlights coming back east.

There was only one seat in the van. Red Rosa had commandeered it. Tyrone and Floyd squatted beside her, hanging on to whatever provided a grip. Red Rosa had told the men that they didn't have any sense at all when it came to driving a stolen truck and they would get them all arrested for sure. They didn't have any answer for that, because they knew it was true. And only Red Rosa had a license, a valid one. That had settled it.

"She said that that statue is as tall as Wilt Chamberlain!" said Floyd, not so much to change the subject but because it was on his mind. "You seen it yesterday, Tyrone. Is it really that big?"

"Bigger. It stands up on this turtle with great big ruby eyes. And it got arms like a octo-puss."

"The turtle?" asked Floyd, confused.

"No, man, the statue! It some kind of Indian god."

"A god?" The idea made Floyd a little uneasy.

"A Indian god. It just a hunk of gold as far as we is concerned."

"Tell me again how much gold it is!" Floyd decided to focus on the material world.

"Ain't just the gold, man! It got more rubies than anywhere else in the whole world! All the rubies in India!" Tyrone smiled a hungry, greedy, toothy smile and his eyes looked far off. Off where, he didn't quite know. But India was a long way, he was sure of that. "Them rubies was pried out of a thousand idols' eyes." He had seen something like that in a movie, he thought.

7

"Shit!" said Red Rosa. Traffic had come to a complete stop again and she had almost slid into the car in front.

"It's the truth!"

"What's the truth?" Red Rosa asked irritably.

"That's what Vi said. 'Bout them rubies."

"We're going for the gold. The rubies are nothing but trouble. Have to have a fence and he won't give you but a nickel on the dollar. We can melt down the gold ourselves."

"Yeah! A ton of gold! Set us up on easy street!" Floyd understood gold; he wasn't so sure about gemstones.

"Vi says it's only a little over a half a ton. But that's heavy enough. Are you and Tyrone sure you can move it?" Red Rosa, at eighty-seven pounds, had a hard time thinking about weights like that.

"Sure thing, Red! Me and Tyrone can do that easy! It about like a piano."

"I got it all worked out." Tyrone explained. "The bed of the caterin' cart just come up level to that platform they got the statue on. We just push it over into the cart and put the cover over it. Easy as pie!"

"Roll it right outta there!" agreed Floyd

"You're sure it's going to fit?"

"Shit, Rosa. I told you a hundred times, I measured. It fit fine."

Red Rosa maneuvered the truck over a lane when they lost the curb lane in front of the Hubert Humphrey Building. A car honked at her, but she ignored it.

"You gotcha gun, Rosa?"

"In my bag."

"Hey, now," Floyd protested, "I thought we wasn't going to go strapped. Those museum guards, they search us for sure."

"They won't search a lady. Capitalist guards are stupid."

"Well, I donno—"

"Don't worry about it, Floyd. It's my ass, not yours."

Floyd thought about that for a city block, then dismissed it. He had other things on his mind. "What chu goin' to do with your share, Tyrone? I'm for goin' somewhere I can lay on the beach all day. Where it ain't ever cold. Heard about a place called Nassau. It's some island, and supposed to be real nice. 'Course they say they can't come getcha in Rio. What they speak in Rio?"

"Spanish. Don't you know anythin' Floyd?"

"Portuguese," Red Rosa corrected.

"Anyway, it ain't English. I'm goin' to stay right here in D.C."

"You crazy man, Tyrone! They catch you for sure."

"I'm goin' to start me a new religion, shave my head, and put on one of them yellow bed sheets, like them Hari Krishnas. It the right thing to do seeing as how all that gold came to us from India. And then I'm goin' to lay around all day long, smoke pot, and make love with all my little-girl con-verts!" Tyrone shook the inside of the truck with his laughter and grabbed at Red Rosa's blue-jeans-protected crotch.

"Cut out that shit, Tyrone! I'm trying to drive!"

"Hey, little woman! This Tyrone you're talkin' to!"

"Fuck off," Red Rosa said tiredly.

They passed under the arches connecting the two halves of the Department of Agriculture, and Red Rosa swung the wheel, using the full length of her arms, to make the turn north onto Fourteenth Street. As they crossed the Mall, they could see the light gray bulk of the Smithsonian's National Museum of History and Technology through the mist. They crept toward it.

"Jeezus! Rosa! You can't turn in there!" Tyrone grabbed the wheel and wrenched it from Red Rosa's grasp. The van aborted its turn into the museum's exit gate and continued down the sidewalk and through a Park Service trash container before bouncing back into the north-bound curb lane. A line of cars slid to a halt as they reentered Fourteenth Street and the two motorists closest to the truck leaned on their horns.

Red Rosa rolled down her window and leaned out. "Fuck off! Fascists!" she yelled.

"Hey, little woman! Now who's goin' to get us arrested!" Tyrone laughed.

Back in the traffic, the van continued down to Constitution Avenue and turned in front of the museum. Slowly, they made their way along the block to the south-bound ramp that led back to the Mall alongside of the Twelfth Street tunnel. Tyrone directed Rosa to turn in at the service entrance to the museum. The gate guard, seeing it was a catering truck, elected to stay in his shelter, out of the drizzle. He waved them through.

Red Rosa drove the truck down the steep descent into the bowels of the building and to the loading dock. "Let me park it, Red!" Floyd insisted.

"I'm going to do it," she said evenly. She stood up at the wheel so she could see out better. But then she couldn't work the pedals. So she sat back down and came in by dead reckoning. She put only minor dents in the bodywork.

If the guard at the loading dock thought that the driver was suspiciously inept, he forgot all about it when he saw Red Rosa climb down out of the big van.

Tyrone and Floyd already had the back of the van open and were pushing out the empty catering cart. "Catering!" said Red Rosa to the guard.

"Hold up a minute!"

"We're late. We got to get set up!"

"I got to check." The guard read "Capitol Hill Hospitality" off of the side of the truck and returned to his office to look through his papers. There was nothing there. "Don't have nothing on no Capitol Hill Hospitality."

"Well, call the guard office. We got a contract to cater the India exhibition opening. It starts at five o'clock!" Rosa reached into her shoulder bag and pulled out the Smithsonian's letter accepting their bid. She waved it at the guard.

Red Rosa paced impatiently while the guard verified the caterers with headquarters. Tyrone lit up a marijuana cigarette. Floyd looked around to see if there was anything else worth stealing.

Eventually, the guard let them go, by then having forgotten to look inside the empty cart. It was just as well. Red Rosa hadn't given much thought to what she would do if he had looked. She might have shot him or she might not. She had intended to play it by ear.

With his friends following, Tyrone rolled the cart under the half-lowered overhead steel tambour door and turned into the main east-west basement corridor. After another eternity, the door opened to the freight elevator and they waited while a crew of carpenters pushed out their carts. Everything was taking longer than expected. Red Rosa looked nervously at her Mickey Mouse watch.

"Goddamn, Rosa!" Tyrone whispered as they alighted on the first floor. "That's that Mr. Henry. He the one man we don't need to see!" Tyrone ducked his head down as best he could in his tuxedo jacket collar and Floyd looked the other way. Red Rosa's hand reached instinctively into her shoulder bag and fumbled for the butt of her police special.

Henry Scruggs hurried along, on his way to the Exhibits Design Office, downstairs. At the sight of Tyrone and Red Rosa, he pulled up short. Those two were unmistakable, Tiny Rosa with her short dark hair and those little Coke-bottle-bottom glasses, and tall Tyrone with his huge Afro and mutton-chop sideburns. He didn't immediately recognize Floyd. It had been months since he had seen him, and Floyd's scraggly, sand-colored ponytail was unremarkable.

Henry blinked. He decided he was hallucinating. Tyrone, Violet's Tyrone, was in evening dress and pushing a huge covered catering cart. He was followed by Red Rosa, dressed as an ordinary seaman on the North Atlantic run, and one of the others from Hazel's party, also dressed in either black tie or a funeral suit. Henry dredged up the name from his rather hazy memory of that night—Fred? No, that wasn't right, it was Floyd.

"Tyrone? What are you doing here?" Henry demanded.

"Catering, man. We're catering this thing this evening."

"But I thought it was Capitol something. That's it, Capitol Hill Hospitality. Silly name for caterers."

"Don't knock it, man; that's us! We got the low bid, man. Now if you excuse us we got to go set up." Tyrone gave a shove to the heavy cart and the procession moved on. Rosa looked at Henry curiously, straight in the face. There was no hint of recognition. Floyd looked ahead, avoiding Henry's amazed look, and carried a box of something. A box containing an axe, actually, just in case Tyrone's measurements of the statue were wrong.

"You think old Henry's going to cause trouble?" Tyrone asked Red Rosa. "He seen us."

"It's just as well he did. Now we know where he is. But I'll fix him if I have to."

They ignored the guard standing between the exhibition entrance and the Constitution Avenue entrance. With long practice, the guard ignored them. She was busy, anyway, with her hand counter, clicking in a large group of visitors who had just alighted from a bus.

"Where is it?" Floyd hissed as soon as they had the cart safely past the barrier and in the gallery.

"Over there on the stage. See, in the corner—" Tyrone's words failed him.

Spotlights illuminated the stage of the little wooden structure diagonally across the large, dark blue room, more than seventy feet from where they stood just inside the gallery. The lights illuminated an empty stage.

"Shit!" said Red Rosa.

"Goddamn!" agreed Tyrone.

"Where is it, Tyrone?" Floyd asked again. A wailing note crept in.

The three of them made a frantic and futile search in all the places where the golden statue could be. That was really only in back of the stage, but they also tore through the bolts of colorful Indian fabrics and other handcrafts displayed against the north wall of the gallery. Nothing there could possibly have hidden Wilt Chamberlin, in gold or not.

"Somebody done beat us to it!" Floyd finally decided.

Red Rosa slapped her little hand on the side of the cart. "Let's get the fuck out of here before the capitalist pigs blame us for it!"

 **Two**

Almost a year earlier:

It was already below freezing and the temperature was dropping rapidly even though it should have been the warmest part of the day. Henry scrooched down his head between his shoulders and leaned toward the cold wind that swept across the Mall. He pressed his elbows against his ribs to keep his jacket from flapping. He should have worn his overcoat when he had come to work this morning, but the sun had been shining and the wind had been slight.

"Jeezus," yelled Blake, "it's not even Christmas yet!" His dark gray linen suit snapped in the wind.

"You gentlemen don't dress properly," Bhagat Gupta shouted above the wind. Bhagat wore an elegant midnight blue overcoat and a homburg, which he held onto his head with one gloved hand.

"All my winter stuff's in storage. Washington's supposed to be warm in December." Blake was just in Washington for a few days on consultation. He was on the staff of the American Embassy in New Delhi.

"It is warm," lied Henry, his teeth chattering, "your blood has gotten thin in India."

"It has nothing to do with the thickness of your blood. Indian blood is just the same as anybody else's." Bhagat spoke a bit stiffly, in his fine London University accent. He was a graduate of the Courtauld Institute of Art.

"Let's cut across the grass, it's closer." Adair Blake turned off the new pebbled walkway toward the National Museum of History and Technology. "Shit!" His heel sank down into the wet sod; icy water poured over the counter of his shoe. He hopped back onto the pathway and pulled off his shoe to drain it. He held onto Henry's shoulder with his other hand to steady himself in the wind.

"It's been raining for the past two weeks," said Henry "That's another thing you're not used to."

"It rains plenty in India. Just not this time of year. Anyway, it's supposed to be frozen. It's cold enough." Adair had his shoe back on and was squishing uncomfortably toward the museum.

"Give it time. It was almost seventy yesterday."

Henry and his guests hurried over the now-slippery terrace and into the front door of the history and technology museum. The blast of warm air instantly fogged Henry and Bhagat's glasses. Henry took his off and groped his way uncertainly across the entry hall to the information desk, where he signed in his guests and got them visitors' badges.

Henry got a stony look from the elevator operator until he remembered to pull out his own laminated Smithsonian I.D. card. On the forbidden-to-tourists fifth floor, they walked briskly out of the elevator and down the left-hand corridor to the executive dining room. It was almost noon and tables would be filling up fast. The dining room wouldn't take reservations for fewer than four, and Henry had elected to take a chance on space rather than invite someone else from the Foreign Affairs Office to go along to make up a foursome. Henry had no representation money, so he had to take his guests somewhere cheap, where he could afford to pick up the check. He wasn't about to take the cultural counselors of the Indian Embassy (Washington) and the American Embassy (New Delhi) to a Dutch treat luncheon.

There were actually two tables left. Henry grabbed Bhagat's hat (to the Indian's surprise) and tossed it onto one of the

14

chairs. He marked another place with his still-foggy glasses and led his party to the buffet line. Chicken again. Henry could eat any amount of chicken.

Adair cupped his hands around his coffee cup after it was brought to the table by the waitress. "Jeezus," he exclaimed again, "I may never get warm! Why doesn't the Smithsonian connect all the museums by tunnel?"

"It would cost money. We don't do things that cost money."

"Ask the fuckin' Congress for it! They got their own subway to get between buildings."

"Actually, we have a tunnel between the Castle and the Natural History Museum. Nobody uses it. It's only for steam pipes and rats."

"I guess rats got more sense than you guys." Adair was still in a foul mood.

"And there is another tunnel that runs under all the buildings on the north side of the Mall. But it's got Tiber Creek in it. It's supposed to be big enough for streetcars. If it weren't full of water, of course."

"Henry, I think Adair has a good idea. You could run barges between the buildings. You would have to deepen the one the rats use, of course. Is it actually under this building?"

"The Tiber Creek tunnel is; at least it runs along the north edge. Tiber Creek was originally a surface canal that ran along this side of the Mall until after the Civil War. It took barges from the end of the Chesapeake and Ohio Canal along what is now Constitution Avenue, then to the foot of Capitol Hill where it skirted around the south side and then went more or less south to the Anacostia River at Buzzard Point. Tiber Creek was buried when the marshes on the Mall were drained a hundred years ago."

"Fascinating," said Bhagat. "One doesn't think of Washington having so much history. It is such a new city, relatively speaking."

"That, of course, is just Indian condescension." Adair was still prepared to pick on anybody but he was warming up. The edge was going out of his voice. "I suppose we would be like that if we had been here for six millennia and painted our saints blue."

15

"Henry," Bhagat got down to business, ignoring Adair, "we would like the Smithsonian to hold a sesquicentennial exhibition on the life of K. V. Chandra."

"Chandra? Not Gandhi?"

"Gandhi was born in 1869; his centennial was a few years ago. Everybody observed it; even the Smithsonian had a small exhibition. But nobody is doing anything about Chandra."

"Who is he?"

"Everybody knows who Chandra is," said Adair, who had some small reputation in academic circles as an Indian scholar.

"I don't." Henry had thought about lying, but he decided he would be immediately caught. He hated being caught with things like that.

"I apologize for Henry, Bhagat. You can easily see why the Foreign Service sent him over here to the Smithsonian. I assure you that most Foreign Service officers are well acquainted with Indian history."

"There is nothing worse than the snobbism of India Service people, Henry; don't pay any attention to Adair. Hardly anybody knows about Chandra outside of India. And of course Pakistan." Bhagat was not about to risk antagonizing Henry. Even though Henry was only on loan from the State Department to the Smithsonian, Bhagat thought it likely that Henry could make or break the Indian Embassy's chances to hold the exhibition. Henry didn't share his confidence.

"The lives of K. V. Chandra and Mohandas Gandhi," he continued, "had many parallels. Of course, Chandra was born two generations earlier, at a time when the British raj was still very much in control and only a few people could imagine that India could ever achieve full independence from the U.K. Most Englishmen could not understand why India should even want independence."

"We could have explained that to them," said Adair.

"That is a common misunderstanding." Bhagat had no compunction about offending Adair Blake. "The British looked upon Americans as Englishmen, or at least they did in the nineteenth century before you took in all those Irish immigrants and freed your blacks." Bhagat did not regard himself as a black though some Englishmen might have thought otherwise. "Englishmen who had gone wrong, but nevertheless as kinsmen capable of governing yourselves. They had no such opinion of the Indians. We were a people to whom they had brought law and indeed civilization. We should therefore be properly grateful for these white man's blessings." Bhagat did not quite regard himself as white, either.

"Chandra had a Scottish grandmother and with the help of family connections was educated at the University of Edinburgh. Despite his lineage, what you might call a whitey in the woodpile, he was still a high-caste Brahman. His was a very wealthy family. Not, of course, comparable to the wealth of the princely families, but considerable all the same. He was destined to be an important man if he assumed his duties and didn't offend the British raj unduly." Bhagat tasted his chicken and made a face. He looked around the table for some sauce to go on it. Seeing none, he poked the chicken with his fork, dispiritedly, as if urging it to metamorphose into *ragan josh* or at the very least into chicken *tika,* and continued.

"Upon his return from Scotland, Chandra settled on his family estates for several years, married, and had his first and only child, a daughter. Then something happened, happened to him personally. He never said what it was and there has been much speculation, but it is only that, because nobody really knows the truth.

"In about 1848, he walked away from his family and his wealth and in a sense became a true Brahman, a priest. Of course Chandra was unusual in that he advocated not Hinduism but what some people today might call, for want of a better term, ecumenical humanism. It also had a certain secular character."

"Humanism is becoming a bad word in America," observed Adair, "and secular is positively nasty."

"More's the pity. Chandra wandered across India, which in those days included Pakistan and Bangladesh, urging reconciliation of Hindus and Muslims, state education, abolition of class distinctions, and independence from Britain. Only because Chandra above all preached ahimsa, or nonviolence, did the

British tolerate him. Even so, he spent many of his remaining years in prison, where he, like Gandhi, learned to make sandals and to make cloth. It was really his idea, not Gandhi's, that India should find her salvation in her domestic economy.

"Chandra was fortunate to have had his first extensive period of imprisonment during the period of troubles in 1857, or the British would certainly have blamed him for the mutinies and would probably have killed him. This would surely have happened despite his pleas for ahimsa.

"Gandhi is today generally given credit for enlarging the concept of ahimsa to include love and self-sacrifice and turning nonviolence from a negative concept into a positive virtue. But during Chandra's famous (in India, at least) journeys in the years 1866 to 1869 to the British administrative centers, the rudiments of the idea of noncooperation, or nonviolent direct action, which came to be known as *satyagraha* in Gandhi's time, were present in many of his speeches. These speeches, and the fact that he pursued the British to their annual retreat to Simla, something that was simply not done, brought about his arrest again and incarceration for a dozen years. While he was imprisoned and personally silenced, he was transformed from being a man in the news to being a legend in his own time. That is, of course, a cliché, but it properly describes Chandra. He had been jailed before, but it was this imprisonment following his trek across India that ingrained him in the Indian consciousness.

"Chandra must have provided much of the philosophical bedrock upon which Gandhi built. As a young man, Gandhi met Chandra at least once before he went to London in June of 1888 to study law. This would have been about 1887, or possibly in early '88. As I have suggested, there is reason to believe that it was Chandra, not the British Fabians, who first turned Gandhi toward the humanitarian mission he was to pursue, first in South Africa and finally and most importantly, in India.

Had Chandra conceived of the hunger strike, India might have achieved her independence a half century earlier. But he did not, and it was left to Gandhi to embarrass the British into letting India go."

"That's nonsense." Adair had returned to the table with another plate full of chicken. He had no patience with hunger strikes. "The British would not have given a shit if Chandra had starved himself to death; in fact they would have been relieved. I'm surprised they didn't suggest it to him. And if he had gone on a hunger strike, with communications the way they were in the nineteenth century, he would have been dead before anybody in the outside world would have heard about it."

"I suppose you're right, Adair. Nevertheless, the hunger strike is highly symbolic for Indians, since famine is often abroad in the land and the spectre of starvation haunts even the wealthiest Indian. That is something the well-fed British never understood. As I said, the British were only embarrassed. They never felt what Gandhi's self-starvation meant to Indians—Hindus and Muslims alike."

"Gandhi didn't succeed in unifying India." Adair could not resist poking holes in Bhagat's exposition.

"No, there were overwhelming forces involved. But Gandhi probably prevented open warfare."

"For a time."

"Yes, for a time. But to get back to Chandra. He achieved, at least among the Hindus, an almost godlike status. He was called the bodhisattva. That means, literally in Sanskrit, one whose essence is enlightenment. It is a name for those who are believed to have abandoned the achievement of nirvana because of their love for humanity. You see, he had given up caste, family, wealth—"

"We understand, Bhagat. Even Henry probably does, remarkable as that may be. Let's get on with the exhibition."

"Yes, of course. The sesquicentenary of Chandra's birth is approaching, and to observe it, we would like to see a museum exhibition held at the Smithsonian Institution. The American Government committed itself to such a Chandra exhibition at the same time it agreed to hold the Gandhi Centennial exhibition."

Adair looked up from a greasy chicken leg. "Not exactly. The agreement was made years ago by Vice President Hubert Humphrey during the Johnson administration. Humphrey was at the time running for president. He lost the election. If Humphrey

19

had been elected, you might be able to say you have an agreement. But he didn't and that was years ago, anyway."

"The present administration doesn't seem to like our non-aligned foreign policy," Bhagat told Henry, "is what Adair is trying to say, and they are taking it out on our cultural exchanges. I don't know why. Perhaps it is because Westerners still view pacifism as a negative rather than a positive force. I suppose that you understand your government better than I do, Henry."

Henry cleared his throat. It had been some time since he had had occasion to say anything. "No, I find the U.S. Government just as baffling as you do, Bhagat."

Bhagat smiled. He knew he had his exhibition.

"There will be no official funds for the Chandra exhibition, Bhagat. If Henry wants to put on the exhibition, then we have no objection, but the Government of India and the Smithsonian will have to foot the bill."

"I understand completely, Adair, but I'm afraid that nobody in New Delhi will. After all, at the last Indo–U. S. Subcommission meeting Mr. Cooper did promise that the American side would live up to its cultural exchange obligations. Everybody presumed he was speaking for the State Department since he was head of your delegation."

There was a silence that neither Adair nor Henry was willing to break, so Bhagat continued. "However, we need not quibble about small things. We are perfectly willing to go more than half way. My government will provide everything necessary for the exhibition. The Smithsonian need only provide space and, of course, install the objects. It will cost very little and the Smithsonian will not find India ungrateful. On the other hand—" Bhagat left the rest of the sentence to be completed by his luncheon companions however they saw fit.

Adair seemed determined not to comment, so Henry took the plunge. "I'm sure we can work something out." Actually, Henry wasn't sure at all, but he understood what Bhagat meant by grateful in the double negative. What Bhagat was saying in his own way was that if the Smithsonian did not put on the Chandra

20

exhibition, it was likely that the Smithsonian would never get the Indian Government to approve another project in India.

All foreign research in India had to go through an elaborate, multilevel approval process which, as often as not, resulted in disapproval or no action at all. If it were only the Smithsonian's own research that was involved, the Indian Government's displeasure would be serious enough, but the Smithsonian also acted as a granting agency for the so-called Special Foreign Currency Program that funded much of the American basic science and other scholarly research being conducted in India. Some $200 million worth of Indian rupees, generated by past sales of agricultural commodities, were available for cooperative research between the two countries. A consortium of twenty-three American universities had established the U.S. Foundation for Indian Research, which for almost a decade had been more than 80 percent supported by Smithsonian SFCP Indian Rupee grants. In addition, many other institutions came independently to the Smithsonian for money for their South Asian studies.

A displeased Dr. Bhagat Gupta could easily bring to a halt the South Asian research of dozens of these American universities and other scholarly institutions. There were already many Indian officials who felt that such Western scholars simply perpetuated a sort of intellectual colonialism in India. Cutting off Smithsonian-supported Indian research would play as well in New Delhi, Poona, Madras, Bombay, and points East as it would play poorly in Washington, Cambridge, New Haven, and points West. It would bomb at the Oriental Institute in Chicago.

Henry tested the grass on the way back across the Mall to the Smithsonian Castle. The wet sod was already frozen. The wind had picked up and Bhagat was now holding on to his homburg with both hands. Adair Blake's longish hair was blown forward like a flying jib. Pushed by the north wind, all three ran across the grass.

* * *

"Gerald, we are going to have to do the Chandra exhibition, that's all there is to it."

"How do you know the Indians would quit approving our

21

research if we don't? Did Dr. Gupta say so?" Gerald Blackman, head of the Foreign Affairs Office (FAO) was making a pro forma argument to Henry.

"No, and I don't know it, but I sure as hell feel it. What do you think?"

"I think they'll close us down," Gerald admitted. He had been hoping for some sort of objective reason that he could use with his higher-ups in the Smithsonian, but he got nothing like it from Henry. But since Gerald's office had responsibility for the Foreign Currency Program, he knew very well that the Indians needed little excuse to quit approving projects. Even if the Indian Science Office and the University Grants Commission didn't quit giving approvals, the Central Bank of India could simply quit authorizing the expenditures of funds from the blocked American rupee accounts. It would have the same effect.

Gerald let out a long and mournful sigh. He picked up his phone and dialed the secretary's office. "Hannah? This is Gerald. Mr. Scruggs and I need to meet with the secretary."

"Yes, as soon as possible."

"Yes, I suppose we can wait until tomorrow."

"Nine-thirty, then." Gerald hung up as Henry looked at him, aghast. He hated early morning meetings, and tomorrow especially, since it was certainly going to be snowing.

* * *

The next morning Henry walked to work. Driving was out of the question. The snow had accumulated almost seven inches and the forecasters were predicting another four to six inches before it tapered off to flurries. The day's high temperature of twenty-four degrees had come at midnight and it was now down to seventeen, making the snow, that which was falling, dry and drifting. The high winds that had begun yesterday were picking up the fallen snow and blowing great clouds of it that often obscured that which was still falling. In Washington, a storm like this was infrequent in January or February and almost unheard of before Christmas.

Everyone was caught by surprise. The city had made no effort through the night to keep the streets clear as the heaviest of the snow fell, and now after a dark gray daybreak there were so many stalled cars that the streets were impossible to plow.

A liberal leave policy had been declared for nonessential government workers. That meant that most civil servants could stay at home without prior arrangement, though the day would be charged against their accumulated annual leave. Henry would have gladly spent eight hours of his annual leave to be able to stay indoors. Make that eighty hours. He would have spent half of it in bed with Phoebe and about noon or maybe one o'clock they would have gotten up and made grits and eggs and some thick-sliced bacon if the electric power didn't fail. If it did, then they would stay in bed, which wouldn't be so bad either. But there was that damn 9:30 meeting with Gerald and the secretary.

As it was, Phoebe was at home alone in bed and it was well after ten by the time Henry slipped and slid to the dark red stone Smithsonian Castle. At the east door, the night guard was held over for the day shift and looked as though he didn't mind not having to go home through the snow just now, especially since he was on time and a half. He told Henry that nobody was in the secretary's office yet.

Though Henry didn't know it, he needn't have hurried. It would be more than an hour before a four-wheel-drive guard force vehicle would bring the secretary to the Castle.

Henry took the stairs to the basement and then went another half flight down into the tunnel that connected the Castle with the Arts and Industries Building. The bitter cold penetrated the tunnel and pooled there. He could feel it up to his knees, like wading through invisible snow. On the other side, he climbed the sixty-two steps to his tower office, too tired to count the steps as he ascended, and managed to put on his teakettle to heat before collapsing in his desk chair. Somewhere in a desk drawer he had stashed away a package of pecan twirls yesterday. Just in case. He rummaged around for his breakfast, then took off his snow-filled boots and swiveled his chair around so that he could put his feet on the radiator to thaw.

The Foreign Affairs Office occupied the low tower, or pavilion, at the northwest corner of the Arts and Industries Building, familiarly known as the A&I. From Henry's window, he could

23

look out to the north through small arched windows onto the Mall, and across it, to the National Museum of Natural History, almost invisible now in the blowing snow. By standing with his nose against the glass, Henry could have seen the corner of the Smithsonian Castle to the west. But he was unwilling to take his feet off the radiator, so all he could see was the unabated storm dumping more snow onto the Mall and, on a bookshelf to the right of the window, he had a clear view of his telephone answering machine. He stretched out an arm and punched the replay button. Nothing. Gerald might have tried to call from his home in Friendship Heights, but nobody could tell because the lines always went down out toward Montgomery County when there was heavy snow.

The teakettle got itself together to whistle and Henry reluctantly got to his feet. Enough feeling had come back to his feet for them to ache when he put his weight on them. By holding onto his desk, he managed to make it around to the other side to the teakettle. He looked into the teapot. Ugh! He dumped yesterday's tea leaves and the remaining half a cup of cold tea into the wastebasket. It made a mess, so he averted his eyes and set about to reload the pot with fresh oolong. He poured in the hot water and cleared a place on his desk for the pot. A stack of files fell off the desk and into the wastebasket. He fished them out and brushed off yesterday's tea leaves and placed the files on the carpet where they could dry off. He poured out the dregs of yesterday's tea from his Japanese earthenware cup, this time into the sink, and gave the cup a perfunctory rinse.

Back in his chair, Henry took a bite of pecan twirl and washed it down with oolong. He leaned back in his chair and cradled the hot mug in his hands. The feeling was beginning to come back to his fingers. He would have to get some mittens if the rest of the winter was going to be like this. He hated mittens, but gloves were no good when it was icy and you had to keep your hands out of your pockets for balance.

The first of the snow had fallen on warm pavement and had melted, but it had then quickly refrozen, making it treacherous underfoot—or under wheel for that matter. Henry thought for a moment with morbid satisfaction what the Beltway must look

24

like with cars turned every which way, often joined front to rear, side to side, and probably top to bottom. *Blechsalat,* the Austrians called it. Tin salad. It happened often enough in wintertime on the Vienna-Salzburg autobahn.

His socks were beginning to steam as the moisture evaporated. They smelled a bit like wet dogs. Stank, he corrected himself. G.B.S. had put it nicely, he thought: "Madam, you smell; I stink." Or was it Dr. Johnson? It must have been Dr. Johnson, now that he thought about it. Shaw would never have admitted that about himself.

He looked at his watch and sighed. Somehow it was already 11:06. He got to his feet again and padded uncomfortably across the none-too-clean carpeting into the large west room where the Special Foreign Currency Program (SFCP) lived. He wiped the condensate off of one of the windows and peered out. In the Castle, across the way, the secretary's office was still dark, but there was a light on in an interior room. Hannah must have made it to work. He should have expected it. Henry walked back to his desk and picked up the phone. There was a dial tone. At least the Smithsonian's own exchange was working. He dialed 5005.

"The secretary's office."

"Hello, Hannah? This is Henry."

"Mister Scruggs. You were supposed to be here at nine-thirty." Hannah was cold to Henry. She still held it against him that her former boss, Secretary Whitfield, had been forced to resign several years ago. Whitfield had brought Hannah Norton with him when he came to the Smithsonian from the California Institute of Life Sciences. She had been in love with Whitfield for years. It was unfortunate for Henry, and even for Hannah, that she had been unable to transfer this love to the new Secretary, Lily Vernon, whom she regarded as an interloper who had probably conspired with Henry to do in Whitfield. Such was of course not the case. Henry had done the deed all by himself.

"I was here at nine-thirty but there was nobody in your office," Henry lied.

"You came in after ten. I checked with the guard."

"Well, I was almost on time. As near as makes no difference."

That was obviously not a satisfactory answer, but Hannah let it pass. "Well, you better come over here now. The guards are bringing Secretary Vernon in, in a Jeep."

Henry struggled to put on his shoes. His feet seemed to have swollen, or his shoes shrunk. Probably both. He poured a second cup of tea and quickly drank it down. The pot was already cooling and the rest would not be fit to drink by the time he returned. He stuffed the last of the pecan twirls into his mouth and washed the stickiness off his hands while he chewed and swallowed. He started off down the stairs, counting: sixty-two, sixty-one, sixty, fifty-nine—

* * *

Hannah was a trim, compact little woman given to wearing conservative and slightly old-fashioned suits with frilly, feminine blouses peeking out. The rumor was that she had been a W.A.C. Sergeant Major during the war. That fitted how she dressed—regular Army on leave. Her idea of jewelry was a pair of artificial pearl button earrings, and occasionally, for festive occasions, a small brooch pinned to a lapel. The one she usually wore looked like crossed pistols until you got up really close. She did her hair á la Claudette Colbert and despite a mien of some severity, she managed to be quite attractive in her own way.

Henry sat down on one of the silly, undersized Victorian chairs in the secretary's outer office and looked for a magazine to read. There was nothing on the little side table except an out-of-date copy of *Forbes* magazine. Henry spurned it; he didn't have any money to invest. He folded his hands to warm them up and contemplated Hannah.

Henry tried to imagine he was in love with Hannah and she with him. He tried to project the intensity of emotion found in love just before the parties thereto have surrendered to one another. Henry felt his eyes moisten as he imagined that there was no other woman, at least not for him. After a time, Hannah began to feel—to feel, well, something. She began giving Henry quick, curious glances, dropping her eyes immediately back to some work on her desk after she saw Henry staring at her. Little, rapid movements betrayed her growing discomfort.

Henry imagined closing his mouth over hers and their lips

melting together. Hannah squirmed. Henry imagined closing his mouth over each of her ears in turn and removing her pearl earrings with his teeth before pushing his tongue into her inner ear. Hannah got out of her chair and hurried into an adjacent file room to look up something or file something, she didn't care which.

Before Hannah returned, there were footsteps in the hall and the outer door was opened. Lylene Vernon, bundled up in a down coat and fleece-lined boots, came in with Gerald Blackman following close behind, dressed in a snow-covered wool overcoat and a plaid scarf.

"Henry!" exclaimed Secretary Vernon, "I'm glad you made it. Gerald said you could get in by yourself but I thought we should have picked you up at home." Lily (nobody called her Lylene unless they were saying something nasty behind her back) Vernon liked Henry, or at least she gave him some of the credit for her having been chosen as the first woman Smithsonian secretary. After Henry's revelations of several years ago, the Board of Regents had been determined to find a post-menopausal female for the job in the mistaken belief that this would ensure that no scandal could possibly involve the new administration of the Institution.

Lily Vernon was just turned sixty and had served with distinction at the Smithsonian as assistant secretary for History and Art, and as director of the National Collection of Fine Arts. Before coming to the Smithsonian she had been for many years curator of Nineteenth and Twentieth-Century Painting at the Museum of Fine Arts in Boston.

Lily not only shattered the sex precedent but she was also the first art historian ever to be appointed Smithsonian secretary. Not everybody was pleased, needless to say, particularly in the oldest and strongest Smithsonian bureau, the National Museum of Natural History.

"Did you drive in, Gerald?" asked Henry incredulously.

"Dr. Vernon was kind enough to give me a ride."

"But you live almost in Maryland?" Henry had never actually seen Gerald's house because he had never been invited, but Gerald always said that was where he lived. The secretary, on the other hand, lived in nearby Cleveland Park. Cleveland Park lay in the hills above Georgetown and just west of Rock Creek Park. Though close to downtown Washington, Cleveland Park was a residential area of sometimes quite hilly streets, often impassable in heavy snow.

"The secretary was kind enough to pick me up."

Well, then, Henry thought to himself. You could have picked me up. I'll remember that, Gerald.

Lily took off her down coat and held it out to Hannah without looking at her. Hannah accepted it sullenly. Henry wondered how long it would be before the secretary had a new secretary. Lily beckoned Henry and Gerald to follow her into the inner sanctum.

Sanctum it was. Every Smithsonian secretary since Joseph Henry had occupied these rooms. Secretary Henry had moved into the rooms as soon as the Castle was ready for occupancy, before the Civil War. Or War between the States, as Henry Scruggs preferred to call it. Joseph Henry probably just called it The War since he lacked twentieth-century perspective.

Though Lily was the first woman secretary, she was not the first resident female. Joseph Henry's wife and daughters had actually resided in these rooms.

Henry (Scruggs) always felt the weight of all this history whenever he visited the secretary's offices. It was noticeable in the outer office where Hannah sat. It grew stronger as you passed through the small room where the secretary's executive assistant (absent today, like most sensible people) had his desk, and was almost overpowering in the southeast corner room, the secretary's personal office.

"Henry, Jerry [Jerry?!] and I have already discussed the Indian problem, and I think I understand the chain of events leading up to your meeting yesterday with the Indian cultural counselor and whomever it was from the State Department. I gather that you agree with Jerry that the Indians will freeze our Foreign Currency Program research if we don't do their exhibition."

"Well, Gerald knows more about it than I do because he attended the Subcommission meeting in New Delhi in May—"

"I told the secretary that the Indians had gone on record that they expected better cooperation from the U.S. side in non-SFCP research. The State Department people assured them that there would be satisfactory support for Indian activities in the U.S. Maybe you can explain why they are dumping it on us. You ought to understand it since you work for the State Department." Gerald was twisting the knife because Henry had recently asked if the Smithsonian would pick up his salary. Henry had been on loan from the State Department for almost two years and would soon have to go back to an uncertain future at the fudge factory if he couldn't get hired by the Smithsonian.

"You have to understand how the State Department operates," began Henry mysteriously. "They never have any money for any sort of cooperation unless it has been planned in advance and has gone up to Congress as a line item in their budget request. That means that they can never make on-the-spot commitments because they never have any money to back them up. They do it all the time anyhow and hope somebody else will pick up the check. They look for suckers like the Smithsonian, suckers with something to lose if they don't reprogram funds to meet State's obligations."

"I should think the State Department would have something to lose if they can't fulfill their promises."

"No, ma'am. The State Department never has any real programs; the programs always belong to other agencies. I suppose in an extreme case the other country might break off diplomatic relations when we fail to make good on a promise, but there's no way the Indians would do that over the Chandra exhibition. I think. However, the Indians are bound to be more upset than usual about the Chandra exhibition. They think the current Administration has reneged on its promise to do the exhibition because we don't like India's nonaligned foreign policy. They think we're trying to tell them what to do, and they really hate that. Makes us seem like the British. It is hard to disabuse them of that notion because they are probably correct."

Secretary Vernon closed her eyes, unwilling even to think about American foreign policy and how it was perceived abroad. "Why does the State Department expect us to have enough money to meet their obligations?" she asked, not really expecting an answer.

"I can tell you that," answered Henry. "Agencies with a lot of experience with State pad the hell out of their foreign activities budgets just in case. Congress is used to it."

"Good God! Did Secretary Whitfield have to put up with things like this?"

"It's not so bad, ma'am. Mr. Gupta told me that the Indians would prepare everything and we only have to provide an exhibit hall and unpack things. It will be cheap. Gerald has probably got enough petty cash in the office account to handle it."

Lily gave Henry a weary look. "Henry, how long have you been at the Smithsonian?" No answer was expected, so she continued. "Well, I've been in the museum business for years. I can tell you right now that nothing that happens in a museum is ever going to be cheap. There's nobody here competent to be curator for an Indian exhibition and guest curators are expensive. I'm not sure we can find the money."

"I hope we can. I more or less promised Mr. Gupta and the State Department that we'd do the exhibition."

"You what!?" This was a chorus of Lily and Gerald.

So it was that Henry found himself appointed guest curator for the Chandra sesquicentennial exhibition.

He was to become learned in a country he had never seen and about a culture that he had experienced no deeper than the chef's special dinner at the Gaylord Indian Restaurant. He was given to understand that if he expected to join the staff of the Smithsonian, he had to prepare an exhibition that would elicit critical acclaim.

Henry called Bhagat Gupta as soon as the telephones were working again. "Hello, Bhagat? The exhibition is on!"

"I'm delighted, Henry!"

"I have tentatively booked a hall in the Museum of History and Technology. We have the space from the first of August next year until March fifteenth. With three weeks for installation, and throw in a week for contingencies, we ought to be able to open sometime in November and close at the end of February."

"Wonderful! Perhaps we can hold our Republic Day reception there. That would be January twenty-sixth."

"We don't have much time and we won't have a professional curator at the Smithsonian, so you are going to have to get the exhibition to me in a form that's ready to install."

"Don't worry, Henry, old friend! Everything is ready. I can have it here in three months." Bhagat Gupta was of course lying through his teeth.

 **Three**

Phoebe was sitting cross-legged in the Saarinen womb chair when Henry returned. The fireplace had already consumed most of the small supply of last year's logs and was blazing away at a needless rate. Henry had been intending to order another cord of wood, but now the price would be at least double. It might be cheaper just to move to Key West for the rest of the winter. Phoebe was protecting herself from the heat of the fireplace with numerous layers of sweaters. Henry pulled off his boots and padded over to the fire and sat on the floor between it and Phoebe's chair.

"You're blocking the heat," Phoebe complained.

"Fix me a drink and maybe I'll move. Eventually."

Phoebe joined Henry on the floor with two glasses and a bottle of Mortlac. She handed him a can of peanuts for him to pop the top. The ring hurt his chilled fingers and the can slipped out of his hand but landed upright on the carpet, spilling only a few peanuts.

"Can you hold your glass or do you want me to feed it to you?"

"I think I can manage. You should have gone to work today. It wasn't too bad. Rather pleasant, actually."

"Liar. The radio says it's dropped to twelve degrees and now they don't know when it will stop snowing. If ever."

"Is that why you decided to burn up all our wood?"

"I thought it would melt the snow in this end of town. Are you hungry?"

"Of course I'm hungry." Henry pulled Phoebe to him and started groping under all the sweaters for the person probably underneath.

"Stop it! Your hands are still cold! I meant for food. I made some lasagna."

Phoebe seldom cooked, even more rarely now that she had taken up with Henry, who regarded the kitchen as his personal preserve. The kitchen would be a disaster area now, of course, with all the pans and things put in the wrong places. That is presuming Phoebe had cleaned anything up, which was un-likely. Nevertheless, Henry felt especially favored. Phoebe must have gotten out of bed by noon and all for him. And herself, of course.

The lasagna was actually quite good. Lunch had been a stale machine sandwich, the Smithsonian Commons dining room never having opened because of the storm. So he was hungry. But beyond that, the lasagna had been in the oven for hours and had gotten quite crusty, making the cheese taste like raclette. Somehow Phoebe had not burned it. Probably the weather had been just too cold.

"Were there many people in the Castle?"

"Hardly anybody. The secretary and Gerald were brought in by the guards in a four-wheel drive. And Hannah made it, of course. I didn't see any lights upstairs in your office."

"Bodde stays home if it even rains hard. He always says he is working on a case and since he's the boss nobody can argue with him. I think he watches soaps on the TV." Phoebe didn't like Hayward Bodde very much. Bodde and Phoebe Casey had both been assistant general counsels and Bodde had been the more senior of the two so, all things equal, it was reasonable he would have been promoted to general counsel. But Phoebe didn't think so. "Men! They stick together!" she had said at the time, ignoring the fact that Lily Vernon had made the appointment.

The plates were abandoned in the sink with Phoebe's unwashed pans as the last of the logs turned to ashes and Phoebe and Henry retreated to the bed to keep warm.

"Isn't that a better way to keep warm?" Henry asked.

"Mmmm," replied Phoebe.

Henry stretched out into regions of the bed that hadn't yet gotten warm. It was icy out there. He hastily retreated to Phoebe's vicinity.

"I know an even better way to keep warm," said Phoebe.

Henry was immediately interested. "Tell," he demanded in as seductive a voice as he could manage.

"A Caribbean cruise," she replied.

That was not what he had in mind. "I don't know if I can get away. How much does it cost?"

"It's free."

"Free! I'm sure I can go. I've got plenty of leave."

"Not you. Me. Besides, it's fully booked."

"What are you talking about?"

"There's a Smithsonian Associates New Year's cruise in the Caribbean. Twenty-one days. Tommy invited me to go along."

"Who the hell is Tommy?" Henry sat up, heedless that he was pulling the covers away from Phoebe.

"Tommy Beckler. He runs the Associates' tour program. He invited me to be one of the Smithsonian staff representatives. He said I was a responsible person. All I have to do is help get people where they're supposed to be on time, and cope with emergencies. Things like that. And I get all expenses paid." Phoebe yanked the covers back over her.

"You can't. I have plans for us during the holidays!" That was a lie. Henry never made any kind of plans in advance. He didn't like plans and particularly hated going out on New Year's Eve.

"Too bad! I'm going," Phoebe said firmly. "Anyway, I'm not leaving until the end of December. You can keep your plans for Christmas."

"Then I'm going, too! I don't trust Tommy What's-his-name."

"You can't. I told you it's fully booked and there is a long waiting list."

"I can be a staff rep."

34

"They don't have room for any more. I only got it because someone else had to cancel."

They argued through the night. Much of the time Phoebe spent with her back to Henry and the covers wrapped around her. Henry was chilled by the cold night air and eventually got up and put on a heavy sweat suit to keep warm. It was a losing battle.

* * *

Nothing much happened until after the end of the year. At least, nothing much that was properly the subject of this book. The snow, which had seemed to promise Washington a rare white Christmas, had quickly melted when the wind direction changed and nearly two inches of warm rain were deposited on top of everything. Slush clogged the storm drains and icy water came over the sidewalks. The usual last-minute Christmas shopping was interrupted by frantic searches for rubber boots, and Christmas came and went on a Saturday, hardly noticed.

Henry had stayed healthy through all the bad weather and Phoebe's usurping the bedding, but now that in Christmas week it had warmed up to more seasonable weather, he decided to catch a cold. He stayed home drinking tea and whiskey, alternately, while making undersized crumpets with rings improvised from chicken-soup cans. Phoebe went back to work, which was just as well because the problem of Tommy's cruise had still not been resolved to Henry's satisfaction.

Henry would have stayed put until the new year if he had not run out of fig preserves and had to go out looking for some. He tracked down a new supply at Magruder's.

The effort of the search for preserves awakened his sleeping conscience and he returned to the Smithsonian on the Thursday before New Year's to find it almost deserted.

Phoebe had departed the evening before, trying unsuccessfully to contain her excitement and to pretend she was sorry to leave Henry. Even Henry knew, though he wouldn't admit it, that he had been lousy company for the past several weeks and it must be a relief for her to get away.

* * *

Henry wandered around the third floor of the tower. Deputy FAO Director Ronald Hipster was making what looked like a crocheted bedspread out of paper clips. A large pile of empty paper clip boxes was heaped around his box-filled wastebasket. Dreamy Weekes was in the SFCP office, working on the peer reviews of proposals for the January meeting of the Advisory Council on Systematic and Environmental Biology. When she saw Henry she suddenly switched her expression from studious to sensual. Dreamy worked hard to keep up her image. Henry lured both Ronald and Dreamy off to lunch.

They walked through the nearly empty Great Hall of the Castle. Rows of giant columns joined by Romanesque arches marched along with them. In the center of the hall, a large, over-decorated Christmas tree had been erected to provide a holiday atmosphere for the almost nonexistent staff and visitors.

On the double doors leading into the west wing and the Commons, a neat but small white card announced that the buffet in the Commons would be closed from Christmas to New Year's. A call to the Museum of History and Technology (MHT) dining room got a recorded announcement to the same effect.

They fetched their coats from the office and went out hunting for a restaurant. The slush was almost completely gone; it lingered only in the few places where the midwinter sun did not shine. It had turned cold again and the ground was frozen except where the bright sun had thawed the surface. Dreamy huddled between Henry and Ronald to keep warm and for the time being Henry would have forgotten all about Phoebe had it not been for his simmering envy of her midwinter vacation in the Caribbean. They careered toward Chinatown, where the restaurants were bound to be open.

"Ronald, you might as well go home after lunch," Henry told Hipster with some firmness after they had ordered their food, "I will be there to answer the phone in the unlikely event that anyone calls." Henry had wanted to make Dreamy ever since he had arrived in the Foreign Affairs Office almost two years before. Now that Phoebe had apparently abandoned him, and without so much as a backward glance, Henry saw his chance.

Dreamy Weekes was Dorothy Dandridge eternally playing

Carmen Jones ("I go for you and I'm taboo"). Henry sat at the table, neglecting his *bung-bung* chicken and staring at Dreamy. Dorothy came in and out of focus until Dreamy disappeared entirely, leaving Henry at the table with Dorothy Dandridge. Henry blinked and Dorothy was Carmen. She was still wearing Dreamy's sweater and it didn't suit her at all. Henry changed it for something more décolleté. There! That was better! While he was at it, Ronald Hipster became a pile of coats thrown over an extra chair, eating its General Tso's chicken. For a moment, Henry was Dusty Miller and he rippled his fighter's muscles. All he could manage was a shrug, but it caught Dreamy's attention.

"Henry? Henry! Your lunch will get cold, honey."

"Huh?" Henry struggled out of it. "Oh, my lunch. It's already cold. It's supposed to be." Henry arm-wrestled his eyes and got them down to his plate.

"Henry? You sure you're all right?" Dreamy was more amused than concerned.

"This is my first day back. I ran out of figs." Henry's mind was wandering a bit. "I mean I had to go out for more preserves and maybe I came back to the office too early."

"You do look a bit peaked."

"And Phoebe's gone."

"Poor baby!" said Dreamy, falsely solicitous. She didn't like Phoebe. "Is he afraid to stay by himself?" Dreamy slipped into small children's third person and pouted her lips with promise. Had Ronald been anybody but Ronald, or perhaps Henry, he would have laughed. He helped himself to some of Henry's *bung-bung* chicken.

"She went on a Caribbean cruise. With the Associates. She's supposed to be helping with the group but I think she did it to be with that Tommy Who's-it." Henry felt Dreamy's leg rub up against him. It could have been that she was simply stretching, but Henry was overcome with anticipation.

Henry ate his *bung-bung* chicken with enthusiasm. Truth to tell, he had been feeling a bit languid. The electricity from Carmen's leg had given him a shock treatment. He reached for the *bung-bung* chicken platter to refill his plate but Ronald had already emptied it. It was just as well, he thought. It is better not

37

to eat too much before sex. Henry wondered whether the restaurant had private rooms and how he could ditch Ronald.

After lunch, Henry insisted they take a taxi back to the Mall. Mustn't get too tired, he thought. "Ronald, we can drop you at your parking lot. Dreamy and I will cover the office this afternoon." Dreamy's smile had moved on from simple promise to federally insured guarantee.

"No, I'd better stay, Henry, I'm in charge of the office. You can go on home and I'll stay." It was uncharacteristic. Ronald didn't usually make sacrifices where the office was concerned. Had Carmen rubbed his knee as well?

"Ronald, I insist. I have to get caught up with my work anyway. You go on home."

"Go home, Ronald," said Dreamy. "Henry doesn't make such an offer very often. You better take advantage if it."

Henry's pulse pounded in his ears as they got out of the taxi in front of the Arts and Industries Building. Even Dreamy was trying to get rid of Ronald. He wondered where they would do it. In the central room on the floor, he decided. That would be away from the windows and if they got caught, well—they just got caught.

"Well, okay, I'll go on, then. But I've got to go up to the office to get my rubbers."

Rubbers! Henry hadn't thought about that. Not Ronald's silly overshoes, of course, but the other things. But Dreamy would be on the pill, of course. And if not, then they would cross that bridge when they came to it. Henry suppressed an involuntary shudder of conscience. All the same, Henry decided, he should get some (not overshoes) to keep in his desk for just such emergencies.

Dreamy started up the last flight of steps, the narrow, twisting, iron steps that led to the top of the tower. They were steep and Dreamy was long legged. That put her fundament practically in Henry's face as he followed her. It also put his in Ronald's face, but he didn't think about that. Neither did Ronald, for that matter, if anyone cared. Dreamy had taken off her heavy coat and was taking her time, swaying from side to side, her clinging skirt conforming to every muscular contraction. Henry thought about Dreamy climbing the stairs forever but decided he would just die if another flight of stairs were, magically, to be added.

Upstairs, Ronald showed little inclination to leave. One of his rubbers was missing and while searching for it, Ronald found several petty things he felt needed doing. Then there was the paper clip bedspread. Henry scooped it up and dumped it behind a bank of file cabinets. He hunted up the missing galosh and handed it to Ronald while removing several papers from Ronald's desk with the other hand. "Now, scoot! If you are here two minutes from now, I'm going to leave with Dreamy and you'll be stuck here until five-fifteen."

Ronald got to his feet with molasses-like slowness and struggled into his overcoat. He couldn't find his left sleeve. Henry twisted his arm around rather roughly and poked it into the sleeve. He gave Ronald a push toward the stairs and Ronald started shuffling off, rather confused by it all.

Henry held his breath until Ronald got to the first landing, then he looked around through Dreamy's open door. She was not sitting at her desk where he could see her. Perhaps she was back by the file cabinets getting into . . . something more comfortable.

Henry heard the door open and close at the foot of the stairs. Thank God! God had to be on the side of fornication because it just naturally led to more subjects. That was something Henry had long ago decided and he didn't think about it now only because his mind was more on Dreamy's body than on the reasons he was being favored by God.

Goddamn! Henry abruptly shifted from approving his Maker to outright confrontation. There were footsteps on the stairs. Was Ronald coming back for something? Henry would kill him. Without a word, Henry would drop Ronald with a Green Beret karate chop. Or maybe he would disembowel him with his Swiss army knife. Dreamy might get off on blood. He would use the crosscut saw blade or maybe the can opener and there would be blood everywhere.

Two heads appeared on the stairs. Neither belonged to Ronald. One was American and the other was Chinese. Henry knew them both. He decided to transfer his allegiance from God.

"Scruggs, we've got to talk to you!"

"I can give you an appointment for tomorrow morning, Dr. Thames. How about ten o'clock?" At that, Henry was making a sacrifice. He did not usually like to set appointments before eleven.

"Now! You've got to do something now!"

Henry didn't like Mason Thames, and not just because Thames didn't know how to pronounce his own name the proper way, *Temms*. Thames was a lizard expert with the National Zoo. He had the personality of a lizard—hostile and unblinking. Actually, it was hard to tell whether Thames really was a member of the staff or was just using the Smithsonian name. He traveled all over the world studying endangered varieties of lizards and supported himself with all sorts of grants and other contracts. He had originally come to the Smithsonian as a predoctoral fellow and had stayed on as a postdoc. Henry doubted that any of his research money actually came from the Smithsonian now, but the Zoo wouldn't say so as long as they were getting publishable research from him under the Smithsonian's name.

Thames had originally come to Henry's attention when he dragged in Tsing, Tay-min, a sometime student he had met in Venezuela or some place. Miss Tsing had accompanied Thames back to the United States, entering as a tourist authorized to have a thirty-day visit. Thames had brought her to see Henry on day twenty-nine and had demanded that Henry make the Immigration and Naturalization Service extend her stay. "How long?" Henry had asked.

"As long as she wants to stay. Make it two or three years, preferably indefinitely. I'll be responsible for her," Thames had replied. Henry had asked Tay-min what she intended to do in America, but Thames wouldn't let her reply. It had taken most of the day (with Henry missing lunch for which Thames would never be forgiven) for Henry to find out from an evasive Thames that she was just his girlfriend, it wasn't likely they would get married, and she wanted to learn about lizards because that was what Thames did and a Chinese woman always took an interest in her husband's (boyfriend's) business.

40

After Thames wormed it out of Henry that a student visa probably had the most flexibility, Thames badgered the Zoo's research director (over the phone) until he accepted Tay-min as one of the Zoo's students—at Thames's expense. Working out the finances took another hour. Henry never did find out how much money Thames had for Tay-min's support. Eventually he had just given up and prepared the student certificate (form I-20) showing her as receiving full room and board (one side of Thames's bed and an occasional Big Mac) from private sources. The immigration officer had been suspicious, but had accepted it.

"What's the matter now?" Henry settled down behind his desk and looked critically at Tay-min. She wasn't so bad; in fact she looked pretty good in her tight blue jeans, but she wasn't a patch on Dreamy. Damn all lizard people. Maybe if he pretended to have a heart attack they would leave. But probably not.

"Tay-min has been ordered to leave by tomorrow."

Henry swiveled his chair around and opened his student file drawer. He pulled out Tay-min's folder. "She should still have another six months—until June."

"Show him, Tay-min."

Tay-min pulled her passport out of her knapsack and held it out for Henry. Henry leafed through to the latest INS stamp. It was dated two weeks ago and was from Miami. "You went out of the country!"

"We just went to the Cayman Islands. They put that stamp in when we came back. They wouldn't give her but two weeks."

"That was because she doesn't have a student visa in her passport. You have to start all over again when you leave the country. I told you last summer that she couldn't use her tourist visa again and she had to get a visa to match her student status if she traveled abroad."

"That was impossible. There wasn't any consulate in the Caymans."

"That doesn't alter the fact that she had to have a visa. You should have come back by way of Jamaica."

"Well, it's too late now. You've got to do something."

41

"INS won't change her back to student when she deliberately ignores the need for the proper visa."

"I don't see why you can't do something." Thames sat there stubbornly. Tay-min smiled at Henry uncomprehendingly. She looked a little like a lizard trying to be pleasant.

Henry thought about the possible alternatives. The least attractive was to go down this afternoon to the INS offices and plead on Tay-min's behalf. And tomorrow, New Year's Eve, would be unthinkable. Nobody at INS would be doing anything. Tay-min would just have to depart. Depart! Now there was an idea! "Dr. Thames, when are you going out of the country for more research?"

"In March. There is the Pacific Saurian Congress in Papua New Guinea."

"Will Tay-min go with you?"

Thames assured Henry that Tay-min went everywhere with him. That was just fine. Henry explained how "voluntary departure" was the solution. INS could delay an alien's departure for up to six months if the alien had some sort of excuse and would leave without a hassle at an agreed-upon date. Henry typed out the proper sort of excuse—an official Smithsonian request asking for a delay until the scheduled March departure—and hurried them off to INS to get there before it closed. Even if INS turned them down, Henry could get the door locked and the office lights off before the lizard people could possibly get back to the tower.

Henry went down to the foot of the stairs to see that they definitely left and to lock the door. Thames had to be given all sorts of assurances that voluntary departure would work. Henry swore it would. He was locking the door when Dreamy appeared behind him, dressed in her coat.

"You can catch my phone, too, Henry. I won't be in tomorrow. Happy New Year!"

"Aren't you going to stay? I thought we might have a drink or tea or something." Henry was horrified and scrambled for some reason to keep her from going. "If you should get any calls, I wouldn't know what to say. SFCP questions are always so technical." Henry looked at Dreamy desperately.

"I'm sure you can think of something. Well, I can't keep my husband waiting." Dreamy started to squeeze by Henry.

"I thought you were separated?"

"We're back together at least for the moment. Nobody wants to be alone at New Year's. Ta'." Dreamy was gone, leaving Henry with a faint whiff of her perfume.

* * *

Nineteen seventy-two arrived on Saturday. Henry greeted it glumly. Phoebe was to be gone for a miserable twenty-one days. Dreamy had come back on the third of January and Henry was mad at her. He wouldn't speak to her. Her conscience may have bothered her a little bit because she went out of her way to be nice in a sisterly sort of way. He threw himself into his work and, by the middle of the second week of the new year, had his desk cleaned of pending work except for the file on the Indian exhibition. He couldn't put that off any longer, so on January twelfth he opened the Indian exhibition file to see where he ought to begin.

 **four**

Henry looked through the Chandra exhibition folder. It was pretty thin—a memorandum of his meeting with Gupta and Blake, another memorandum he had written following his meeting with Secretary Vernon, and a copy of an old (1967) cable from the State Department to the American Embassy, New Delhi, regarding Vice President Hubert Humphrey's discussion with the Indian ambassador about the Gandhi centenary and Chandra sesquicentenary. The pink piece of paper (outgoing cables were pink, incoming cables were white in those days) was brief, to the point, and unambiguous (rare in a State Department cable then, uncommon even now), though lacking in details. It said that the Vice President had committed the United States to sponsor major museum exhibitions in Washington commemorating these events. Just how the exhibitions were to come about was to be worked out later, presumably after Humphrey succeeded Johnson as President.

Not much to build upon. Henry tried to imagine what the Indian Government might send now that the mistrustful Republicans were in power and no official U.S. funds were to be forthcoming to support the exhibition. The Indians might send anything, but the odds were high that whatever they sent would make more sense to Indians than it would to anybody else. Full of obtuse philosophical quotations, Henry thought. He was going to have to pin down Gupta soon for some answers. He also had to have a talk with Fat Dog. In fact, if he were to avoid being caught in the middle, he had to get Gupta and Fat Dog together.

Henry picked up the Smithsonian phone directory and looked under *F* for *Fat*. Nothing there. He turned back to *D* for *Dog*. Nothing there either. He closed the book and looked at the date on the cover. It was published after Fat Dog came to the Smithsonian, but the directory's entries were probably prepared earlier. Henry opened the directory again and looked under *B* for Fat Dog's predecessor. He, at least, was listed. Henry propped the directory open with his elbow, picked up the phone, and dialed.

"Director's office." The receptionist didn't say "Fat Dog's office." Henry wasn't surprised. She probably couldn't say it without laughing.

"This is Henry Scruggs. I would like to talk to Dr. Fat Dog."

"The director is in a meeting. May I have him call you?"

"Actually, I need to set up a meeting with him and the Indian cultural counselor. It's about the Chandra exhibition."

"Yes. I know he wants to talk to you about it."

Henry got a number of possible dates and called Gupta to see if any suited him. They settled on Wednesday afternoon, next week.

* * *

It was seasonal for January when Henry left the office the evening before his meeting. Cold, clear, and dry. And dark, though being almost a month past the winter solstice, a suggestion of twilight remained. The air was clean and he didn't mind the walk across the Mall to his car. The Corvair started easily. It, too, didn't much mind the cold. Henry was going to be sorry when it got too old to be reliable transportation. He should have gotten one of the '69s before they were all gone. Damn Nader for murdering the Corvair! What does he know about automobiles? Henry hoped once again that General Motors would get Nader. He thought about sending an anonymous letter.

Speaking of people he'd like to get, there's Phoebe. He'd

45

heard nothing whatsoever from her. She had said she'd be away three weeks and that was today. Or maybe tomorrow. He didn't know whether to count the day she left. She could have written. Cruise ships are always doing things like posting mail for you. She couldn't possibly have any excuse. Except the obvious one that he had not been very much on her mind. Damn Tommy Whoosit.

Henry lived on nearby Capitol Hill, on northeast Maryland Avenue. In nice weather it would have been silly to drive such a short distance, about twenty blocks. But "nice" meant "warm," which it wasn't and what with waiting for traffic lights and detouring around the Capitol, that was at least a forty-five minute walk. Too long to be out in twenty-two-degree weather.

But it was only a short drive and he was home before the car's heater was warm and before he had a chance to get heated up with exasperation at Washington's late rush-hour traffic.

The first thing he noticed when he opened the door was the fire blazing away in the fireplace. His new supply of firewood wouldn't last a week at that rate. He had had to settle for what local scalpers call a face cord. That was only about half a real cord, being about two feet deep instead of four, and was a way to jack up the price when wood got scarce.

Without looking over the high back of the Saarinen settee he knew Phoebe was there. He couldn't smell her perfume for the wood smoke and besides, his nose was too cold, but nobody else had such a callous disregard for the cost to his wallet and the nation's forests. "I thought you were going to stay south for the winter," he said.

"I thought about it."

"Why did you come back?"

"I missed TV."

Henry couldn't think of anything to reply to that. Phoebe never watched TV. He fixed himself a drink—a big one—and sat down in a chair where he could see Phoebe. She had a book in her hand, but the title was against her. "You didn't write or anything," he complained.

"I forgot to pack a pencil." That had to be a lie. A lawyer without a pencil?! "I don't recall getting any message from you.

People in movies are always getting telegrams delivered to the boat."

"I never go to movies." That was a lie, too. Henry loved going to movies. When she didn't say anything, he dropped the subject in favor of one calculated to cause even more trouble. "I had to spend New Year's Eve with Dreamy. I hope she didn't leave any of her things in the bedroom." Phoebe disliked Dreamy possibly even more than vice versa.

"Does she take American Express or did you have to pay in cash?" It was not really a question. She went back to her book. Henry noticed she was turning pages faster than she could possibly read them.

* * *

By the next day Henry and Phoebe were more or less reconciled. So Henry was in a reasonably good mood when he went into the meeting with Bhagat Gupta and Dr. Fat Dog. Fat Dog's office was on the south side of the fifth floor of the National Museum of History and Technology. Henry and Bhagat were kept waiting for half an hour in the windowless inner room with the director's secretary. Then they were shown in after the director buzzed on the intercom. Henry thought that didn't bode well. If you keep a foreign diplomat waiting when there is a specific appointment time, then you should come out of your office to apologize. Anything less was rude.

Dr. Fat Dog was reading some sort of papers when they entered and the secretary told them to take a seat. He read through to the end (Henry decided they were memoranda on the Chandra exhibition) and then he looked up. "Good afternoon, gentlemen," he said without much conviction.

"It is so nice of you to receive us, Dr. Dog," said Gupta with a reasonable facsimile of warmth and sincerity, as might be expected of a diplomat. Henry immediately felt better.

"Fat," said the director.

"I beg pardon?" Gupta was confused.

"Fat. My name is Fat Dog. Dr. Rufus Fat Dog. I am an Indian. A real one. An American Indian. I am a Cowanee. That is a branch of the Cherokee Nation."

"Yes, of course. Dr. Fat. I am an Indian, too. A real one as well, from the Republic of India. I take it you are an anthropologist?" Everybody always assumed that. If an American Indian ran a American history museum, it must be because he was an expert on tribal history or some such Indian-studies specialty.

Fat Dog gave up on his name and turned his attention to his credentials. "I am a physicist. MIT. This museum includes the history of science and technology as well as other sorts of history."

"Ah, I see, I see," said Gupta, attempting, halfheartedly, to rise above his gaffe.

"This Chandra exhibition is hardly appropriate for this museum. We are only concerned with American history, not Asian or anything else."

Gupta blanched through his walnut skin. "Does this mean that you won't—"

Fat Dog interrupted. "No, no, the secretary has ordered us to hold the exhibition and we will do so. None of our other museums will admit having suitable space available at the time you want it."

Gupta was smiling again. He really didn't care too much what Fat Dog thought as long as the exhibition was safe. "I am very glad there is no problem."

"I didn't say there wasn't any problem. The secretary just told us to hold your exhibition. She didn't say that we should abandon all control over it."

"Control over it?" asked Gupta apprehensively.

"It is Smithsonian policy to retain control over the content of any exhibition which we present in any of our museums. Who is preparing the Chandra exhibition?"

"The Ministry of Culture. I'm sure it's in very competent hands."

"That may be," said Fat Dog doubtfully. "Nevertheless, we shall have to send someone to India to see. Since your government is supposed to be paying for all the expenses, I presume that there will be money available for this travel and for any necessary consultant fees?" This was a demand, not really a question.

48

"I can go," offered Henry. "Then there won't be any need to pay for a consultant."

Gupta thought about it for a time. "I am sure we can cover travel through the excess currency program."

"Using Smithsonian excess rupees, I suppose," said Fat Dog with a touch of sarcasm.

"Exactly."

"Well, I guess I don't mind that because it won't come out of my budget. And if we have to, I suppose we can make somebody on our staff available."

"I said—" began Henry.

"It will have to be a professional," interrupted the director. "Mr. Scruggs is State Department, so he won't do."

"I quite agree," said Gupta disloyally, "a State Department representative would be regarded as an interference. It would have to be a professional museum person. May I suggest someone on your staff?" The director said nothing but looked up expectantly. "There is a young lady in, I believe, your exhibits department. I have met her a few times and she seems to have quite a feeling for things Indian. East Indian, that is. Her name is Strauss—Violet Strauss."

* * *

Henry saw Gupta to the Constitution Avenue exit of the museum and returned to the staff elevator. Showing his badge, he descended into the basement where he asked his way to the exhibits department. The wide corridor was crowded with odd bits of exhibitions, some not yet completed, or already used and now being stripped, or in some cases you simply couldn't tell what they were. Peculiar bits of stuff that could be found only in a museum basement. Since coming to the Smithsonian, Henry had been amazed at how much time and effort and stuff went into exhibits and for how short a time they were on view before things were thrown out to make room for something else. The public was seldom aware of this waste. As far as they were concerned, the show they saw on their last visit was now just gone and something else, probably unexpected, stood in its place.

Of course there were still some old halls that hadn't changed since Methuselah was a pup but there were fewer of these with each passing year. Museums were once quiet, almost moribund places of dusty reflection. Now they were pulsing, integrated machines geared to showtime.

Henry was not completely convinced that the change was for the best. It might be exciting to have new things thrown at you at carefully thought-out and programmed high speed, but there was also something missing. That something, Henry thought, was the sense of individual discovery. He remembered how it had felt as a child to hunt out and identify an object almost hidden in the great piles of odds and ends that used to fill the Smithsonian's museums. Even when the find was unlabeled, it still might stimulate imagination in a way that could not be equalled by objects in today's carefully planned exhibitions.

It probably depended upon how you learned. For people who wanted to be taught what to think, the new museums were probably fine. But if you wanted to go your own way, a good pile of miscellaneous junk was best, anytime.

Ahead, at the end of the north-south corridor, just past what appeared to be an eight-foot-high cut-away mock-up of a ship's engine gearbox, was the door to the Conservation Analytical Laboratory. As he drew closer, Henry could smell the various reagents and other chemicals employed by the mad scientists within, in their crowded and inadequately ventilated space.

To the right of CAL was the door to the Exhibits Design unit. The designers were equally as crowded and equally as mad as the conservation chemists, but they didn't smell as bad, at least not out here in the corridor. The messier parts of the office of exhibits, including production, photographic, paint, and car- pentry shops, were removed to other parts of the building's basement.

The receptionist in Exhibits Design ignored Henry. He stood in front of her desk and she sat there rather primly, he thought, staring down at some papers. She couldn't help but see him. He cleared his throat but that didn't do any good either. Perhaps she was used to having men come in to stand there staring at her and occasionally clearing their throats. Henry could see that if it hadn't been wintertime and if she had been wearing the sort of summer clothing that some women wear, there would have been something to stare at. He would have to check that out next June.

"Hello," he ventured. Henry tried to pitch his inflection so the conversation could go any direction. She had to be curious. Almost all women were curious.

She looked up. "Did you want something?"

"Well, I'd like to see—" Just then the phone rang and she immediately picked it up and announced, "Exhibits, Miss Farrell." Henry thought that he should have called first. He stood there while Miss Farrell discussed something about time card entries. She appeared to have little patience and eventually put down the phone harder than strictly necessary. She looked back at the papers on her desk.

"I'd like to see Miss Strauss," Henry said without waiting for any particular sign of Miss Farrell's attention.

"In the back," said Miss Farrell without looking up.

The back was a pair of rooms crowded with drafting tables, stools, cabinets, racks of felt-tip pens, dirty coffee cups, full ashtrays, and all sorts of pieces of paper taped or pinned to every conceivable surface, showing floor plans, perspective drawings, photos of objects, cartoons, exhibition production schedules, vacation postcards, and you name it. Smoke lay in stratified layers in the room. Henry's bronchial tubes constricted spasmodically. He coughed to clear his lungs. It didn't do much good. He went into the first stages of an asthma attack.

Most of the people who might be presumed to work there were absent. The rest—and there were three of those—were doing various things. An untidy, slightly plump black man of about Henry's age was working on a drawing. A half-full glass of red wine and a paper plate with the remains of a sandwich were on top of a low filing cabinet beside his chair. A large but not fat red-haired white man, who Henry put at about six foot four and in his thirties, was sitting on a high stool with his feet flat on the floor. A small young woman was more or less sitting in his lap except that his lap was more or less standing up so she was actually leaning against him. His large, ink-stained hands were wrapped around her, at bosom level. She looked flushed but not particularly embarrassed.

"Uh, Miss Strauss?" Henry wheezed and waited for her to reply. He hardly knew where to go from there.

"Who are you?" Miss Strauss (Henry presumed) asked.

"Henry Scruggs." Henry sounded breathless, which he was.

"Well, la-ti-dah!" was her comment. But she must have decided that Henry was somebody because she removed the redhead's fingers from her breasts and moved away from him until she was standing up straight. She was taller than Henry had at first thought. Maybe five foot three. She stood there looking at Henry. It was as though she had walked in through his eyes and was looking around inside. Her expression announced her as being amused at what she saw in there. It was uncomfortable and more than a little intimate.

Henry tried to remember why it was that he had come into the exhibits office. Exhibits. Oh, yes. "I wanted to let you know about the Chandra exhibition. We're going to be working together on it."

"We are? What is a chandra?" She had a naturally mocking voice. An edge of hardness to it.

"It is a who, not a what. Chandra was an Indian—philosopher, I guess you would call him. Sort of like Gandhi."

"I haven't heard anything about it."

"It has just been decided. I have just come from a meeting with Dr. Fat Dog and Mr. Gupta, the Indian cultural counselor. Mr. Gupta suggested having you work on the project."

"You mean Baggy? He recommended me?" Miss Strauss almost squealed. Perhaps it was her way of laughing. Henry decided she was more than a little manic.

"I guess so. His name is actually Bhagat. He said you knew about Indian culture and things like that." Henry sat down without being invited. He had to get his nose below the worst of the stratified smoke.

"I'm what you might call an expert on Indian hemp."

"You mean—?"

"Mary Jane. Grass. You know, pot."

"I know about it. But I don't think it has much to do with K. V. Chandra. He was more of an ascetic than that."

"Don't you believe it! Those Indians get high all the time! I know from experience." Miss Strauss smiled comfortably.

Henry noticed for the first time that there was something else in the air besides tobacco smoke. He looked in a nearby ashtray. The butts appeared to be hand rolled.

Violet Strauss introduced Henry around. The pudgy, industrious black man was Hy Boone. He looked up briefly to give Henry a sympathetic grin and then went back to his layout for something the captions on the drawing said was a laser exhibition. The tall, big-boned groper was Cyril Rochester. He grunted at Henry good-naturedly. Henry decided that their names were mixed up. He didn't know why, then it occurred to him that it was probably because of Jack Benny's straight man, Rochester, but then it might also be because the redhead looked like he ought to be out wrestling with large bears instead of with small though apparently willing women. Henry had a coughing spell that lasted until he ran out of air. He sat down again gasping.

"You don't look so good, Henry. Are you having a heart attack?" Miss Strauss looked unexpectedly solicitous.

"It's the smoke," Henry croaked, "it bothers my asthma."

"Let's get you out of here," suggested Miss Strauss, "it is a bit thick in here."

Miss Strauss led Henry out into the corridor and into the conservation laboratory next door. "Are you sure it isn't a heart attack? Have you ever had one before? You might not know. A lot of people just drop dead before they realize anything serious is wrong with them." She prattled on happily as she continued past the conservation laboratory's receptionist without stopping and into one of the inner laboratories. She ignored the people who were working at the benches, and picked her way past strange-looking equipment until she came to a collection of gas cylinders chained to the wall. She took a hose from a green one and handed it to Henry while she turned on the regulator valve. "Here, Henry, breathe some of this."

Henry was gasping and was beyond protesting, so he put the hose in his mouth and inhaled. He felt immediately better. He stood there inhaling the gas until he began to be light-headed.

Miss Strauss took it away from him. "It's just oxygen. I come in here all the time when I've *overindulged.*" She laughed at herself.

When they were out in the corridor again, Henry felt better, but he still had a good case of asthma. He needed to get home and take a Tedral. "Perhaps we can get together in the next day or two to talk about the exhibition," he said hurriedly, since she seemed to be set on leaving the museum.

"What you need now is a drink. We can talk about it at Clyde's." Miss Strauss grabbed Henry by the arm and dragged him toward the elevator. Resisting was out of the question.

* * *

Henry got as far as Georgetown and Clyde's front door and refused to go in. Not only was it heavy with smoke but the noise level was unbearable. "I'm sorry, Miss Strauss, but I don't think I could survive going in there."

"We'll just have to work up to it, I guess. Stick with me and in a few weeks I'll have you so you can go anywhere." She laughed uproariously at the thought, apparently, of some of the places she might take Henry. "Besides, I'm Violet."

They looked around Georgetown, but didn't see any place that wasn't both noisy and poorly ventilated. Henry drove Violet back across the Rock Creek Park bridge and uptown to the Madison Hotel. It was rush hour with no parking on Fifteenth Street, so Henry said to hell with the expense and pulled into the hotel garage. They proceeded into the cocktail lounge at the Madison. "Jeezus, Henry, this is like a morgue!" Violet said, but she sat down and Henry ordered a whiskey sour (suppressing a shudder) for Violet and a decent double Scotch for himself.

The Madison was the sort of place Henry liked. For one thing, it was quiet and civilized. For another, you could order Scotch without any danger that you might be served something that the distillers were only willing to identify with initials. Henry had long ago become convinced that good Scotch always sailed under the full name of the place where it was born, or at the very least, its maker.

After his first double he was beginning to be able to breathe again. It always seemed to work that way. He supposed that the alcohol relaxed the bronchial passages. Clever of Violet to know

54

this—seemingly instinctively. "About the exhibition," he began, "we have to get it together in less than a year. I'm afraid you may have to go to India to coordinate with the Indian Ministry of Culture."

Violet was immediately taken with the idea. Henry suspected that here was a girl who was game to try anything new. They had several more refills and talked about Chandra. Or Henry did. Bhagat's assurances to the contrary, Violet didn't appear to have ever heard of Chandra. Henry began to wonder what it was about India that Violet was so knowledgeable. But she picked up on what Henry said and bubbled with ideas.

"Let's go to my place." Violet dropped that into the conversation without preamble. They had gotten very cozy on the Madison lounge's circular settee, but they had still been talking business, more or less. To be candid, Henry's attention had been wandering from what Violet was saying to just Violet—her mouth making funny and rather attractive shapes while she talked. He was saying things that didn't quite make sense. Or maybe they did, he wasn't sure. It was probably the whiskey.

Henry paid up and they helped each other toward the door. It was quite cold on the sidewalk and Henry's lungs constricted again at the shock. This was a bit sobering and somewhere a part of Henry's mind began working properly and it told him to leave the Corvair parked in the garage and to take a cab. That probably accounted for their safe arrival and thus to some degree for the events that were to flow therefrom.

Violet's place was a row house on Hillyer Place. It was tiny. The front door opened into a living room so small that Henry's piano would have filled it completely, leaving no room for furniture and barely enough space to get around to the small staircase or the door leading to what appeared to be an eat-in kitchen capable of handling dinner parties of two. Henry took comfort that the tall redhead probably wouldn't fit into the house at all. As it was, without the piano, there could have been a couple of chairs. Instead, there were rugs and cushions strewn about on the floor in front of a fireplace that could accommodate maybe two sticks of firewood at a time. The one very low table held a hookah with two hoses and some odds and ends.

And the dog. There was a large dog, an English sheepdog. Henry could see the reason why there was no furniture.

"Herbert! Get down, Herbert! This is Henry. You are not to eat him! Bad dog!" Herbert, the dog, was either trying to wash Henry's face or to bite his nose.

"Nice doggy!" Henry said from his position squashed between the door frame and Herbert. He took hold of Herbert's paws and set them firmly on the floor. Herbert turned and rubbed his body against Henry, giving his fleas a chance to transfer to a new host. Dogs instinctively knew that Henry attracted fleas. Something in his body chemistry, no doubt. Of course Henry, being an allergic person, reacted violently to any kind of bug bites.

Henry helped Violet off with her coat. She gave him an impatient look. She wasn't used to gentlemen, apparently. Odd, since she knew Bhagat. Maybe he wasn't a gentleman around her. Keeping one eye on the dog, Henry looked around for a place to put her coat (to do both was a bit like working out billiards problems), but Violet took it from him and hung it on a nail behind the door. There was a second one for his. Definitely a two-person house, tops.

Violet set Henry to lighting a fire. She disappeared upstairs and in a few minutes returned wearing a loose but heavy cotton exercise suit. "What do you want to drink?"

"What do you have?"

"Anything you want."

"I'll have a Scotch on the rocks."

"Actually, all I've got is gin."

"I thought you said—"

"I can fix you anything you want as long as you don't mind gin in it."

"Oh." Henry asked for a Bloody Mary. He settled down on the floor in front of the fire. Of course, everywhere in the room was in front of the fire. He tried to get comfortable. First he sat with his legs straight out in front of him and his arms stiff to the floor, propping up his back like a letter *A*. Actually an upside-down letter *V* since there was no bar through it. But he couldn't drink his Bloody Mary that way, so he changed to a cross-legged sitting position. That worked for a few minutes and he got down half his drink but then his legs started going to sleep so he changed again, this time onto his stomach, propped up on his elbows, the way he used to read the Sunday funnies as a child (and sometimes as an adult). That gave him limited arm motion, but by craning back his neck he could continue working on his drink. He had gotten fairly comfortable when Herbert stepped on him and started nosing around his behind. "Go away, Herbert," he said uncomfortably.

"I'm afraid Herbert is gay," said Violet. She loaded the hookah with something from a lacquered box and lighted it. Bluish smoke drifted toward Henry.

"Tell him I'm not a dog." Henry waved away the smoke.

"It wouldn't do any good. Herbert doesn't know he's a dog. He's never been around any dogs, at least ones that look like he does. Here, have a puff." Violet handed Henry one of the hoses.

"Thanks but I don't think I'd better. I don't smoke. Why didn't you give him a name like a real dog. Rover comes to mind. Or Fido. Those are good dog names. Then there wouldn't be any confusion."

"I named him after my shrink."

"After your shrink? You have one?"

"I quit going. The dog Herbert is an economy. This way I can talk to him all the time and it doesn't cost anything."

"Yeah, but your dog can't talk back." Henry was taken with the idea but he felt there had to be something wrong with it.

"My shrink never talks either. The best ones don't. You have to do all the talking. Of course I don't think my shrink would sniff your ass, but on the other hand, you never know. He's pretty strange."

Henry drained his glass. "I'd better get going. I've got to get home and take something for my asthma. I don't think Bloody Marys work as well as whiskey, or maybe it's Herbert. I'm allergic to dogs. Particularly long-haired ones." Henry was having real trouble breathing again. Even Violet must have been able to hear his wheeze. He refrained from mentioning the smoke because Violet might take it personally. He started to get to his feet.

"Don't go!" Violet gave him her most inviting look. Henry

looked at her and thought about the long trek to his car, that is if he could remember where he had left it. Oh, yes, at the hotel. He subsided back onto the floor. "What do you take for asthma?" Violet asked. "I've got a regular drugstore upstairs."

"I can't imagine you'd have it. I take Tedral. That's a mixture of ephedrine, theophylline, and phenobarbital."

"Well, go look in the bathroom. I know I've got phenobarbital and maybe the others, too."

"Are you an asthmatic?" Henry was surprised, considering her home and work environments.

"No, I'm just a collector. Of course I could be out of what you want. I like to experiment, and they go pretty fast."

Henry climbed the stairs. They were steep and he was getting alarmingly short of breath. Maybe Violet was right and it was a heart attack. He put his hand against his chest and something seemed to be beating. He was all but convinced that the climb would be futile.

The upstairs was all one room except for the bathroom and an open closet with hanging space and shelves. There was no furniture. The bed was a large mattress and there were piles of clothes and bedding here and there around the room.

He looked in the bathroom. There were all kinds of added shelves and cabinets as well as the usual built-in mirrored cabinet over the wash basin. Toiletries, medicine bottles, and mysterious packages covered almost every available surface and filled every shelf and cabinet. Violet must drink mouthwash instead of water. There were even mounds of medicine bottles piled on the floor in corners, and some of those closest to the shower had lost their labels.

Though his first inclination was to run, the prospect of finding some sort of relief and his incaution of having had too much to drink led Henry to poking through the bottles. He found a number right away that were barbiturates of one sort or another, mostly rather old or suspiciously undated. He pocketed one with eighteen-month-old phenobarbital. He found a loose label that said ephedrine and there was an unlabeled bottle by it that looked right for ephedrine. He could see where a label the right size had come off after repeated splashings. With misgivings, he added it to his pocket. He continued his search.

There seemed to be dozens of tranquilizers and mood-altering drugs and there were odd things Henry didn't think people used anymore—paregoric, laudanum, and lots of substances Henry didn't recognize but which had all sorts of cautions on the labels. Here were some amphetamines and something called levodopa, and of all things, chloral hydrate. Henry thought he remembered that was knockout drops. He'd better watch what Violet put in his drink. Odd, most were prescriptions with names of patients that weren't Violet—men's names he didn't recognize. Perhaps Violet had worked in a pharmacy and had simply collected prescriptions people hadn't called for. Of course she would have to have worked in a lot of different drugstores, judging by the names of those that had filled the prescriptions.

Here was the tranquilizer corner—Equanil, Miltown, Bamo (??), Demerol—Henry wasn't sure but he thought Demerol perhaps didn't belong in that group.

Aha! Theophylline! Several years old, but there it was. Henry added it to his collection and returned to the floor below. He took one of each with another Bloody Mary. Bloody fool, he thought, as he looked again at the questionable ephedrine.

They were well into the third round of drinks when Henry looked at his watch. Herbert had given up on Henry, evidently deciding he was straight, and had gone to sleep in front of the fire. Henry was beginning to breathe more freely and had found that by sitting on a cushion he was able to cross his legs without cutting off all the circulation. Violet was leaning against Henry and Henry was trying to decide whether she wanted him to put his arms across her front or whether she would at least tolerate it. He had some time ago decided that when she had gotten into something more comfortable, it had not included underwear, at least not of the restricting kind.

Anyway, he could see things going in a direction, even if they were only thoughts, that made him feel guilty about Phoebe. Not very guilty, but a little bit. So he asked whether he could use the telephone. He would call Phoebe up and tell her some sort of lie about working late, not that she deserved it after running off on her Caribbean cruise.

The phone was in the kitchen, fighting for space among containers of dog food, full and empty. He called Phoebe. Phoebe wasn't home yet or had decided not to answer the phone. He returned to the living room and scratched a real or imaginary flea on his ankle.

They got comfortable again. Henry was beginning to feel the accustomed light-headedness he associated with Tedral. It wasn't only his head. He was a piece of baloney floating between two slices of light bread. He was becoming very relaxed in that characteristic way that left a small part of his brain nervous and alert, but disconnected from any other part of his body. His hands, acting without his guidance, resumed their slow encroachment on Violet's bosom while his eyes went their separate way, staring into the flickering fire. Violet stuck the mouthpiece from one of the hookah hoses in his mouth and he inhaled deeply. That, too, didn't seem to have anything to do with what else was going on. His lungs didn't constrict, but seemed to welcome the smoke. His biological systems were in a state of anarchy.

Henry felt that he was turning over slowly between his two slices of fluffy bread. He had never tried marijuana before and perhaps it was that or maybe it was the mixture of asthma drugs and the gin. Probably it was everything put together and maybe even Herbert's fleas had their effect.

He had confirmed that Violet didn't have on a bra when there was a commotion behind him. He looked around with some irritation to see that Herbert, the cheap shrink, was swatting the door. It was as near a scratch as he could manage. He woofed, making a hoarse, ragged sound.

Violet groaned. "Herbert wants to go out. I should have walked him when we came home. Poor baby," she said to Herbert, "Henry will take you out."

"I'll open the door. I am sure a psychiatrist can take care of himself outside. He can knock when he wants back in."

"He would get lost. He has a terrible sense of direction. You'll have to walk him. I'm not dressed." Violet slipped her jersey up from between Henry's hands and her front. Henry couldn't, for the moment, think of anything to say.

Herbert woofed again, this time louder. It would have shaken the furniture had there been any. As it was, it shook Henry to his feet.

A decidedly dizzy Henry was pulled by Herbert and pushed by Violet out the door. Off they went with instructions to bring back fast-food hamburgers and fries and not to forget Herbert's share. There was a cold drizzle that shocked Henry awake and it had gotten very dark. Cold as it felt, it must have been warming up because it wasn't snow. Henry wanted to head for the lights of Connecticut Avenue but Herbert had other ideas, so off into the dark toward Twenty-first Street they went. Instinctively, at first, Henry worried about muggers, but then he decided that anyone reckless enough to try it would be buggered by Herbert. Serve them right.

It was a whole different society out here in the mist and dark. Henry passed a number of pretty girls out walking their attack dogs. They smiled at him and their dogs lunged against their leashes. If he had been walking by himself the girls would have looked suspiciously at him and hurried on after their dogs had mauled him a bit. Apparently, large, awkward, fuzzy Herbert was a guarantee of Henry's bona fides. Or perhaps they all knew Herbert and were really smiling at him, not at Henry.

After numerous stops including several reverses to places previously sniffed, Herbert found the spot he liked on the steps of the Phillips Gallery and voided his bowels. Henry looked the other way and pretended he didn't know what was happening. He wasn't about to try to drag that animal over to the curb.

Henry left Violet's place long after midnight. He felt elated but finally properly guilty. He had been gloriously unfaithful to Phoebe. He wouldn't have missed the last six hours for anything he could imagine. If it hadn't been for the goddamned dog, he might have stayed forever.

Violet was noisy when engaged in what, for reasons Henry could never understand, is called making love, and it had upset her dog psychiatrist, who dealt with it by jumping ponderously up and down on the bedroom floor and woofing hoarsely. When at last Henry and Violet had grown still, Herbert had stood licking Henry's bare feet with his large wet tongue. Herbert's idea of buggery, Henry decided.

five

"You stink!" Phoebe rolled over and put the covers over her head. She didn't bother making a pretense of looking at the clock. She already knew it was almost three in the morning.

"I just had a shower," Henry protested.

"A shower! Since when have you got a shower in your office?"

"I mean before I went to work this morning," Henry lied. Or sort of lied since he had taken a shower that morning too, but it wasn't his most recent one. "And I wasn't in my office. I had to meet with the exhibits designers over in the history and technology museum." Henry wasn't going to get trapped by that. Phoebe knew he wasn't in his office. She would have called there and gotten the answering machine.

"Who is she? I can smell her on you!"

"They use lots of lacquer and things like that in exhibits. It makes the whole place smell funny."

"Liar! I know drugstore perfume when I smell it! You've also been smoking pot. That's particularly stupid for somebody with asthma."

"I was with two people. Violet and Herbert. It was strictly business."

"Business I can believe, though I'm not sure what they call it when they make a business of group sex."

Henry spent a cold night on the settee. It wasn't long enough (the settee, not the night) for him to straighten out, but at least Herbert was miles away.

*   *   *

Before Violet could be sent to India, Henry had to get hold of some money. As Gupta suggested, the money had to come from the Smithsonian's Special Foreign Currency Program.

Writing up the Chandra project as a research trip to India was a tall order. The SFCP was managed by Henry's office, the Foreign Affairs Office, but that didn't mean that Henry could get the money just for the asking. Everything had to go through an advisory council made up of scholars—mostly academics— appropriate to the field of study. Project proposals were judged competitively and the advisors weren't fond of giving money to the Smithsonian's own pet projects if it could be put to better use by their university colleagues. Most of the academics came to the advisory councils convinced that second-class scientists at the Smithsonian were already ahead of universities in feeding from the public trough, and the mediocre quality of some of the Smithsonian's in-house project proposals only served to reinforce that belief.

Henry cooked up something about research on Chandra that sounded good if you were totally gullible and knew as little about the subject as Henry did. He thought about asking Dreamy to submit the proposal to the astrophysics advisory council, figuring that they might approve it rather than go to the trouble to find out that it was nothing but the droppings of the sacred bull. Besides, the deadline was already passed for submitting proposals to the anthropology council, which should have considered it.

But Dreamy had a better idea. She tore up Henry's proposal and wrote out a one-page request for research development money. That was money to go over to India to get information needed for a project proposal. She got a couple of council members to bless the request. She was very good at leading men on without having to deliver on her obligations.

So it was that Henry got travel and per diem money in India for Violet, subject to approval of the Indo–U.S. Subcommission on Education and Culture. The Subcommission was to meet in early April and might or might not rubber-stamp the Smithsonian travel-money award. That gave Henry ten weeks during which he and Violet had to decide what they really wanted from the India trip.

* * *

Henry took to stopping over at Violet's place after work almost every day. He took the precaution of taking a Tedral (a real one, not one concocted from Violet's pharmacy) each afternoon. It was sufficiently numbing that he almost didn't notice the bites of Herbert's fleas.

It was on the third visit. They were lying on Violet's mattress in the bedroom with Herbert between them like a shaggy bundling board when Violet put the question to him: "Get me some pills, Henry." A command, actually.

"What kind of pills?" He was afraid he knew already—opium, codeine, morphine, Benzedrine, something like that?

"Those things you take."

"You mean Tedral? They're only good for asthma. You don't have asthma."

"I might discover a new use for them. Get me some. And I need some sleeping pills."

"Sleeping pills? I don't have a prescription for anything like that. I have the opposite problem—staying awake."

"Then ask your doctor for some."

"What kind?" asked Henry doubtfully. "He'll think it's funny if I ask for a particular kind."

"Oh, any kind as long as it's a barbiturate. Make sure he gives you something strong."

"Why don't you ask your doctor for some?"

"I'm already up to my limit with him. Besides, he has some idiotic idea I might commit suicide." Violet laughed as though the idea were hilarious.

"Suicide!? What makes him think that?" Henry's stomach suddenly felt hollow and queasy.

"I suppose it's because I tried it once. Actually twice, but once he knows about. That's when they locked me up." Violet raised herself over Herbert and looked down at Henry, naked and smiling. It made her look beautiful. Beautiful and crazy.

* * *

"Doctor, I need to renew my Tedral prescription."

"You must have been taking a lot lately. The drugstore just called me a few weeks ago about a refill."

"I've been spending a lot of time with a sheepdog. And besides, I lost my pill bottle. Somebody stole my jacket," Henry lied.

Dr. Pilky looked at Henry, trying to make up his mind about him. "Well, okay," he decided, "but you shouldn't take too many of these. The phenobarbital in them is addictive. It would be better if you quit seeing the dog." He reached for his pad and wrote out a prescription.

"And, uh, doctor—"

"Yes?"

"You better give me a prescription for some sleeping pills, too. Something strong," Henry blurted out. "I haven't been sleeping very well recently."

Dr. Pilky looked back through Henry's file before he answered. "No, I don't believe that would be such a good idea. Not while you're taking the Tedral. Anyway, you've never mentioned having sleeping problems before. Try some warm milk. It's probably only temporary."

Thus dismissed, Henry went back to Violet with only the Tedral. She sulked for a while but after several trips upstairs and several runs of the hookah, she was her old manic self.

To ensure that he was back in Violet's good graces, he took her out shopping. One thing he had learned living with Phoebe was that shopping, if you could stand to do it, always made things better. Shopping with Violet had the same result, though it was rather different in all other respects. Violet was a pure impulse buyer. They came back with fire engine red shoes from Massey's and four pairs of incompatible green stockings. Henry insisted on some warm lounging pajamas with a convenient zipper in the right place.

* * *

It was perhaps a week before Phoebe got sick and tired of Henry and changed the locks on the doors to Henry's house. He came home to find a stack of suitcases sitting on the front porch. A cursory check showed that she had packed an adequate selection of his winter clothing. That there were no summer things seemed to indicate that she thought there was a possibility that he might come to his senses, eventually. He rang the doorbell, but there was no answer. He thought he saw a living room window curtain move ever so slightly. But it was dark and 2:00 A.M. so he couldn't be sure.

Every time that he left Violet's place, she always said, "Don't go," and hung on him with her mouth all soft and inviting. She used her bosom like a sponge, soaking him up, holding him there. It was a bit disquieting, therefore, when he returned to her place an hour after he left it, but laden with all his baggage. She had taken something and was groggy. Perhaps her uppers had crashed. "Goddamn, Henry, you woke me up." She turned her back on him and climbed the stairs to bed.

Living with Violet was distinctly different from stopping by for drinks, drugs, and sex. For one thing, hers was a household without books, magazines, or newspapers. Not even TV. Not to mention furniture. There was just Violet, pot, other drugs of one sort or another, Herbert, and more Violet. And now Henry. Oh, yes, and the radio. Violet had a clock radio that played constantly what Henry thought of as elevator and supermarket music. Henry had tried to turn it off the first time he had gone to bed with Violet but she had pitched a fit. She wouldn't say why she wanted it on all the time but Henry was beginning to think that she might have some sort of auditory hallucination that she blocked out with constant sound. Henry decided that if he could put up with Herbert, he could stand the damn radio. At least until spring came and he could sleep outside.

But otherwise, it was a household of suspended animation. Nothing happened except the aforementioned activities. Henry missed his piano and had he been candid about it, he was beginning to miss Phoebe. You could talk to Phoebe about something other than whether something felt good or bad, as the case may be.

Henry called up Phoebe at her office. She wasn't answering the home phone anymore.

"Phoebe? Don't hang up!"

"I don't want to talk to you."

"But it's about my piano. I want to come get it."

"I'm holding it for ransom."

"You're already holding my house for ransom!"

"I was given that in the separation agreement."

"We never had any agreement. You just took it."

Click. Henry heard a dial tone.

Henry tried to get back to work, but he wasn't having much luck. He fixed a cup of tea to use to wash down his late-afternoon Tedral. It was Friday and Henry couldn't imagine what the weekend was going to be like. He hadn't ever spent a weekend with Violet. The mid-February weather was cold and raw, but perhaps they could go somewhere and not just lie on the floor and drink and smoke pot and engage in sex. Henry was tired of pot. He couldn't tell that it had any significant effect on him except to aggravate his asthma. He was now up to three twelve-hour Tedrals a day and losing ground. For the first time in his life, he really couldn't sleep. Perhaps he ought to go back to see Dr. Pilky. He had laid in a supply of Scotch so he would have something decent to drink, but perhaps that was a mistake. He really couldn't function too well with so many pills and so much hard liquor.

"You are going to meet some of my friends tonight," Violet announced on the way home.

"Humph!" Henry said. He was so spaced out that he had run through a red light and had gotten a ticket. His first moving violation in all the years he had been driving. The cop had bawled him out. Unnecessarily, Henry thought. He felt bad enough about it already.

Henry decided that it was unfair to blame his lapse on Violet. He would try to be nice. "Your friends? I would like to meet them." That was patently untrue. Unless they were as good in bed as Violet, Henry couldn't imagine why anybody would want to meet a bunch of pot-heads—particularly twenty-year-old singles. "They haven't been over," Henry continued to pursue it.

"They've been staying away. They don't feel comfortable around establishment people."

"And I'm an establishment person?" Henry never had thought he was. He was a liberal Democrat with atheist and anarchist tendencies. He believed in the divine right of revolution.

"You were, but getting kicked out of your house has made you one of us. One of life's losers." Violet smiled chummily.

Henry wasn't sure why Violet thought he ought to feel flattered.

*   *   *

Violet dressing up to go out proved to be the same as Violet getting undressed for an evening at home by the fire: woolly trousers, a sweater six sizes too big, and no bra. Henry put on the sort of clothes he would wear to cut a Christmas tree in the woods: corduroys and a turtleneck. But Violet made him change back into a suit with a tie and a vest. "I want you to look nice for my friends," she explained.

"But you aren't dressed up," he complained.

"I don't have to impress anybody."

Henry's asthma was getting worse. He was breathless and took an extra Tedral to be on the safe side. He was sure everybody would be smoking. Something. Three hours apart on a twelve-hour pill. Too close, but he needed it. The theophylline in the Tedral was making his heart race.

Henry wanted to drive, but Violet wouldn't hear of it. "You are already zonked. I'll drive."

"You will be 'zonked' before the evening is over. You always are. I won't get any worse. The Tedral will wear off."

"I'm used to driving half out of my mind. So I'll drive. You can ride in the back if you're nervous." Violet had never mastered a manual shift and couldn't begin to handle the Corvair's four-on-the-floor, so they took her car, a dented Datsun automatic. They sailed forth into the night. Fortunately a dry, clear one, though cold.

Their destination was a house on Capitol Hill, not far from Henry's own house, the one Phoebe had expropriated. Violet parked illegally, as usual, and they descended a few steps to an

English basement apartment, the usual sort with one long room, a kitchenette and a bath. A white man with an Afro answered the door. "Whoozis?" he asked Violet.

"This is Henry. Henry, say hello to Burt."

Henry extended his hand. Burt looked at it and then again at Henry. He didn't take it, but turned and said to the people inside, "It's Vi and some old guy." He led the way into the room.

There were two others there, one rather pretty and wholesome blond girl who had been dressed by her wicked stepmother and a young man with a ponytail and sideburns. They were introduced, respectively, as Hazel and Floyd. Hazel seemed to be at home and was serving drinks from a well-stocked bar. She asked Henry what he wanted. He looked at the labels. Mostly house brands. Something said it was Scotch and had a pretentious name. He asked to have some poured over ice. Hazel put in a cube and filled up the glass, a big one.

The apartment looked to be furnished from the Salvation Army Store, the one on the alley with the cheap stuff, but at least there was something to sit on. Henry found a place to sit on the bed. It had not been made up.

Henry did a quick appraisal of the group. At forty-four he was just about twice as old as any of the others. True, he had been letting his hair grow, but it would take a while before it got unfashionably long. Right now it only looked as though he needed a haircut. He was never going to look like these young men because his hair was too far gone on top. Besides, he wasn't really sure what sort of person Violet wanted him to be.

In a little bit, Henry began to understand why Violet did without furniture. Having something to sit on kept your head up in the pot smoke. Henry had declined to smoke, but it didn't seem to make any difference. He was getting distinctly light-headed. He sat there and smiled, trying to look interested in what the others were saying. They were talking about people he didn't know and nobody offered any explanations.

During Henry's second drink, others arrived. This time there was Tyrone, a black with a real Afro, and Red Rosa, a small, dark, intense young white woman wearing an androgynous sweater, a minimal leather miniskirt, and small round glasses. They brought numerous packages which, when unwrapped, turned out to be food. Fancy party food, and lots of it. And more bottles. This time some Red Label and White Label. Rosa and Tyrone settled on the bed with Henry.

Tyrone dug a small pipe out of his pocket and lit up. Prevailing winds brought the smoke directly by Henry's nose. He took a big drink in hopes it might immunize him.

"What you do, man? You an artist?"

Henry shifted uncomfortably under Tyrone's gaze, but he couldn't move much because of Rosa. "What makes you think that?"

"You got a little bitty beard, man. Like you gotta make some kind of a statement but you don't want to frighten nobody." Tyrone stroked his dense thicket of sideburns unconsciously. Henry expected a fox or a rabbit to run out. Or a covy of quail.

"This is the best I could do. I'm not very hairy, I suppose."

"No, you sure ain't," said Tyrone sympathetically. His gaze became fixed on Henry's receding hairline.

Henry thought of it as receding, but to be truthful, he might have admitted it looked more like low tide. "I'm not an artist. I work for the State Department."

"Oh, you do, huh?" It was obvious Tyrone considered this a conversation stopper. He sat silently, one hand extending behind Henry to fondle Rosa, who was drinking vodka and smoking something. Tyrone dragged on his own pipe and clouds drifted in toward Henry from both sides.

Henry felt he ought to say something. After all, they were Violet's friends. And, if things continued as they were going, they would eventually be his friends. Henry repressed a shudder and tried again. "It's all right, I'm leaving the State Department. I didn't approve of our Vietnam policy and now I think we're being stupid about Cuba." Henry racked his brain for something else he ought to disapprove, but he was getting too muzzy from the pot smoke to think clearly.

"Yeah? What's Vietnam?"

Henry ignored that. Everybody knew what Vietnam was. At least everybody over thirty. Tyrone was baiting him. "What do you do?" Henry was baiting Tyrone, now. He expected Tyrone was unemployed.

"Catering, man. I'm in catering. I pour out drinks at parties for you rich honkeys."

"Why do you do that?" Henry was curious. He couldn't imagine Tyrone in black tie behind the bar at an embassy party.

"I like to spit in the glasses of the rich and powerful." Tyrone paused a moment to let Henry's stomach flip over. "And I like to be close to a good supply of booze."

That made sense. Henry looked around. The liquor supply looked like the stuff liquor wholesalers pushed off on catered affairs. Stuff good enough not to drive away business but stuff with a high markup. "Is that where the food came from?"

"Yeah. We had some shrimp, too, but it begin to stink."

Henry decided to skip the food except for things like crackers and cheese. The density of smoke was increasing greatly. Hazel put on a record of folk rock from the mid-sixties. Henry didn't mind that too much. He hated most other kinds of popular music, but folk rock was different. Without counting he poured his third drink. He started talking to Rosa.

"How do you know Violet?" he asked. The bed sagged a lot and it pushed him together with Rosa. It would have been unthinkable to try to ignore her. Tyrone had drifted over to the bar and had not made it back, having now, apparently, the hots for Hazel.

Rosa turned toward him and blew smoke at him from about six inches away. "We were roommates."

"In college?"

"Do I look like a fucking college girl? In a mental hospital."

"Oh," said Henry and tried to think of what to say next. Rosa saved him the trouble.

"I was named for Rosa Luxembourg. Sometimes people call me Red Rosa. My parents are Communists."

"Oh," said Henry again. He was silent for a minute. "How interesting."

"My parents don't give a flying fuck about anything. I don't either. Except for free love. I like that part." Rosa's hand went exploring for Henry's zipper.

"Why were you in the hospital with Violet? If you don't mind my asking," Henry hastened to add. It did the trick. For the moment it distracted Rosa from making a direct assault.

"Suicide," she said matter-of-factly. "Except Violet is only an amateur. I tried six times. I almost succeeded twice." Rosa pulled up the sleeves of her sweater and turned over her wrists. The undersides were badly scarred.

"Why did you want to—to do that?"

"I'm not going to live long anyway. I don't want to get old," she said contradictorily. She looked at Henry to see if she had hurt his feelings, but evidently decided she didn't care.

"I want you all to come to my abortion," said Hazel out of the blue. "As soon as I can arrange it."

"Girl, they'll never let you stop that baby," said Tyrone. "It's gonna be a fine striped chile."

"Half-black babies aren't striped, silly, they are gray or maybe it's brown," replied Hazel.

"Tell them you're going to kill yourself, then they'll let you," advised Rosa. "That's what I do."

Violet got them off that subject by passing among the guests holding something in a cupped hand. "Hold out your drinks, everybody, it's pill time." She plopped a pill into each glass.

Henry automatically held out his glass and then covered it with his other hand. "No, I don't think I'd better."

"Oh, come on, Henry, don't be a party pooper." Violet pulled his hand away and dropped something in his glass. He watched it while it slowly dissolved. What the hell!

* * *

Henry didn't remember much after that. His arms felt like they were strapped down. He forced his eyes to open. There was a gray haze in front of him. My God, he thought, I've gone blind! He turned his head a little and something moved in front of him. He tried to focus his damaged eyes on it. It appeared to be a clear plastic tube. Without his glasses he couldn't see very well, anyway. Something was bothering his nose. He wrinkled it up. It was sort of numb, but there seemed to be something clipped to it.

For the first time in it seemed like weeks he could breathe

73

reasonably freely. He inhaled deeply. Whooee. It made him light-headed. He waited a few minutes and when his head cleared he tried to sit up. There were things hooked to him. He forced his right arm to move. It was terribly tired, leaden, even, but he got it to move and he felt around him. There was a little tent of some sort over him.

"He's awake, nurse," said a voice far away. It was a familiar voice but he couldn't place it. There was a commotion and the gray plastic tent was lifted. A woman replaced it and a hand fiddled around his nose and adjusted something.

"Good afternoon, Mr. Scruggs. Nice to have you back with us."

Henry tried to say something but his lips and throat were too dry. The strange face disappeared and in a moment it returned with a paper cup, which it put to his lips. Henry tried to drink, but most of the contents spilled. The cool water felt good in contrast to his splitting headache. Headache? Had he had a stroke or something? The nurse disappeared again.

The tent moved again and this time there was Phoebe's face. It smiled at him. "Well, Henry, have you finally come to your senses?"

* * *

"Where am I?"

"Not very imaginative, Henry. I should have thought you would have said something more original."

"I'm not trying to entertain. I'm just trying to find out where I am."

"Intensive care. Do you know who I am?"

"Of course I know who you are, Phoebe. That doesn't have anything to do with my not knowing where I am. I want my piano."

"Well! That's a relief. They thought your brain might have been damaged."

"Why, for heaven's sake?"

"The rescue squad said you weren't breathing. After the accident."

"Accident? I don't know anything about any accident!"

"Well, you were certainly there. There when little Violet tried

74

to take a shortcut through the Capitol grounds. She tried to jump the west fence with her car. She failed. I don't know why, she was flying high enough."

"Was—was she hurt?"

"Bruised a bit but she had already had a general anesthesia, so I doubt she felt anything until the day before yesterday."

"Day before . . . how long have I been here?"

"This is Monday. They brought you in on Friday night."

"Good lord! Is Violet in the hospital?"

Phoebe looked annoyed at Henry for asking. "She's got a nice private room at the city jail."

* * *

Violet got out of jail before Henry was released from the hospital. There had been a preliminary hearing for which Henry was asked to give a deposition. He could honestly say he didn't remember anything. Since he hadn't been driving, it wasn't his car, and there had been nothing incriminating in his pockets, he had not been charged. They had made up for it by charging Violet with everything they could think of. Fortunately for her, all they could think of were things like drunken driving, reckless endangerment, destruction of government property (the Capitol grounds and fence), having an uninspected vehicle, and a revoked driver's license. Had they sampled the contents of her stomach, they could have added to the list considerably. Had she not already dropped off Tyrone and Rosa, they could have expanded the list to include cocaine.

* * *

Phoebe had not been back since she saw that Henry was not going to die right away. Henry was allowed to recuperate in peace except for the busybody nurses. Finally he finished his cortisone series and was weaned to theophylline. Together, they cleared up his lungs, but the theophylline made him as jumpy as a cat, not to mention the urinary problems. However, the extra exercise was good for him and he was clearly on the mend.

He was dressed and waiting for the doctor to authorize his release when Violet came by to see him. "Henry, you look terrible. Did you have a heart attack?" Violet always liked to suppose the worst. "Maybe you'd better stay in the hospital."

"What the hell kind of pill did you put in my drink?"

"Which one?"

"At the party. You put one in everybody's drink. What was it?"

"Is that all you remember?"

"Of course that's all I remember. It must have knocked me out."

"Well, it's just as well, I guess. It wasn't anything particular. Just something to cheer you up. You were so gloomy you made everybody nervous."

"I wasn't gloomy! I was just having a talk with that girl, Rosa."

"I'll say you weren't gloomy. You were the life of the party! But only after the pills, of course."

"If you knew what was going on why did you wreck the Capitol grounds? You could have gotten us killed!"

"It's your fault! I was just trying to save you, you ought to be grateful! You acted like you had died. I thought you had had a heart attack. You are the right age for it. I was just trying to get you to the hospital. I thought there was a way to get through the goddamned fence!" Violet laughed. She thought the goddamned fence was funny.

"I'm sorry." Henry didn't feel like arguing. "Just take me home. I think I'll even be glad to see Herbert." Henry sighed, wondering whether he ought to revise that last bit.

"I don't think so, Henry. I don't think it would be such a good idea for you to stay at my place anymore."

"Not stay—!" Henry was at a loss for something to say.

"You don't really fit in. They didn't want to come over to my house before they met you and now that they have it will be worse."

"But—"

"You can't expect me to give up all my friends for someone so—so middle-aged!"

"It was the goddamned vest. I told you it was wrong."

"Face it, Henry, you're miscast as my lover."

Henry sat on the bed in a state of shock. He could feel his face fall. Wrinkles grew where rosy cheeks had gone before.

"Don't look so sad, Henry. You had a good time while it

lasted. Nothing is forever. You can go home to Phoebe. I'll make her take you back."

* * *

Henry moved into a furnished room. Phoebe sent him a postal change of address card—filled out for Point Barro, Alaska. Henry found it right away on the map; he had looked at the farthest place served by the U.S. Postal Service.

The last weeks of February were very hard. If there had been nothing to do but drink and have sex at Violet's place, there was now nothing to do but drink. Henry tried doing his drinking at singles bars, but the liquor was expensive and lousy and a singles bar is nowhere to be if you don't want to talk to anybody. He went out and bought a case of toothpicks and a case of Duco cement and started working on a model of the Firth of Forth railway bridge. During the nights he glued toothpicks together and during the days he sat in his office peeling the dried cement off of his fingers.

Henry had completed the first arch when the Indo–U.S. Subcommission met and approved Violet's trip to India. He called Bhagat and told him it was a go.

"I heard, Henry. It is the best time for an American to go. It is still *shishira,* the cold season."

"I doubt she will feel the need of any more cold weather."

"It will seem warm enough after Washington. Particularly in the south where she will need to go."

"Yes—well, we should get together with Violet and brief her on the trip. She will need to know whom to see in India."

"No, I don't think it will be necessary."

Henry was silent a moment. Had Violet been in touch with Bhagat? "I still think she needs to talk to you," he probed.

"I can talk to her on the plane. I'll be going back to India with her."

Henry couldn't very well complain. It was a good idea if Bhagat was willing to do it. Henry agreed to have the Smithsonian's travel office make the reservations.

Henry got them on a PanAm flight to New Delhi only days before Violet was to come to trial for the Capitol-grounds incident and before a warrant was to be issued for her because of a long string of unpaid parking tickets she and the Datsun had accrued before it met its end on the Capitol fence.

* * *

The call came at 10:14. It was unexpected. Henry's phone had only been in for less than two days and nobody knew his number, and more to the point, nobody cared. Nobody except whoever was ringing now and must have gone to a lot of trouble to get the number from the phone company. Of course it was probably a wrong number. Henry wiped the glue off of his fingers and picked up the phone.

"Hello?"

"Henry! Is that you?" It was Violet and she sounded a long way off.

"Of course it's me—I," he corrected himself. "Are you in India already?"

"I'm in London!" Violet was shouting into the phone. Henry decided she must be at a public phone.

"I gave you a ticket to New Delhi. That's where you're supposed to go!"

"I'm going. Baggy and I have a few minutes in London."

"Sweet of you to call," said Henry with just a touch of sarcasm.

"Listen, Henry? You've got to do something for me!"

Henry was silent, waiting. He feared the worst.

"Henry, are you there?"

"Yes, Violet. What do you want me to do?"

"You've got to rescue Herbert. I forgot all about him. You've got to keep him while I'm gone."

"Where is he? In your apartment?"

"Yes. You have to go get him now. The poor baby is probably frantic!"

"I don't have a key. I gave it back to you." Henry was prepared to let Herbert starve.

"Break in, silly!" Violet paused. "Oh! Henry? They're calling our plane. We've got to go. Bye!"

Henry stood there holding the now-dead telephone. He slowly replaced it on its cradle. He cursed. He would feed and water Herbert. Look at the time! And he would have to walk him, but take him in? Never! Henry put the cap back onto the Duco

78

cement and surveyed his bridge. What wouldn't Herbert do with that?

There was little traffic on that cold February night, so Henry made good time to Violet's apartment. He used a credit card to get in the door. Quieter than breaking a windowpane and required no repairs.

Herbert knocked Henry back against the wall. He was glad to see him so he let him live. For the moment. Herbert didn't seem in immediate need of going for a walk and a casual inspection revealed that this was because he had found a substitute for the sidewalk, in the kitchen. Henry started to clean it up and then decided that after it had dried for a few weeks, it would be less odious. And Violet would have to deal with it so it wouldn't be odious at all.

He fixed Herbert his supper and sat down on one of Violet's cushions to wait for Herbert to eat. Then he and Herbert went for a walk through the dark and cold. All the pretty single blondes with their shepherd attack dogs were apparently snug in their little apartments round about Dupont Circle. They were probably in bed with young single men whose boxers and Dobermans had guaranteed their acceptability. Henry was going to have to think about getting a dog. Perhaps a plastic one on wheels that he could pull along behind him when he went hunting for those girls.

In the meantime there was Herbert. He would just have to stay by himself tonight. There must have been plenty of nights when Violet had not made it home so he must be accustomed to it by now. Tomorrow Henry would see about a boarding stable.

 **Six**

"May I sit down?"

The Commons was already full, with people lined up outside waiting, and Henry was sitting by himself at one of the little tables in the north bay. He knocked over his chair getting to his feet.

Phoebe sat down as casual as you please. "Thursdays are always crowded it seems."

"It's because all the docents come in for training on Thursdays. They like to eat in the Commons, God knows why."

"It makes them feel like a part of this hallowed institution."

"A Smithsonian T-shirt would be easier on the digestion."

"Maybe. I never ate one." Phoebe sat there for a while watching the line at the buffet. It had stacked up waiting for the louts in the kitchen to refill the hot entrees but now it was moving again. She got up and hurried over to get in line.

Henry watched her go. He wondered what it was he saw in Violet. Raw sex and madness, he supposed. And women didn't have any monopoly on being fickle.

The Commons was a large room situated at the west end of the Castle. The Castle itself was a Norman-Romanesque, red stone building, designed in the 1840s by James Renwick. Ren-

80

wick chose as his model the ancestral English castle of the Dukes of Northumberland, for the very good reason that James Smithson, who endowed and gave his name to the Smithsonian, was the illegitimate son of Hugh Smithsonian, First Duke of Northumberland (actually, First Duke in the Third Creation, an odd feature of English titles we won't go into here).

Viewed from the outside, the Commons looked for all the world like a chapel of almost church proportions, with an altarless apsis on the north, or Mall, end (an error in siting, of course, perhaps the reason why the Smithsonian has remained over the years somewhat disoriented from the church) and a rose window on the south.

This room had recently been reborn as a sort of university commons, or dining hall, on the occasion of the establishment of the Woodrow Wilson International Center for Scholars in the center and west end of the Castle. Even though the regular Smithsonian staff rather overwhelmed the WWICS scholars at lunchtime in the Commons, the place managed to keep a sort of cloistered, university atmosphere.

Henry always sat in the apsis if he could. It had nothing to do with religious feeling; it was closer to the buffet.

Phoebe returned and sat down again. Henry had given up on his short ribs, which were mostly bone and fat. He made a sign to the dessert-and-drinks lady across the room who understood immediately that Henry wanted her to save him his usual piece of chocolate truffle pie before it was all gone. He suppressed a qualm about the choice he was soon going to have to make between chocolate and his current suit size. He settled down to wait for his dessert and tea, and to watch Phoebe eat. She ate like a lady, but a businesslike lady with an orderly mind. Violet ate—he tried to picture Violet eating. Sensual and impulsive, that was it. But greedy and sloppy. Of course, there were times when Violet would ignore food entirely. She ignored it in her kitchen, for example, and her impulses might just as well be not to eat as to eat. Henry remembered his week with Violet. He was always either hungry or eating when he wasn't hungry. It had been quite upsetting.

He was sorry Phoebe didn't have mashed potatoes with gravy

and peas. Nothing told you more about a person. A really orderly person would arrange the potatoes like a volcano with gravy for lava in the crater, and would construct a levee around the base to protect the peas in case the gravy should come pouring down the mountain while the potatoes were being eaten. Properly done, each forkful of potato would be dipped in the little lake of gravy. At the other extreme, everything gets mixed together. Gravy on peas. Ugh! As a child, Henry had enjoyed digging a tunnel under the gravy so that at the last moment it would come rushing out all at once to be caught in the dam at the base. He supposed he was fundamentally disorderly. Perhaps that is what explained Violet's attraction.

Phoebe eyed Henry's pie when it arrived. In fact, she couldn't take her eyes off it. Henry took his unused spoon and scooped off the point, the best part, and gave it to her. Her eyes grew wet. She curled up her tongue and used it to lick off little bits of the chocolate from the spoon. She alternated licks with sips of coffee. She was stubborn about the coffee. Henry had tried to win her over to tea but had long ago given up.

"Henry, I can't keep a boy separated from his piano any longer." Phoebe dug into her pocketbook and came up with a shiny brass key. She plopped it down in front of Henry. "You can pay for my lunch." She dabbed her mouth daintily with one of the Commons' totally nonabsorbent napkins and left, having exacted her last bit of retribution.

Henry ordered another cup of tea and heedless of the people waiting for tables, sat a while in the Commons pondering things, mostly his piano. He would start with the *Wiener Urtext Edition* of the Haydn sonatas. No, the J. C. Bach *Opus 17 Sonatas* would be a better place to begin. He would sneak off from work and get home early so Phoebe wouldn't hear how badly out of practice he was.

* * *

Henry returned to his office in the A&I tower. Violet had been gone almost a week. Time enough for something to have happened. Indeed, the 2:00 P.M. mail delivery brought a State Department telegram. The telegram had been several days getting to Henry. The State Department sent routine cables over to the

82

Office of the Secretary by the regular messenger run the day after they were received. Hannah would send the cables on to Henry by interoffice mail, whenever. Thus Henry usually got cables in his hands two days after they were received in Washington unless Hannah mislaid them. Things of cosmic importance were handled in the same way except that the desk officer at State would call Henry and read him a copy. That is, if he got around to it.

Violet's message was not cosmic. It barely qualified as routine:

UNCLASSIFIED

TO: SECSTATE, WASHINGTON, D.C.
FROM: AMEMBASSY, NEW DELHI
SUBJECT: SMITHSONIAN - CHANDRA EXHIBITION

DEPARTMENT PASS SMITHSONIAN, ATTN. HENRY SCRUGGS:

SMI REP. VIOLET STRAUSS REQUESTS EMB. PASS FOLLOWING MESSAGE: QTE.

1) HENRY, YOU WOULDN'T BELIEVE INDIA. BAGGY SAYS REAL INDIA IS IN VILLAGES. SUGGEST YOU EXTEND MY TRAVEL ORDERS ANOTHER THREE WEEKS PLUS US DOLS 2,000 EQUIVALENT INDIAN RUPEES FOR LOCAL TRAVEL AND THINGS SO I CAN VISIT AND TAKE PHOTOS.

2) CALLED ON MINCULT YESTERDAY. THEY UNAWARE OF CHANDRA PROJECT. SAID THEY WOULD LOOK INTO IT.

3) IN MEANTIME I AM PRACTICING YOGA EXERCISES FOR INCREASING MAITHUNA PLEASURE AND BAGGY IS SERVING AS MY SHAKTI AND SHOWING ME THE NEW DELHI TOURISTS NEVER SEE. YAB-YUM. HENRY, DO YOU KNOW ANYTHING ABOUT TANTRIC SEX AND EROTIC MYSTICISM? ABOUT KAMA KALPA? IT CERTAINLY MAKES YOU UNDERSTAND WHY THERE ARE SO MANY INDIANS. YOU AND PHOEBE OUGHT TO TRY IT. THAT IS IF SHE HAS LET YOU BACK INTO HER BED. BAGGY AND I CAN BE REACHED ROOM 65 OBEROI HOTEL NEW DELHI UNTIL THURSDAY. IN THE MEANTIME I HAVE TO PRACTICE MY VYOMAPADA-UTTANA-BANDHA. KEEP YOUR MULADHARA CHAKRA DRY. VIOLET ENDQTE.

It took Henry a while to simmer down. Damn Bhagat and his exotic Eastern sex. Naturally Violet would go for that. She would go for anything new that was a thrill. He tried to put it out of his mind but his curiosity got the better of him and he went over to the reference library in the Natural History Museum to look for a copy of the *Kama Sutra* and something on Tantric terms. He was sorry he did—damn that Violet!

Still, Violet's advice wasn't completely bad. There were some things it might be interesting to try as long as Phoebe didn't get the idea it had been Violet's suggestion.

As for Violet's demand for more travel support, Henry was going to forget she asked. If she was hungry, he would hear from her more often.

* * *

It was good to be back with his piano again. He found he wasn't much worse than usual. Either that or his standards had decayed along with everything else touched by Violet. Anyway, after the evening of Bach (J. C.) and Haydn, he was ready to celebrate. He went out Saturday morning and bought the best tape-recording equipment he could find and afford and went home to spend the rest of the weekend with the Mozart four-hand sonatas. He had in mind to record one set of hands on tape and then to play duets with himself.

The results were pretty bad. In the first place, Henry had always been rather casual about keeping the strict time that is essential to playing duets. Second, it was hard to hear the tape recorder over the piano, so playing the second part was about like playing it without accompaniment.

Phoebe stood it as long as she could and then went out shopping even though it was a raw, rainy day. After a while, Henry gave it up and prepared medallions of veal poached in Marsala wine to make it up to Phoebe. There was no use antagonizing her while he was still on probation. Phoebe couldn't resist good food.

* * *

Another week went by. The weather was getting warmer and everyone, it seemed, looked for reasons to be outside. It was, as a matter of fact, Henry's best time of year. The weather was not so cold that it aggravated his asthma and not so warm that it made the trees bloom and bring on his spring hay fever. He took to walking to work, arriving well before eleven A.M.

"Here you are, Scruggs," Gerald said one morning when Henry came lightly up the stairs, glowing with his renewed vigor.

84

"Your little piece wants her money," Gerald said nastily. "I suppose drugs are expensive even in India." He held out a State Department telegram to Henry.

Henry declined to look at it until he had plugged in his teakettle. While it heated, he collapsed in his chair (his physical renewal was only skin deep) and read the telegram:

UNCLASSIFIED

FROM: AMEMBASSY, NEW DELHI
TO: SECSTATE, WASHINGTON, D.C.
SUBJECT: SMITHSONIAN - CHANDRA EXHIBITION

DEPARTMENT PASS SMITHSONIAN, ATTN. HENRY SCRUGGS:

SMI REP. VIOLET STRAUSS REQUESTS EMB. PASS FOLLOWING MESSAGE: QTE.

1) HENRY, WHERE IS MY MONEY?

2) GOING TO LIVE IN AN ASHRAM FOR A FEW WEEKS. BAGGY SAYS IT IS ONLY WAY TO GET UNDER SKIN OF CHANDRA. APPARENTLY IN ASHRAMS YOU STAY HIGH ON HASHISH ALL THE TIME AND TRIP ON OTHER SENSUAL DELIGHTS. YOU CAN REACH ME CARE OF ADAIR AT THE EMBASSY.

3) SENDING YOU 14 ROLLS EXPOSED FILM VIA AIR POUCH. YOU HAVE TO SEND ME 35 ROLLS FILM IMMEDIATELY. 25 ROLLS PAN ATOMIC-X AND 10 TRI-X. SEND 36 EXPOSURE ROLLS ONLY. HARD TO CHANGE FILM WHEN YOU ARE HIGH.

4) WHILE I THINK OF IT, MY T/O AMENDMENT HAS TO INCLUDE BANARAS AND TRIVANDRUM. BAGGY SAYS I SIMPLY HAVE TO SEE THEM. LOVE, IN MY FASHION, BUT DON'T LET IT GO TO YOUR HEAD. OTHER LOCATIONS OKAY. VIOLET. ENDQTE.

Nothing else was heard from Violet for two weeks. Henry called Bhagat's office at the Indian Embassy but they would only say Bhagat was on home leave and they didn't know when he would be back.

The pouch shipment of film arrived ten days after Violet's cable. No letter was enclosed. Henry took the film over to the photo lab in the History and Technology Building, where it was developed right away only because Henry threatened to do it himself. Ordinarily, they liked to age any kind of work order

85

until the emulsion peeled off the film. A few stabilization prints showed that whatever else Violet had been doing, she was sending back some dandy pictures of India. Henry fancied himself a photographer, but Violet's photographs of people were ones he could never have taken. They were too intrusive. Henry didn't know how Violet could go up to strangers in another culture and take such intimate photographs. Actually, he did know how Violet could do it. She had that sort of personality. She could go up to God or the Devil, it didn't matter which, and take a picture of Him brushing his teeth (if such beings have teeth, of course).

Knowing he shouldn't, Henry went anyway to Dreamy to beg for more travel money. Violet seemed determined to stay and she was producing useful stuff. He had to make sure Violet could afford to be an honest woman if she chose to, which she probably wouldn't. Dreamy approved the travel order amendment and handed it back to Henry with a look that said he was creating obligations that would haunt him later.

Whatever Violet was accomplishing, it wasn't what she'd been sent to India to do. There was still no indication of what, if anything, the Ministry of Culture was doing about the Chandra exhibition. Of course, Henry could fill up the exhibit hall with Violet's photos. They might make a better exhibition than would something produced by the Indian bureaucracy. Henry shuddered at the thought of what the Indian equivalent of the United States Information Agency (USIA) might think fitting for an American museum audience.

* * *

It was time to send a cable to New Delhi and remind Violet of her mission.

UNCLASSIFIED

FROM: SECSTATE, WASHINGTON, D.C.
TO: AMEMBASSY NEW DELHI
SUBJECT: SMITHSONIAN - CHANDRA EXHIBITION
ATTN: CAO ADAIR BLAKE

SMITHSONIAN REQUESTS FOLLOWING MESSAGE FROM HENRY SCRUGGS BE PASSED TO VIOLET STRAUSS: QTE.

1) HAVE YOU BEEN BACK IN CONTACT WITH INDIAN MINISTRY OF CUL-TURE? IF NOT, PLEASE DO SO AT ONCE.

2) ESSENTIAL THAT WE BE INFORMED OF DETAILS CHANDRA EXHIBITION PLAN AND THAT YOU REVIEW CONTENT AND REPORT YOUR FINDINGS SOONEST.

3) IF INDIANS NOT DOING ANYTHING ABOUT CHANDRA, YOU MUST COME HOME IMMEDIATELY AND WE WILL CANCEL EXHIBITION.

4) ANY VISITS TO OTHER PARTS OF INDIA MUST COME AFTER COMPLE-TION MINCULTURE ASSIGNMENT.

5) YOUR FILM HAS ARRIVED AND HAS BEEN DEVELOPED. PICTURES ACCEPTABLE. WILL POUCH FRESH FILM AS SOON AS I CAN GET IT FROM PHOTO LAB. SIGNED HENRY, ENDQTE.

For days there was no answer from Violet. Something must have happened to her. The silence was ominous. Henry was on the point of telephoning Adair at the embassy but had decided to wait one more day. Then he heard from Violet again.

UNCLASSIFIED

FROM: AMEMBASSY, NEW DELHI
TO: SECSTATE, WASHINGTON, D.C.
SUBJECT: SMITHSONIAN - CHANDRA EXHIBITION

DEPARTMENT PASS SMITHSONIAN, ATTN. HENRY SCRUGGS:

SMI REP. VIOLET STRAUSS REQUESTS EMB. PASS FOLLOWING MES-SAGE: QTE.

1) HENRY, I AM ASKING ADAIR BY PHONE TO SEND THIS CABLE. I AM FLOATING ABOUT THIRTY FEET OFF THE GROUND AND EVERYTHING LOOKS AND SOUNDS FUNNY. ADAIR SOUNDS LIKE A MUNCHKIN BUT MAYBE IT IS JUST THE INDIAN TELEPHONE SERVICE. HENRY, YOU HAVE TO COME TO BANARAS, VARANASI, OR WHATEVER IT IS CALLED. HENRY, IT IS NIRVANA!

2) HENRY, THE MINISTRY OF CULTURE PEOPLE AREN'T WORTH A FLYING FUCK. ADAIR WILL EXPLAIN IT ALL; I CAN'T CONCENTRATE VERY WELL RIGHT NOW.

3) HENRY, BEFORE YOU GET MAD AND CANCEL THE EXHIBITION, PAY ATTENTION TO WHAT I HAVE TO SAY. MY PHOTOS ARE GREAT. WE ARE GOING TO MAKE A SHOW PEOPLE WILL REMEMBER FOR CHANDRA'S BICENTENNIAL OR WHATEVER BIRTHDAY IT IS. JUST LEAVE IT TO ME.

4) THE BEST IS LAST! BAGGY HAS LOCATED A SOLID GOLD LIFE SIZE (ALMOST) STATUE OF CHANDRA. IT MAKES HIM LOOK A LITTLE LIKE A

BEARDED BUDDHA, BUT IT IS BEAUTIFUL! HE IS RIDING ON A TURTLE OR MAYBE IT IS A TORTOISE, I DON'T KNOW. IT HAS THIS BELT COVERED WITH ALL THE RUBIES IN THE WORLD! HOLD ON TO YOUR HAT! WE CAN BORROW IT FOR THE EXHIBITION! GET THE MONEY! WE HAVE TO HAVE IT!

5) I HAVE TO HAVE MORE FILM. I KNOW I HAVE THAT STRAIGHT. DON'T KNOW WHETHER MY CAMERA WILL TAKE PICTURES OF THE THINGS I CAN SEE FROM UP HERE BUT I'LL TRY.

6) I AM OFF TO TRIVANDRUM WITH BAGGY. CHANDRA SPENT HIS LAST YEARS THERE IN A SEA-SIDE VILLA WITH A MISTRESS HALF HIS AGE. YOU CAN RELATE TO THAT, HENRY. OVER AND OUT, VIOLET ENDQTE.

7) FOLLOWING IS MESSAGE FROM BLAKE TO SCRUGGS: QTE:

8) MINCULTURE HAS LOCATED MAN WHO IS WORKING ON THE CHANDRA EXHIBITION. IT IS GOING TO BE MOSTLY REPRODUCTIONS OF SKETCHES, PAINTINGS AND A FEW PHOTOGRAPHS OF CHANDRA AND SOME MODERN PHOTOS OF PLACES IMPORTANT TO CHANDRA'S LIFE. JAILS WHERE HE WAS IMPRISONED AND THE LIKE. THE MINISTRY WILL ALSO SEND YOU SOME BACKGROUND INFORMATION ON CHANDRA'S LIFE. YOU WILL HAVE TO PUT IT ALL TOGETHER, I'M AFRAID. SORRY ABOUT THAT BUT WHAT CAN YOU EXPECT FROM A BUNCH OF INDIANS WHO DON'T KNOW ENOUGH TO LIVE IN THE WESTERN HEMISPHERE.

9) THE STATUE VIOLET MENTIONED WAS MODELED FROM LIFE BY ONE OF CHANDRA'S FOLLOWERS, S.S. AGARWAL, AND IS NOW IN A PRIVATE COLLECTION. IT HAS NEVER BEFORE BEEN OUT OF INDIA. YOU WILL HAVE TO INSURE IT FOR U.S. DOLS 10,000,000. THAT IS JUST FOR THE VALUE OF THE GOLD AND THE RUBY GIRDLE. THE LATTER IS INTEGRAL PART OF SCULPTURE AND CONTAINS MANY LARGE CABOCHON CUT ANTIQUE RUBIES. THE ARTISTIC VALUE IS PRICELESS. INDIAN OWNER INSISTS INSURANCE BE PAYABLE IN U.S. DOLS, NOT RPT NOT IN RUPEES.

10) BECAUSE OF WEIGHT OF GOLD, AIR FREIGHT WILL DOUBTLESS BE COMPUTED ON WEIGHT RATHER THAN VOLUME BASIS. IT WEIGHS 1,100 POUNDS. I WILL ASK BHAGAT TO APPROACH AIR INDIA FOR FREE SHIP-MENT. HE WILL HAVE TO ARRANGE FOR THE STATUE'S EXPORT, ANY-WAY.

11) YOU MAY POUCH FILM TO ME AND I WILL FORWARD IT TO MISS STRAUSS. IF YOU WILL ACCEPT MY GRATUITOUS COMMENT, MISS STRAUSS IS RAPIDLY CHANGING THE IMAGE OF A STAID INSTITUTION THE SMITHSONIAN HAS LONG ENJOYED IN INDIA. SIGNED ADAIR BLAKE ENDQTE.

Henry made an appointment for the next day to see Dr. Fat Dog. Then he went over Violet's negatives and spent the evening in his own darkroom making sixteen-by-twenty-inch prints of two dozen of the most interesting. The light in India, Henry decided, must be marvelous. The prints had a fine luminescent quality. They justified an exhibition of their own regardless of what came from the Indians.

Fat Dog was ready to cancel after reading the New Delhi cable. He was also ready to chew off Henry's ear. But he, too, was won over by Violet's photos. Particularly after Henry reminded him that Secretary Vernon had ordered him to put on the exhibition.

"Isn't it nice," Henry had said, "that Miss Strauss has made such fine photographs. Now the secretary won't regret having ordered you to hold the exhibition. It was a brilliant stroke of yours assigning Miss Strauss to the project. If you don't mind, I will include a memo to that effect when I send the secretary copies of Violet's pictures."

Henry's memo requesting insurance money for the statue was less successful. Here the catcher was the requirement that claims be payable in dollars. If rupees had been acceptable, SFCP rupee funds might have been obtained, though that would have been precedent setting and might or might not have been approved by Dreamy and her advisors. Even after Henry found an insurer who would write a policy for 2 percent, a premium of $200 thousand still had to be paid. That was a lot of money to put into something as invisible as insurance.

It was Doug Cross, the assistant secretary for museums, who came up with the solution. What Henry had to do was apply for a U.S. Government indemnity to cover the statue. This was a new program intended to cover cultural exchanges where insurance costs were otherwise prohibitive. Henry talked to the Bureau of Educational and Cultural Affairs and they agreed to consider supporting his request.

But there was no hope for shipping money. That would have to be in Adair's hands. Henry sent a short cable to Adair advising him about the pending indemnity application and urging him to have Bhagat get in touch with Air India. While it was on his mind, he pouched to Adair as much film as he could get his hands on.

"Mr. Ambassador! Ambassador Scruggs? Wait up a moment!" Hamilton Sealyham hurried after Henry in the Great Hall of the Castle, catching him before he went through the double doors at the east end. "Do you have a moment? If you are not rushing off to the White House or some place like that, I want to show you something."

"Sure, why not?" Henry had plenty to do but just now he wasn't too inclined to get started. He always found Hamilton interesting, which was more than he could say for most of his regular duties. Hamilton Sealyham was director of conferences in the Office of University Programs. He was more or less an anthropologist but he knew everybody in academe and almost everybody else as well. Hamilton usually addressed Henry as Mister Ambassador and introduced him to others as the Smithsonian's Foreign Secretary. It would have been annoying had Henry's real station in life not been so lowly that no one was likely to be confused by Hamilton's banter. Henry followed him to his office.

Hamilton's office was high in the clock tower, and frightening either way it was approached. By land, there were the wide, precipitous crossed stairways leading from the base of the tower. The stairs had tiny, steep treads that reminded Henry of the terror he had felt when he had once climbed the high temple steps at Uxmal. By sea, there was the rocking, creaking ancient elevator to the third floor, prone to entrapment and sudden, sickening lurches.

Once on the third floor, there were two more choices of access to Hamilton's aerie. One was another ancient elevator even more decrepit than the first, and the other was a steel ladder that ascended through holes in the floors above. Once trapped in the elevator, one might not be discovered for months. One slip from the ladder's rung and one might plunge almost forever downward, dying from horror before landing shattered in the corner of someone's office. Henry said a prayer and joined Hamilton in the lift.

"You know Taylor's been in Nepal for months? Cloistered on top of the world, I think they call it. He has taken the cloth, though the best he was able to do was saffron." Hamilton chattered away, unconcerned, as the upper, elder, elevator creaked ever higher in the tower.

Henry unclamped his teeth from his lip. "I haven't seen him since I don't know when. I assumed he had gone somewhere." Taylor Maidstone was another buddy of Hamilton's. He ranged over the earth making films of disappearing traditional rituals and things like that. When Taylor was in Washington, he was a bit like a ship in dry dock with nothing to do and his bottom showing. On such occasions, Henry saw quite a lot of Taylor because Taylor had nothing to occupy himself but gossip and was always good for lunchtime amusement.

Hamilton reached his office and opened the elevator cage door in time to be caught by a phone call. As he talked on the phone he dug in his In box and pulled out a letter written on what looked to be handmade paper. He waved it at Henry.

Dear Hamilton,

Greetings from Nambyang. I have taken up residence in the oldest of the Kaani-hod monasteries which is near here, and I am filming the sex practices that make up the important part of their Hui'paok rite. As you doubtless know, Hui'paok dates from the founding of the sect in the eleventh century and has not been performed since 1926 (both dates according to our calendar, of course) and there are no written documents telling how it should be done. Since this ceremony only comes around every 45 years and the life expectancy of the locals is about 33, it is always touch and go whether anybody will live long enough to perpetuate the old ways.

It appears that Hui'paok will survive this cycle provided a pair of old codgers manage to hang on for a couple more weeks. They have been arguing since I got here about the proper way to conduct the ceremony but neither one can be persuaded to tell anybody else how it's done.

From what I can gather from local gossip, Hui'paok

91

sex is quite something, developing as it has in a celibate community that lets off steam only twice in a century. I'll give you the low-down when I return about the first of December.

If I haven't lost track, income tax time is about here again. I suppose I could borrow a mule and ride over to Kathmandu and get a 1040 at the embassy, but it is a bad time for me to leave right now. Hui'paok could happen at almost any time. The monks don't use any sort of written calendar. The Kaani-lama just announces when the time has arrived.

I have attached a page of figures and I wonder if you could enter them on a 1040 and send it in to IRS. Just sign something that looks sort of like my name. IRS won't care as long as they get the return. I missed filing in 1969 and IRS gave me fits. Don't worry about W-2s and things like that. I can file an amended return after I get back.

By the by, I encountered someone from Varanasi last week and he mentioned that somebody from the Smithsonian—a woman—was in the Varanasi area and was living in what he said was 'a style that promised to bring shame on her family and disgrace upon the Smithsonian Institution.' He was not able to identify her as he had only heard about her from his relatives but he did say that she was supposed to have ridden naked through the city on the back of an elephant.

I wonder if you know who might be in India right now? This woman, whoever she may be, sounds worth a few feet of film for our archives.

Oh, don't try to write to me. The monks don't get mail from anybody and they might not understand. We can get caught up when I get back.

Taylor

"Where is this Nambyang?" Henry asked Hamilton, who had gotten off the phone.

"I don't know exactly. It isn't in my atlas. But I think it is in northern Nepal, near the Tibetan border. Close to God, I should think, or at least one of them. I think that's where Taylor said he was going last year. I wondered if you might know who the Smithsonian woman was that he mentioned. I believe you keep track of such things?"

"It's bound to be Violet. Violet Strauss."

"I don't think I know her," Hamilton said with a touch of surprise, "though she sounds perfectly charming."

"You might not have met her. She's an exhibits designer at MHT. She went to India to do research on the Chandra exhibition."

"Oh, yes, that's this thing you're working on and that's the lady you were . . . ?"

"Isn't there anything around here that's private?" asked Henry with some irritation, admittedly directed more toward Violet than Hamilton.

"Oh, no, dear boy! We're all family, here."

*   *   *

Violet's second shipment of film was, if possible, finer than the first. Most of the pictures had been taken outside of New Delhi, and while Henry had never been in India, after printing the negatives he felt he had spent his whole life there. At first, Phoebe had been annoyed that he was spending so much time in the darkroom with Violet's pictures, but after she had seen some of the results, she joined him. Phoebe did not have bifocals (nor indeed any sort of glasses) so Henry set her to running the enlarger where she could focus much faster and more accurately. She also proved to have a better sense of negative density and exposure values.

In Henry's mind the exhibition was beginning to take shape. Violet had made most of the photos with very fine grain film and these would enlarge quite well. It remained to be seen if they could be blown up as large as Henry wanted. The photos at Banaras were breathtaking. Violet may have been high as a kite but her camera was firmly on its tripod, her lens was sharply focused, and she was judging exposure to perfection. Henry supposed that she was taking some sort of hallucinogen and that unlike most such things, it had productively sharpened her senses.

Violet had photographed in grainier Tri-X, and in uncharacteristically poor light, what could only be the Chandra statue. It confirmed that she was right that the exhibition had to have the statue. The golden figure seemed to glow. Without it the exhibition would have no focal point. It would be a temple without a god. That of course was the key. It had to be something of a place of worship if the sense of what Chandra was, was to come across to the American museum audience.

Henry shuffled through the pictures until he found what he was looking for. Included in these latest pictures was a view of a small structure at the ashram where Violet had evidently stayed. It was just the sort of thing that Henry wanted. He could scale it down and simplify it enough to provide a setting for the statue of Chandra. He could picture the statue there. He could picture the whole exhibition hall and he felt the excitement growing.

* * *

Henry felt more optimistic than he had at any time since he had become involved in the Chandra project. On Monday morning he climbed the stairs to his office with a spring to his step—fifty-three, fifty-four, take two on the landing, fifty-five, fifty-six, fifty-seven, fifty-eight, fifty-nine, sixty, sixty-one, sixty-two! He landed on the tower floor at full stride. The new temporary secretary/receptionist looked at him apprehensively, as though he were perhaps an alien being. No normal person did anything but hang on to the top newel post to catch his or her breath after climbing all those stairs.

"Can I help you, sir?" Henry was late as usual and she assumed that anybody who wasn't in by 9:30 couldn't possibly work there.

"Tea, my good woman! I thirst!" Henry strode past her desk and into his glass-walled office. The temp hurried into Gerald Blackman's office to ask what she should do. Henry plugged in his teakettle as he always did and dumped Friday's tea leaves out of his teapot and into the wastebasket.

He was well into his first cup of tea and was picking the crumbs of a Reece's blueberry doughnut off his lap when the temp came tentatively into his office. "Uh, Mr. Scruggs? Here are the telegrams, sir." She handed Henry a sheaf of cables, the morning's crop.

Henry looked through the collection. Whales. There were always a whole lot on whale conservation and however worthy their purpose, they were never very interesting. He stuck them into an envelope and marked it for the attention the Marine Mammal Division in the Natural History Museum. There was a self-serving USIS message about how well an American specialist had been received during his lecture trip to Japan and Korea. He had spoken about the recent works of Chicago painters and sculptors. The Tokyo public affairs officer got in the prescribed number of self-aggrandizing licks without saying much about the distinguished visitor. Henry marked that one for the director of the National Collection of Fine Arts.

One cable Henry had actually been looking for was a response regarding his inquiry to the American embassy in The Hague asking the science officer to look into a long-overdue loan of proto-Eskimo skeletal material. The Hague said they were sending the Smithsonian request to Bonn, where the science counselor was resident. The counselor could then take care of it during his next visit to The Hague sometime next year. God! Anything to avoid picking up the damned telephone and doing it themselves!

The last cable was one of the sort you always read but which have little to do with your own business. It was from Amconsul (the American Consul) Madras and was action for SCA at State. The Smithsonian was always getting copies of their cables because the distribution boxes were next to one another—SMI for the Smithsonian and SCA for Security and Consular Affairs. Just as often Henry got top-secret cables destined for SMS, some sort of a security agency sitting on the other side of the Smithsonian box. He sympathized. It was awfully boring distributing telegrams.

FROM: AMCONSUL MADRAS
TO: SECSTATE, WASHINGTON, D.C.
INFO: AMEMBASSY, NEW DELHI

SUBJECT: WELFARE - WHEREABOUTS: POSSIBLE SUICIDE ATTEMPT IN TRIVANDRUM BY WOMAN BELIEVED TO BE AMERICAN CITIZEN.

1) CONGEN HAS RECEIVED REPORT THAT A WOMAN DESCRIBED AS BEING IN HER EARLY TWENTIES HAS EITHER ATTEMPTED SUICIDE OR SUFFERED DRUG OVERDOSE IN HOTEL TRIVANDRUM EXCELSIOR. IDENTITY UNCERTAINTY STEMS FROM FACT THAT ALL HER BAGGAGE HAD APPARENTLY BEEN STOLEN BY COMPANIONS DESCRIBED AS INDIANS OF DISREPUTABLE APPEARANCE AND SHE HAD CHECKED INTO HOTEL USING NAME PARVATI, CONSORT OF SHIVA, SOMETHING THE HOTEL MANAGEMENT BELIEVES ONLY AN AMERICAN WOULD HAVE DONE.

2) TRIVANDRUM POLICE BELIEVE WOMAN TO BE AMERICAN BECAUSE LABEL IN HER SOLE REMAINING ARTICLE OF CLOTHING OR OTHER PERSONAL POSSESSIONS (PAIR OF RED HIGH HEELED SHOES) IS MASSEY'S OF WASHINGTON.

3) SUBJECT WOMAN IS NOW IN SEVENTH DAY ADVENTIST HOSPITAL TRIVANDRUM AND CONDITION SAID TO BE STABLE THOUGH SHE IS STILL UNCONSCIOUS. WILL REPORT WHEN AND IF ANYTHING FURTHER LEARNED.

Henry read through the cable three times, looking to see whether any other interpretation might be possible. There wasn't any. He reached for the phone to call Consular Affairs. To tell them to buy Violet a dress and send her home if they could get her on her feet again.

 **Seven**

The Indian Embassy put Henry's call directly through to Bhagat Gupta.

"Henry, dear friend! I've been meaning to call you, but I found things rather piled up on my desk when I got back."

"When did you last see Violet?"

"Oh, I suppose it has been more than a week. Almost two, actually. Is she not back yet?"

"Was she still in Trivandrum when you left her?"

"Exactly so! She should be coming in any day now. I'm not sure precisely when. Haven't you heard from her?"

"A cable from our consulate general in Madras came across my desk this morning. It said something about an American woman's suicide attempt in Trivandrum. They didn't have a name, but it was at the Hotel Excelsior."

"My Lord, Henry! That's where she was staying! But I can't believe it could possibly be Violet. Did they give any details?"

"Only that she was using the name Parvati, Consort of Shiva, and that it might have been a drug overdose. And that the woman had been in the company of rather disreputable persons."

Bhagat was silent for a rather long time. "I suppose it could

97

be she. But I'm sure it would have been accidental, Henry. You know Violet as well as I do. She was—is, I should say—always ready to try new things. Perhaps that is why she is so—uh, creative. In Varanasi she painted her face black and called herself Kali. As it happens, that is another name for Parvati. As you can well imagine, Indians don't quite know how to take Violet. Did the cable say what her condition was?"

"Madras didn't have much information. They say she is still unconscious but they will report anything further that they learn. I assumed it was Violet—for the same reasons you would—and called SCA—"

"SCA?"

"Security and Consular Affairs. Don't ask me why the two go together. I told them it was Violet and that she was on official business for the Smithsonian. If it is Violet and she is able to travel, they will do a medical evacuation."

"Henry, I am so sorry this happened. I should have stayed with her. The Ministry in New Delhi ordered me to come back to Washington but I should have insisted on delaying until she was ready to return."

"I don't see how you could have done that."

"I could have said it was necessary for the Chandra exhibition. That has a high priority in New Delhi."

"Bhagat, we both know how little control anyone has over Violet. The only thing you could have prevented, perhaps, was the theft of her personal possessions. Madras said her companions didn't leave her anything but her shoes. I presume those thieves got her cameras and probably her film. The cameras can be replaced, of course, but the pictures she was taking in India were extraordinary."

"Even her clothes?" Bhagat hummed to himself abstractedly. "Ah, that is India for you. Nothing is wasted. But I have her film. That which was exposed, of course. There is quite a lot of it. She cannot have had very much unexposed film with her in Trivandrum. I'm sure I brought most of the film back with me. I also have some background material on Chandra for you. I'll have a messenger bring all of it over to you."

"Why don't you come over to my office. I need to discuss what is being done in India. Adair's last message suggested that I might have to augment the exhibition somewhat here at the Smithsonian. I have some ideas how it might be possible, provided the core of the exhibition comes from India."

"That would be a good idea. I also have a proposal I would like to try out on you. I could come over perhaps on Wednesday afternoon."

* * *

There had been a lot of rain in late March and early April but now in the third week of April it was drying up and, as if to compensate, Henry's nose was running more or less continuously. This was not Henry's best time of year. He was now on two Disophrol per day, a dosage he would maintain for another three weeks when he would increase to three per day. After yet another week or two, depending on the rainfall, three pills would no longer prevent convulsive sneezing and Henry would have to take to his bed and breathe as infrequently as possible. Even then, if it were cool and dry and the wind blew strongly from the northwest, Henry would have to stuff his handkerchief up his nose to stop the sneezing. At times like that, his sinus cavities felt like they were filled with fiery coals.

Even when things were more or less under control, the sedative effect of the medicines softened Henry's brain and rendered him semiconscious. At the same time, his nervous system was rubbed raw. The best that might be said of him was that he slept fitfully. Day and night.

"You look terrible, Henry!" said Bhagat cheerfully as he sat down, depositing several large packages on the floor beside him. "You Americans don't eat properly. If you cook things in ghee you will never have colds."

"Looks are often deceiving, Bhagat. I feel worse than I look. But it's hay fever and ghee wouldn't help unless I drowned in it. Let's have some tea. It isn't Indian, it's Formosa oolong, but I think it helps." Henry pulled out his sodden handkerchief and wiped his nose. His nose had an unhealthy redness to it and it hurt when anything touched it. It burned when he breathed. Everybody else used Kleenex for sanitary reasons but he had long ago found that he was allergic to the wood fibers in such tissues. The only thing he could tolerate was pure, well-washed cotton. Perhaps silk, but he had never owned a real silk handkerchief. Silk seemed too expensive to buy by the gross. Bhagat looked at Henry's bedraggled handkerchief with ill-disguised distaste.

"Have you heard anything further about Violet?"

"This morning we got an information copy of an April eighteenth message from Madras to New Delhi. Violet seems to be conscious. As soon as she can travel by commercial airline they'll send her home. I hope it is a nonstop flight. There's no telling what might happen if she has to change planes."

"Yes. Well, I'm sure she'll be all right, but I'll speak to our people in New Delhi just in case. Henry, here is the film." Bhagat deposited a good-sized package on Henry's desk. "I had some difficulty getting it through customs without being x-rayed. They wanted to open all the canisters. I threatened them." Bhagat looked as pleased with himself as he was annoyed with customs officials.

"And this is material on Chandra." The second package that Bhagat deposited on Henry's desk was smaller than the first. "It's mostly unpublished material, but there are a few references in books. I think you'll find them useful."

"I hope I won't need them. What are we getting from New Delhi?"

"This is it. Oh, there will be some pictures and things, but there will be no exhibit text of the sort you are going to need."

Henry had half-expected this, but he was still upset. "What the hell do they expect us to do? We understood that we would receive a completely prepared exhibition ready to put in place or hang on the walls or whatever. You told us that!"

"I know, Henry, but that was before the Smithsonian insisted on sending someone to India."

"We only sent Violet to check on the Ministry of Culture, not to prepare an exhibition. She's done a lot of photographs but they are of India and are hardly an exhibition on Chandra."

"Well, the thing is, you used SFCP funds. When the Government of India approves the use of excess currency rupees, it considers them to be the same as a domestic expenditure. And

100

they certainly can't expend funds twice for the same purpose. The auditors would be very upset. So when Violet's trip was approved, they simply stopped working on the exhibition."

"*Herr Gott!*" Henry often lapsed into German when English words seemed inadequate. "I think we had better just cancel the exhibition!" Henry had no authority to do that. Once things had been published in the Smithsonian calendar, cancellations were high-level decisions with much soul-searching.

"I quite sympathize," said Bhagat insincerely, "but I'm sure you can still go ahead with the exhibition. It will be much to your credit—more than it would be if you simply installed an exhibition prepared for you in India. On the other hand, canceling it now would make it very difficult for Smithsonian scientists to work in India. For many years, certainly. And however unjustifiably, the Smithsonian is bound to hold that against you. You personally, that is."

"Damn!" Bhagat was right of course. Henry had been had.

"It need not happen," Bhagat said comfortingly. "Between us, I think that we can put together a very nice exhibition."

"Are you offering to work with me on it?"

"My dear Henry, I have been working with you for weeks now! After all, I escorted Violet to India and located the golden statue of Chandra."

"I have been meaning to talk to you about that. Who is the sculptor, this S. S. Agarwal?"

"Oh, he is very well known! In India, of course. He was very fashionable in the middle of the nineteenth century and did all the important people. Including the British Viceroy. Then he became one of Chandra's inner circle of followers and just quit sculpting. Except for the gold image of Chandra which he made for a rich maharanee to present to Chandra's ashram."

"I still don't know how we can find the money to transport it here. Do you really think it is necessary to the exhibition?"

"It is simply vital. After Chandra's death and the dissolution of his followers, the sculpture became the property of his daughter, and later, her descendents. So you see, it has not been on public view for almost a century. It is the most important existing Chandra artifact. It will make the difference between an ordinary exhibition that anyone could put together and one which will excite international interest. However, transportation is not going to be a problem. I have spoken to the directors of Air India. They will transport it for us. The more important question is the insurance."

"Private insurance would be prohibitively expensive. The Smithsonian has applied for a U.S. Government indemnity. We should be able to get it if our embassy in New Delhi supports our request strongly enough."

"I will ask my ambassador to telephone Adair."

"Maybe it would be better if he called the American ambassador."

"I am certain he would do that if you think it would be better. The indemnity would be payable in dollars, wouldn't it?"

"To be on the safe side, the owner of the statue should make it a condition of the loan. In the unlikely event we had to make good on the indemnity, the American government would certainly try to weasel out by using blocked rupees."

"Oh, my! That wouldn't be satisfactory at all!"

"Then the owner must make dollar payment a condition from the beginning."

"Agreed! Now, about the exhibition text. I think you are going to have to write one. The manuscripts and books I have brought you will be very helpful, but they will be no substitute for a knowledge of Indian history."

"Which you will provide?"

"Yes, in a way. I will provide someone to work with you. My nephew."

"Your nephew?!" Henry was incredulous.

"Yes. My nephew is a historian. I have asked him to come to Washington and he has said he would be delighted to do so."

Henry reflexively shifted back to being a consular officer. "Is he a student?" he asked.

"Yes, at Banaras Hindu University."

"Maybe he could come over as a member of your household—with a diplomatic visa."

"The Smithsonian has a foreign student program, does it not?"

102

"Yes, for people studying museology and things like that."

"That would be exactly right. He has always been interested in museums."

"What about his financial support? I doubt the Smithsonian could provide any. Unless you think we could pay him off with rupees."

"Oh," Bhagat waved away the idea, "that won't be necessary. And he can certainly live with me. We Indians are used to having all sorts of relatives around the house."

With misgivings, Henry arranged for Bhagat's nephew, Somnath Gupta, to undertake a museum internship at the Smithsonian and sent him a form I-20, a Student Visa Eligibility Certificate, so he could apply for a student visa.

* * *

Weeks later Henry stood in the concourse of Eero Saarinen's Dulles Airport terminal and looked out through the tinted glass onto the runways. It looked as though it might rain. He wished to God it were so, but he knew it was just the effect of the tinted glass. Outside, the mid-May sun was blazing down and the humidity was as dry as an empty martini glass. Pollen granules were riding joyously on the back of a steady fair-weather breeze from the northwest. Henry's nose dripped into his fresh but already soaked handkerchief. He hated May. He hated it more than April and much more than June. Swollen membranes outlined his eyes in red. He suppressed a whimper.

Bhagat looked at Henry with the sort of superior sympathy that is affected by the nonallergic. "Are you going to be all right, Henry?"

"No." There was no use lying about it.

"My dear chap, I wish I could do something for you."

"Make it rain." No "please" or other pleasantry such as "oh, don't worry about me, it's only my head that's affected." Henry was beyond that.

Bhagat turned away and watched a Pan American plane landing on the back runway. "I think it's their plane. It shouldn't be long now."

It actually always takes about three times as long as you expect and when those funny Dulles Airport people-transporters pull up to the terminal everybody comes off with such a rush that you can't quite figure out what took so long. Even the flight crew had arrived before Violet walked rather uncertainly out of the vehicle. A gangly brown youth with rimless glasses guided her by an elbow. They made an odd couple. The boy had on Western (European, that is) clothing; Violet was wearing a sari. It looked nice on her except for her being so white. Henry wondered how anybody could have just spent several months in India without getting into the sun. As she came closer he saw that she wasn't pink pale; she was chalk white. Poor Violet, what have you done to yourself? He sneezed.

"Where is Herbert?" Violet demanded.

"Herbert is playing with the other horses. I put him in a stable." Violet looked at Henry uncomprehendingly. "He is in a kennel, Violet. He's just fine."

"That wasn't very nice of you. Herbert hates kennels. I told you he doesn't know he's a dog." Violet was serious. She was quite displeased.

"Herbert and I are both happier apart."

"Henry," broke in Bhagat, after he and Violet had greeted one another with hands placed together in what Henry always thought of as a prayerful attitude, "this is my nephew, Somnath. Somnath Gupta."

Henry started to put his hands together but Somnath thrust out one of his for a handshake. It made sense since his other hand held his carry-on (or is it carry-off?) luggage. "Mr. Scruggs! I am so pleased to meet you! My uncle has told me so much about you!" His English was as formal as Bhagat's, but it lacked the latter's fine University of London accent. "I look forward to working with you! I am eager!" he said needlessly. "And of course with Miss Strauss," he added, remembering his manners.

They stood around while luggage was collected by the Indian embassy driver. Bhagat had volunteered the car and Henry had accepted gladly. Driving may have headed the list of things he didn't feel like doing today.

Violet didn't have much except a rather cheap and small bag the American Embassy must have provided. Henry looked down at her feet. She had on sandals. The red shoes must have been in the bag. He searched around for something to say. "It's warm for so early in the spring," he said.

"Stuff it, Henry," Violet said without any particular inflection in her voice.

The limousine glided silently along the Dulles access road toward Washington. Henry sat on the jump seat and looked at the others, seated across the backseat. Three Indians, one with a pale face. The passengers were as silent as was the stretch Cadillac. Violet had effectively shut everybody up. It was she who broke the quiet as the limousine turned onto the George Washington Memorial Parkway. "We are going by the kennel first to pick up Herbert. Tell the driver how to get there, Henry."

"Why don't we take you to your apartment first and then I can go and pick up the dog?"

"I'm sure Herbert knows I'm back. He is very perceptive. I imagine he is desperate to see me. We are going there first."

"It's all right, Henry," said Bhagat, "we can pick up Herbert first. There's plenty of room. Just instruct the driver."

"Have you seen Herbert? He might be a problem in the car."

"Oh, yes, I know Herbert. He and I are old friends."

Henry capitulated against his better judgment and gave the driver an Arlington address.

But when the dog was brought out from his run, Henry saw that Violet had been right. Herbert jitterbugged all the way out to the car and tried to climb in through the window. Henry pulled back on his leash so that the door could be opened and Herbert shifted his interest to one of the limousine's white-wall tires. He bathed it in yellow urine while the horrified driver looked on in disgust. Henry hoped for Herbert's sake that the driver was one of those Indians who holds all life sacred. Then, again, maybe he didn't hope that.

The ride across the Potomac and into town was chaos. The dog could not be contained in the front seat because he wouldn't stay still enough for the driver to concentrate on traffic. In the backseat, the dog kept up his dance, which Henry now concluded owed more to Saint Vitus than to the more modern jitterbug.

Herbert's violent movements stirred up a storm of dog hair that proved to be too much for Henry's unfortunate nose. Henry erupted in violent, convulsive, and hysterical sneezes. The more he sneezed, the more excited Herbert became, if that were a possibility.

"Henry! Stop it! You're driving poor Herbert crazy!"

Violet screaming was all Herbert needed. He went berserk and woofed thunderously at everybody, including Violet. Bhagat covered his face with his arm as Herbert lunged at him. Herbert's massive jaws closed on Bhagat's necktie and he pulled back, digging his paws into the knees of those seated across the back of the car. Bhagat began to strangle.

The embassy driver hit the brakes. There were several jolts and everybody, including the dog, was thrown against the back of the front seat. Everybody, that is, except Henry who was already pushing open the car door. He fell out onto the street and sat there for a moment, sneezing. He pinched his nose closed, picked himself up, and hailed a taxi. As he got into the cab, he forced his streaming eyes open to look at the embassy car. Everybody was getting out and there seemed to be two cars behind the limousine that were somehow connected with it. The damage appeared to be minor, but Henry didn't care.

The Biafran refugee cab driver looked at Henry in his mirror. "You wish to go to the hospital, yes?"

"No, just away from here. Anywhere will do." Henry closed his eyes and tried to keep from breathing. He took the opposite corners of his handkerchief and began stuffing them up his nostrils. He bit his tongue to control his sneezing. The blood ran salty in his mouth. The cab sped on aimlessly, but Henry didn't care.

* * *

For the remainder of the week, Henry stayed in bed and ate antihistamines like peanuts. He practiced breathing shallowly, breathing infrequently, and breathing through layers of much-washed cotton handkerchiefs. Eventually, he sent Phoebe out to buy a hookah—one like Violet's. He breathed through that and the air bubbled through the water before it reached Henry's insides. With concentration, he could breathe through it, but it was exhausting and he felt continually frantic for air. However, it finally made him so tired that he slept for eighteen hours and that was what brought him back to the living.

That and the rain. It rained at last. Not piddling little dust-settling rain nor hard and too-soon-gone rain, but a wonderful northeast wind that brought in a light but steady rain from the Atlantic. It was Henry's favorite weather. He was the only one who liked it.

* * *

Monday was a holiday and Tuesday was the thirtieth of May. With any kind of luck, humid June weather would be arriving soon, and fat, heavy, hygroscopic pollen grains would sit harmlessly on the ground waiting until the July gully washers would float them into the storm sewers and thence to the Potomac and to the Chesapeake Bay, where they would settle to the bottom where they would interest and confound paleontologists millennia hence.

"Jeezus, Henry," Gerald Blackman, Henry's office director, looked him over with something approaching concern, "You look awful!"

"I am one with Lazarus."

"Yeah? You do look sort of like a diseased beggar."

"Not that one, the other one—the brother of Mary and Martha. You know, the one who got raised from the dead."

"They should have done it before you decomposed." Gerald was not without religious feeling, but it didn't extend to Henry.

The other problem with Gerald was that he liked to call staff meetings at the beginning of the week, at least once every month or two. It made him feel like a supervisor, which he didn't ordinarily feel like, since the Foreign Affairs Office was a place where everybody mostly went their own ways. The problem with Monday meetings (or in this case, the Tuesday after a holiday) was that staff meetings were show-and-tell time. But Monday (or in this case, Tuesday) was too early in the week for anybody to have done anything and last week was too long ago to remember anything particularly interesting. Henry had long urged, to no avail, that the meetings be held on Fridays, preferably at the end

107

of the day when everybody, including Gerald, would be in a hurry to go home.

So it was that on Tuesday everyone dragged chairs into the large central room of the tower and prepared for an ordeal which with any kind of misfortune at all would last long enough to make everybody miss luncheon engagements while Gerald tried to ferret out enough exciting news to look good in his monthly report to the bureau director.

"I have exactly six months, actually six months from tomorrow," said Henry when his time came, "to prepare a nonexistent exhibition on a subject nobody knows or cares about. It is my one chance for greatness. But there is nothing to worry about because I have all the help I need from an exhibits designer who is a suicidal social dropout and from a polite but probably useless Indian boy. I have also passed through my spring hayfever crisis and may live until the first of September if the bad weather holds. Unless of course a mad dog who is as big as a horse and named Herbert finds me first."

"Poor baby," said Dreamy as she crossed her legs and gave Henry a sexy look.

Eight

"I had Violet on both sides," said Henry, "you don't have anything to worry about."

"Well! Really!" Phoebe was shocked. It was a condition not often achieved since she had, after all, gone to law school in the sixties.

Henry became flustered. He had not considered how it sounded. He scrambled to explain. "I meant Violet was like having mumps. If you have a good case of them, it makes antibodies and you acquire a lifetime immunity."

"Are you trying to tell me that Violet turned you off of girls?" asked Phoebe suspiciously.

"No, of course not. You are quite right. Violet was more like Hong Kong flu. You acquire an immunity just to that particular strain."

"Why don't I feel convinced?"

"I'm sure I don't know. But anyway, I've got to work with Violet on the exhibition. It's my job," Henry said as though that explained everything.

* * *

Work on the exhibition was still rather formless. Henry had no clear idea about establishing priorities. He just worked on whatever came to his notice and that was aplenty. He did talk to Dr. Fat Dog and got some work space allocated to him and Somnath. It was impossible to work in the design department with Violet for a lot of reasons, not the least of which was her presence.

He had tried it for a few days, but he found himself unwilling to turn his back on Violet.

"Henry? Are you afraid of me?"

"No! Of course not! Well, maybe I'm a little afraid of myself. But only a little."

"You don't have to be. I don't think of myself as a wife. A mistress, perhaps, but not a wife." Violet had an odd way of saying "wife" so that it cut rather like a knife.

"I'm sure you'd make a fine wife," Henry said, regretting it as he said it.

"No, I lack constancy. You shouldn't expect it of me. You, on the other hand, are a very constant person. That is why you have such a hard time. You are in an inconstant situation." Violet looked at Henry, sizing him up.

Violet had more or less returned to normal and was either teasing Henry or he was becoming paranoid. Probably both. They had more or less agreed on a general design for the exhibition and Henry set himself to writing a script, with Somnath's help. He turned over the fine points of design to Violet, where it was better off anyway. He hoped she would get things done on time. Things always seemed to work out for Smithsonian exhibitions. Of course there usually was a curator involved who knew what to do.

On Thursday, June 29, Violet struck again. Things had been going so smoothly that Henry found it hard to remember what the winter had been like. Even the spring hay fever was only dimly remembered, now that it was hot and afternoon rainstorms regularly washed the city clean. His humor was returning. Perhaps he was even good company, at least Violet thought so to the point of going with him out onto the Mall at midday to see the Festival of American Folklife, which was just gearing up for the Fourth of July long weekend.

It was crowded and Henry held on to Violet to keep them

from becoming separated. In the dust of the Mall, Violet smelled like all those things that ads on TV suggest. Violet was back to using a little of everything. Henry noticed again that particularly live feeling that the waists of young women have. Fat, he thought, on thin—the reason they look good in bathing suits and other places. They wormed their way through the crowd to where somebody was performing what they thought was music of Appalachia. It bore little resemblance to that which Henry had heard when he was growing up in the mountains. Probably invented in New York, he thought. Violet stood on tiptoe and whispered loudly in Henry's ear.

"Let's go to my place and make love for lunch," she said. Nobody around them paid any attention.

* * *

"Don't look so worried, Henry. I won't tell Phoebe." Violet was having her postcoital marijuana cigarette. Henry was sitting as far away as he could manage in Violet's small living room (they had not made it up the stairs to the bedroom) so that he wouldn't have an asthma attack and wouldn't smell (stink) too much like pot. He scratched his ankle that had been discovered by one of Herbert's migratory fleas. "You can go home for dinner," Violet continued. "That's the least I can do. I like Phoebe."

"She doesn't like—"

"Me. Yes. Women don't, particularly, except for a few of the really strange ones. Rosa and Hazel come to mind."

"Did Hazel get her abortion?" Henry hadn't really thought about Violet's friends since the night they tried to drive over the Capitol fence.

"Of course. It wasn't any problem. It's her religion that was really the problem."

"She's a Catholic?"

"Yes. She thinks it's wicked to take the pill."

"But—oh, never mind." Henry decided he didn't want to sort that one out. "Violet, I wonder if it is a good idea for us to get involved again?"

"We're not involved, Henry. I just borrowed you. Men can be boring if you keep them around too long. Like you, Henry, you are boring." Henry started to protest. "Don't look so upset. It's nothing personal. In fact I mean it as a compliment. Any man who is not boring is too dangerous to have around."

"Such as?" Henry felt positively belligerent. He could be dangerous if he wanted to. But he just didn't want to, though he might change his mind if Violet didn't lay off.

"Well, Baggy for example. He is not at all boring but he is quite dangerous."

"Bhagat? I don't believe it." Violet must be teasing him again.

"That's just like you Henry. You pretend to be sophisticated but deep down you are positively naive."

Henry swallowed. Violet could be exasperating. He had a coughing spasm. The dog hairs and the smoke were really getting to him.

"Henry! Are you having another heart attack?" Violet sounded almost hopeful, as she always did when bringing up such dire possibilities. It made her seem a little like a black widow, or was it a praying mantis? Mate with the male and then eat him.

* * *

The script proved to be less of a problem than expected. Usually, the difficulty is in knowing too much about the subject and having to pare things down to fit the limitations imposed by the exhibition. Henry knew so little, however, that all he had to do was pump up the text with adjectives until it fit. Looking it over after it was written, Henry was justly proud of it. It was simple, straightforward, and he had inserted just the sort of adjectives he had heard Bhagat and Somnath use, so it sounded nicely Anglo-Indian.

Shortly after the Fourth of July, a wooden packing case from the Indian Ministry of Culture arrived at the Indian Embassy. Bhagat brought it over to the History and Technology Building; he and Henry opened it on the basement loading dock. It contained several dozen photos mounted on cardboard. The cardboard curved in various directions, making the pictures concave, convex, or sometimes both at once. "From Moline," said Henry absently.

"No, from New Delhi, certainly," said Bhagat.

112

"No, I was just remembering a limerick from years ago."

"A limerick! I love English limericks!" Bhagat put on his jolly face. "They are much more popular in India than so many other English things."

"Irish. At least the name is Irish. But this one isn't one of the great ones. I think it goes, 'There once was a man from Moline, who invented a—a you-know-what machine, both concave and convex, it would fit either sex, and with attachments, those in between.' "

"Very good!" said Bhagat, enthusiastically. "But I don't get the connection."

"Never mind, there probably isn't any."

As it turned out, most of the pictures, once flattened out, could be used. They illustrated the various people and places in the life of Chandra—his jails, his friends and relatives, the Viceroy who gave him so much grief, even the ashram near Trivandrum where he spent his old age—and they served nicely to enliven Henry's text.

Within a few days a second, larger packing case arrived at the Smithsonian, consigned to Henry. It contained a quantity of traditional textiles and other crafts that Violet had deposited at the American Embassy for forwarding and had been months underway by sea freight. So that was where Violet's per diem had gone! She had neglected to mention they were coming. Probably she had forgotten all about them. The things were pretty, at least, and could be used to decorate the exhibit hall. They might go nicely on the north wall. The original idea had been to project photographic slides there with a battery of lap-dissolve projectors, but Violet complained that would be too distracting from the mood of the rest of the exhibition.

Besides, there were going to be pictures aplenty, elsewhere in the gallery. Violet's black-and-white photographs were enlarged beyond all reason. Those made with Panatomic film were successful and were printed on strips of four-by-eight-foot paper, sometimes in as many as three sections to make a twelve-by-eight-foot picture. The enlargements presented problems beyond the simple matter of maintaining sharpness. The photo lab was not equipped to develop more than one strip at a time

113

so it was very difficult to balance the development of the several strips that made up a picture. And mounting was another problem. The prints were wet-mounted on sheets of foam. But as the photographs dried, they shrank, imparting a concave curve to the foam. Henry began to appreciate the problems the Indians had with the smaller Chandra photographs. An experienced exhibits production technician came up with the solution. A blank sheet of photographic paper was wet mounted on the back of the photo panel at the same time the printed sheet was mounted on the front. The panel shrank more or less evenly all over, reasonably flat.

The next problem was with the editorial department. Smithsonian museums have editors who go over exhibits texts and mess them up in the interest of uniformity, style, and catching real or imagined errors and implanting the stamp of the particular editors' idiosyncrasies. Henry's English was somewhat eccentric, even quaint, but it was his own. He spent most of August arguing with the museum's editor. He was at his best because his hay fever was completely in remission. His text was saved because the editor had rented a house in Ocean City for the last week of August and the Labor Day weekend. She was not about to miss her seaside vacation just to impose her will on Henry.

While the production people worked on silk-screening the Chandra text onto two hundred feet of Indian-yellow-painted hardboard, Henry went into seclusion for his fall season of hay fever. This was the short one. With luck, only six weeks. He completed the Firth of Forth bridge the day after Columbus's birthday. The next Monday's business section of the *Washington Post* noted a strange shortage of toothpicks in the Washington metropolitan area.

The middle of November, the gold Chandra arrived. It was preceded by a last-minute demand to raise the insured value to $15 million, to allow for its artistic value. State/CU of course refused and sent a cable to Adair in New Delhi suggesting that the loan of the statue be cancelled. A hurried telephone call came from Adair saying that the statue was already en route and that the owner was willing to accept the $10 million insured value.

The statue came in at the freight terminal at Dulles. It had been originally scheduled for BWI Airport, but Henry decided that in the event of a heist attempt, the limited-access road to Dulles would make escape more difficult. Henry urged Bhagat to have an armored truck bring the statue into the Smithsonian, but Bhagat said he thought a regular Smithsonian truck would attract less attention. "Perhaps what we really need is a garbage truck," said Henry testily. "That would really be inconspicuous." He thought Bhagat was far too unconcerned by a relatively unguarded $10 million.

When the statue was uncrated and sitting on a stage replicating the Chandra ashram, Henry had to admit that it made the exhibition. It glowed powerfully and dominated the room. What did $10 million matter? The statue was beautiful and Bhagat was right. The exhibition would have been nothing without it.

Everything was now in the hands of Exhibits Production and miraculously things seemed to be coming together. Except for a thousand and one little details, of course. But Henry's work was indeed almost done. The one thing left for Henry to do, besides worry, was to arrange for guards for the statue. He went to see the captain of the History and Technology Building guard detachment.

"We need around-the-clock guards in the special exhibition hall."

"You mean for that golden idol thing?"

"Yes. It's a statue. It's valued at ten million."

"You got it insured?"

"Of course. The Government does."

"Then don't worry about it."

"I'd feel a lot better if we had a guard stationed in the hall at all times."

"The building's secure. The guardroom backs up to the hall. There's no way anybody's going to move that thing. It must weigh half a ton."

"A little more, actually. But you would be surprised at what burglars can move."

"Not hardly. But it's not going to happen. Besides, you got the money for the overtime?"

"No."

"Then relax. We guard a lot more valuable things than that in this museum."

"Such as?" asked Henry doubtfully.

"George Washington's false teeth."

"Washington's teeth aren't gold."

"Yeah, but that statue ain't of George Washington." That seemed to settle the matter.

* * *

In the last few days preceding the opening, Henry saw less of Violet. He was beginning to spend some time back in the Foreign Affairs Office, where he made frequent occasion to remind Gerald that money had to be in the office budget if Henry were to avoid having to go back to the State Department sometime after the beginning of the year, which was fast approaching.

But he found himself thinking about Violet a lot. He thought about Phoebe, too. Phoebe and his piano. Violet and Herbert. He switched it about and compared Phoebe and Herbert with Violet and his piano. Either way, Phoebe came out ahead. But he still missed Violet.

From things Somnath said, he gathered that Bhagat was seeing Violet more than casually. Henry suppressed a pang of jealousy and wished him luck with her. Insincerely, of course.

* * *

"You look depressed," said Phoebe. "What has Violet done now?"

"It's nothing she's done. We were taking a look through the exhibit this afternoon and she said she wouldn't be there tomorrow for the opening."

"She wouldn't miss it for the world. Don't worry about it."

"She said she was going to kill herself."

"I doubt it. That kind never really does it."

"I don't know. Violet looked strangely happy. With her that's always a dangerous sign."

"Well, you still shouldn't let it worry you. You're not still in love with her, are you?" Phoebe demanded.

"No! Of course not. The mumps, don't you remember? Or was it the flu? No, I just feel like I ought to do something."

116

"Well, you could report her suicide threat to the authorities."

"What authorities?"

"The police or whatever. Whoever would listen to you. Then they would lock her up. Are you prepared to do that?"

"No, not really." Henry looked at his bridge. "Would you mind if I got a train set? I made the bridge to HO scale. We could confine the tracks to the living and dining rooms."

"You're the one they ought to lock up."

* * *

Except for the cleaning people, the exhibit remained empty and closed until noon Thursday, November 30. Henry spent the morning with Special Events making sure that the meager catering arrangements were on track, and during a quick lunch in the Commons he put the finishing touches on the remarks that Dr. Fat Dog was to make when the guests arrived at five o'clock. Then he hurried over to MHT to meet Somnath in the gallery for a last look around. Violet was there with Somnath. Henry was relieved.

"I thought you said you weren't going to be here," he said.

"Did I say that? Well"—Violet paused, searching for an explanation—"you can't always believe everything I say."

"I'm glad of that." Henry had sort of gotten used to Violet's threats, but not entirely. He thought he had heard somewhere that suicides often threatened for years before they finally did it. Some, possibly Violet, seemed to get a perverse pleasure from working up to the act.

Violet read his mind. "Sometime when you least expect it I'll do it."

Well, that was a relief. He expected it all the time. Henry dropped the subject and they started around the gallery. They switched on the tape loop that would play continuous Indian music. It began with Henry's drum tattoo followed by the sound of a sitar. It sounded a bit loud, but he supposed it wouldn't once the hall was filled with people moving about. Henry tried to imagine that he had just come in off the street and was seeing the exhibition for the first time. Whatever else you might say about it, it looked arresting. Arresting and interesting.

The gallery was large, between tennis and basketball courts in

117

size, but the soft, deep Indian blue of the room pushed out the walls, erased them in an infinity of space, except for the finite narrow band of dense, earth-bound Indian yellow-brown that circled the room, bearing the story of the life of Chandra.

It was a scene upon which crowds of Indian villagers looked from Violet's large photo panels, set closing the angle between the blue walls and the invisible blue ceiling. So that when you read about Chandra, an eternity of Indian souls watched over you and approved.

Diagonally across the room from the entrance to the gallery was a low stage, an open-fronted wooden structure, designed to look like the ashram, the hermitage where Chandra spent his final years.

Centered on the stage, and centered in the light, stood the gold figure of Chandra, the gold, ruby-encrusted image of Vishnu, not all of one or all of the other, but more than both.

"Henry," (Somnath had started using Henry's first name about mid-August) "this is a fine exhibition. You do honor to India and the memory of Chandra. You both, of course," he added politely, with a nod to Violet.

"Thank you, Somnath. But we couldn't have done it without your help." That was not altogether true, but it was the only proper thing to say. Somnath had been useful particularly in making sure Indian names were spelled right and things like that, but the design had been largely Violet's and the text had been Henry's—every word of it.

Violet left them as Henry began reading through the exhibit text in a final (and of course, too late) attempt to find errors and other lamentable lapses. Violet had no patience for reading anything.

There were two or three small typos in the silk-screening, nothing that couldn't be ignored. Such things were inevitable, it seemed. Then, after a final five minutes spent standing in the gallery and soaking in the total atmosphere, Henry turned around to look for Violet. The gallery appeared to be empty. But during a quiet passage in the music, Henry heard someone moving about.

He found Somnath puttering around behind the little ashram

that provided a stage for the golden statue. "Somnath, where did Violet go?"

"I think she probably went back down to the basement. For a smoke, I expect."

"Well, I think I'll go find her." Somnath went with Henry as far as the entrance to the cafeteria, where he said he would have some coffee.

There was nobody in the design unit, which was not in itself unusual. Henry made the rounds of Exhibits Production, the Photo Lab, and other places she might be and finally decided she might have gone to the ladies' room. He settled down in Miss Milly Farrell's chair to wait. After perhaps half an hour, Milly strolled in, back from a late lunch, apparently. Yes, she had stopped by the ladies' room and no, Violet wasn't there. Her manner demanded Henry give back her desk chair and quit asking her silly questions.

He gave up and returned to the first floor. Perhaps Violet had gone there by another way. It was almost three-fifteen when he reached the north entrance foyer. The guard at the door said he hadn't seen Miss Strauss for some time and that the gallery was empty.

Henry thought he would check the snack bar and had gone back to the cross hall when the elevator doors opened and the caterers emerged. Henry blinked. He decided he was hallucinating. Tyrone was pushing a huge covered catering cart. He was followed by Red Rosa and one of the others from Hazel's party. Henry dredged up the name from his rather hazy memory of that night—Fred? No, that wasn't right, it was Floyd.

"Tyrone? What are you doing here?" Henry demanded.

"Catering, man. We're catering this thing this evening."

"But I thought it was Capitol something. That's it, Capitol Hill Hospitality. Silly name for caterers."

"Don't knock it, man, that's us! We got the low bid, man. Now if you excuse us we got to go set up." Tyrone gave a shove to the heavy cart and the procession moved on. Rosa looked at Henry curiously, straight in the face. There was no hint of recognition. Floyd looked ahead, avoiding Henry's amazed look, and carried a box of something.

Henry went on down to the snack bar. He felt the encounter with Violet's friends was ominous. Nothing good had come of it the last time and surely nothing good could come of it now.

There were a few loafers in the lunch room drinking coffee and smoking cigarettes. Henry's nose told him it was tobacco, not marijuana. He had become quite an expert during the past year. But tobacco irritated his nose as much as pot so it didn't really make much difference. Anyway, it confirmed that not only was Violet not there but that she hadn't been there recently. He ambled back upstairs by way of the gent's.

It was four o'clock when he returned to the gallery. He went on in to see how Tyrone and his pals were setting things up. Doubtless they would use the ashram as the bar, or something like that.

He strode into the gallery. No caterers. Where the hell did they go? No Violet either. Maybe Tyrone was catering another opening somewhere. He didn't actually mention the Chandra exhibit, now that Henry thought about it. One could hope. If not, where were his caterers? It was getting pretty late for them to set up.

Kurt, the audiovisual man, was the only person in the gallery. He had a hinged panel open and was looking at the way his tape loop was running. Henry went over to him. "Have you seen Violet?"

"Nope."

"She was here, but now she's disappeared. We open the exhibition pretty soon."

"I just got here. Fuckin' tape!" Kurt tapped the Plexiglas catch box with the handle of his screwdriver to get the tape to fold properly on the bottom. "Some idiot turned it on before I checked it out." He fiddled with it and then evidently decided it was not going to tangle up and shut the panel.

"Must have been the cleaning people," lied Henry. He looked around the gallery. Funny—something didn't look right. It didn't sparkle somehow. Sparkle! "My God!" Henry screeched. "The statue! Where is it?"

"How the shit should I know?" demanded Kurt truculently. He turned and left without waiting for an answer.

120

Henry went over to the low platform where the golden Chandra should have been and stared at the spot. He blinked. It was still not there. Had Exhibits taken it out to clean it? Impossible! It weighed too much! They would have cleaned it right here. Perhaps the platform needed some work done on it? They might have trundled it off, perhaps around to the back. That would have been an awful job! Why the hell do people do things like that? Give a fellow heart failure.

Henry poked around behind the ashram. There was nothing there but some odds and ends—electrical cable, some cans of paint for touch-up, things like that. Henry sat down on the edge of the ashram. His mind was a total blank. He couldn't think. He practiced slow and careful breathing to get himself under control.

It was slowly dawning on Henry that the golden Chandra was really gone. He must act! He stood up and careened toward the door. Outside, he grabbed the street entrance guard, the new one who had come on duty at four o'clock, by the arm. "How long have you been here?"

The guard was clicking her counter for a long line of school-children who were filing in the Constitution Avenue entrance. She doggedly ignored Henry until she had finished. Then she looked vacantly at Henry, somehow avoiding looking him in the eyes.

"The gold statue in there! It has been stolen!"

"You are not supposed to bring anything into the museum, sir. The Smithsonian cannot be responsible if you don't use the checkroom."

Henry frantically tugged out his billfold and pulled out his Smithsonian identification card. He waved it at the guard. "A ten-million-dollar statue has been stolen! Sometime in the past hour!"

The guard was beginning to catch on. She picked up the phone at her station and called the duty lieutenant. In short order the guardroom was empty and the north entry hall was full of guards. Arriving visitors were being denied entry and departing ones were being sent upstairs to use the Mall exit.

Everybody in the north lobby was asking questions. Everybody was milling around and talking at once. And nobody was taking anything down. Henry thought of a Chinese fire drill and wondered why people called such confusion that.

The gallery entrance was on the west side of the lobby between the checkroom and the visitor information desk, with the entry guard's little lecternlike station no more than twenty feet away. Nobody at these locations had seen anybody cart out an eleven-hundred-pound gold statue. One of the checkroom women said she thought she remembered somebody pushing around a large catering cart, but she couldn't swear to it. It was a cold day and she had been busy with coats.

If they were to be believed, the volunteer at the information desk and the two women in the checkroom had all been continually at their duty stations since Henry had last seen the statue and had left the gallery to search for Violet. The guard shift had changed at four, so the Constitution Avenue door guard had not been on duty when the statue had likely been taken. And the earlier shift guard had already left the building.

* * *

Somebody passed the word to the director's office. Dr. Rufus Fat Dog came hurrying up as fast as his rather short legs would allow. He joined the chorus of people questioning Henry.

"When did you last see it?"

Henry looked at his watch. "Just an hour ago. Maybe an hour and a half, I'm not sure."

"Where did it go?"

"How should I know?"

"You're not being very helpful, Mr. Scruggs." Dr. Fat Dog allowed his voice to be censorious.

"Well, I wasn't here when it went. All these other people were. Why don't you ask them?"

"It's not my responsibility to guard things in the galleries or—" began the information desk volunteer.

"Nobody said it was but you still might be a witness." This from Captain Harbuck, head of the South Mall guard units. He had just arrived from the Natural History Museum. "Now, I want everybody who has been in the gallery or in the immediate

122

area of the gallery entrance this afternoon to come with me into the gallery."

"Do you want me to see if I can find all them schoolchildren who came through here, Captain?" asked the late-shift door guard.

"Don't be an idiot, Corporal."

"But what about the opening?" asked Fat Dog. "We have to open the exhibition in less than an hour and the caterers have to start setting up things in the lobby right now."

"I think you have to cancel it. We can't allow visitors in the gallery."

"I'm afraid the caterers have disappeared," Henry was now trying to be helpful.

"Then we're certainly not going to have to pay them." Fat Dog moved happily back to money considerations.

"Ah, Captain, don't you think we had best keep everybody, even the staff, out of the gallery until we've had time to examine the room?" This came from an elderly guard sergeant who didn't look to be overly respectful of the young captain.

"Good thinking, Sergeant! Now where can we assemble everybody?"

"I believe the auditorium is empty," said the sergeant. He crossed the lobby to the east side and opened the door to the Carmichael Auditorium. It was empty, and after guards were posted at the gallery door, the rest of the group filed into the auditorium and down to the seats directly in front of the stage. What had looked like a crowd in the lobby hardly filled the front two rows of seats.

The audiovisual man, Kurt Schindler, and even the cleaning people were sent for. Somnath Gupta was found in the staff toilet. A couple of Exhibits Production people and the assistant director for exhibits had evidently visited the gallery briefly, just before Kurt had arrived. They were sent for. Violet's absence was noted but nobody seemed particularly concerned about her.

If others were in the gallery during the afternoon, they weren't noticed. Everyone made statements, this time taken down, but they weren't at all helpful. Somnath confirmed the first period covered by Henry's statement and Kurt covered the last part. That made Henry feel better but did not bring them any closer to finding the statue. Henry suggested that the guards be asked about the caterers. However, the guards had been changed at four o'clock and the evening-shift guards hadn't seen anything of the caterers.

The only thing that could be concluded was that with the exception of the caterers, nobody except Smithsonian staff had been in the gallery between about two-thirty and four that afternoon. And the caterers had evidently not remained in the gallery very long before they, too, had unaccountably disappeared.

And during that period eleven hundred pounds of gold had disappeared, evidently moved past four people—a guard, a volunteer, and two coat-check women—all of whom should have seen everything that was going on. Henry claimed to have seen the caterers arrive, but they were nowhere to be found now. If they really existed, they seemed to be the likeliest suspects.

While statements were being taken, the head of the Protection Department and his assistant arrived. Colonel McKeown had spent years as an officer in the military police, retiring some time ago at age forty-five. He was hired to shape up the Smithsonian guard force after a GAO audit had found the Smithsonian remiss in protecting the hundred million objects in its collection. Part of its collection of antique firearms had found its way into Washington street crime. Insp. Dawson (Grannie) Apple had been a Philadelphia city police detective until he was hired away by Colonel McKeown to head up the Smithsonian's investigative unit.

"Scruggs!" said Vance McKeown, "I thought you were supposed to go back to being a diplomat!"

"I can't leave, Colonel. There's too much sin at the Smithsonian. You need an outsider or it goes unnoticed."

Dr. Fat Dog pushed his way into the circle of people surrounding McKeown. "Colonel, shouldn't we be notifying the metropolitan police? Right now?"

"We will, sir. As soon as I've had a chance to examine the scene of the crime."

"Well, it's your responsibility. The thief is probably getting away."

124

"He's probably been gone an hour already."

McKeown looked over the statements that had been taken by the MHT guard force. He turned to Henry. "Do you know anything about these caterers, Scruggs?"

"They call themselves Capitol Hill Hospitality. I didn't know who it was when they were hired but I recognized them, at least the ones who showed up today. The head of the group is called Tyrone and he's got two assistants, Red Rosa and somebody named Floyd."

"Red Rosa?"

"Yes. She was named for Rosa Luxembourg. Her family's Communist."

"Good God! How do you know these people?"

Henry explained about Hazel's party, leaving Violet's name out of it.

"And you, State Department!" McKeown shook his head at the sorry plight of hallowed institutions, and got back to the investigation. A search of the crime scene didn't turn up much. There were a few splinters on the wooden platform and the railing on one side looked as though something had leaned hard against it. Otherwise, there seemed to be nothing wrong except that the statue was not there anymore.

A crowd of guests had gathered at the entrance, but their way was blocked by guards. Henry spotted Bhagat Gupta through the glass door and arranged for the guards to allow him to come in.

"What's happened, Henry? Isn't the opening supposed to be at five o'clock?"

"It has to be cancelled, Bhagat. The director is going out in a few moments and suggest that everybody go home."

"Oh, dear! Is somebody ill?"

"Everybody feels a bit sick. Your statue has been stolen."

"No!" Bhagat looked appalled. "But this is a catastrophe! The owner will not understand how such an institution as the Smithsonian could let this happen!"

"We don't understand it either. Somnath and I saw it at about two-thirty and when I came back just after four, it was gone. Vanished, like it never was."

"Well, at least the police have had a chance to get on the trail while it is still warm."

"They haven't been called."

"What! Why not, in heaven's name!?"

"Our Protection Department is still investigating."

Bhagat went striding over to Colonel McKeown and demanded that the police be called in. After the call, nothing happened for three-quarters of an hour and then the police arrived and began taking everybody's statements over again. It was almost seven-thirty when all the possible witnesses were allowed to leave. The tape loop had broken an hour earlier, bringing blessed silence from the Indian music in the gallery and now people drifted away in little groups, leaving a core of city police and Smithsonian investigators who would poke around for most of the night.

"There is one other odd thing, Bhagat."

"Which is that, Henry?"

"I haven't seen Violet since midafternoon."

"That is very odd. I should have thought—"

"It's just that she said something rather silly yesterday. She said she wouldn't be at the opening because she was going to kill herself."

"You must have misunderstood, Henry."

"No, she was quite clear. I thought she was just being dramatic at the time. You know how Violet is. Then I saw her early this afternoon and she said she didn't mean it."

"Well, then, I don't see what you're worried about."

"Then she said she'd do it when I least expected it. Then, of course, I didn't expect it anymore."

"Yes." Bhagat was silent for a long moment. "I see what you mean. Henry, I have a feeling that we had better get over to Violet's apartment."

Bhagat's Indian Embassy car and driver were waiting in front of the museum, illegally parked in the driveway. The guards, long experienced with vehicles having diplomatic tags, were leaving the driver alone. Henry and Bhagat climbed into the Cadillac and Bhagat ordered the driver to go at once to Violet's house.

* * *

Herbert was sitting on Violet's door stoop with his nose to the front door. He was whimpering. Bhagat reached over him and tried the door. It was locked. "She must not be home."

"I don't think she would ever go away and leave this idiot dog outside. When you went to India, she locked him in."

"That is true, Henry, but she wouldn't leave him outside if she were inside, either."

"Something's wrong, Bhagat. We had better go in. Give me room; I can open the door." Henry got out a credit card and used it to push back the door latch.

Herbert pushed his way past them and bounded around the little house as though he were looking for Violet. Eventually he settled down in the kitchen and stared at his dog dish. He sat there waiting impatiently for somebody to feed him. Being out in the cold so long had given Herbert an appetite.

Bhagat and Henry took more time to look around the house. Violet was definitely not there, but somebody had been. Of course there wasn't much furniture to upset but somebody had been looking for something, poking around in everything. Not that Violet was tidy enough for it to make much difference except that the clothes in her closet were all off the hangers and the cabinet doors were open.

"Oh, dear," said Bhagat, "something isn't quite right."

They fed Herbert. Since he appeared to have been outside for hours, they decided he could do without his evening promenade. Before they left, Henry wiped clean the dog-food can and the can opener and on his way out wiped the doorknob, pulling the door to with his handkerchief over the knob. Bhagat smiled his approval.

 **Nine**

"Henry?" Phoebe looked up from her book. "You're late. It must have been a good opening." Phoebe had declined to attend. It was Violet's big night and she would rather see it later, thank you very much. If at all. In the ordinary course of business she could ignore Violet, but being at a ceremonial event such as the opening and having to be polite to her was more than she could manage. Not just yet.

Henry struggled out of his coat and dumped it in the chair nearest the door. It was an old coat he had bought when he was living in Austria. He had wanted to buy a new one this year, but Phoebe had told him he had to buy another chair, first, since he never hung anything up. There wasn't room in the living room for another chair, so Henry kept his old coat. When the weather got warmer he would remember to lose it. Actually, that had been one of the disappointments about living with Violet. She didn't have any chairs at all. The coat wasn't on his mind now. A drink was. He fixed uncommonly large drinks for himself and Phoebe. He sat down in a heap.

"What are we doing?" she asked. "Celebrating your exhibit opening?"

"It didn't open. Somebody stole the Chandra statue."

"Stole it! Why that thing must weigh—"

"Over half a ton." Henry explained about the theft.

Phoebe was intrigued. She pumped him for details. She was beginning to look pleased—there was a crime to solve. In law school, Phoebe had always imagined a career as a criminal lawyer—part investigator and part courtroom strategist, a sort of Perry Mason lawyer. After graduation, however, she took the first job offered and concentrated on paying off her student loans. So much for the prime-time TV life. Still, the hankering lurked, unfulfilled by the product licensing agreements, construction and services contracts, and deeds of gifts that filled her days.

"And I think Violet has disappeared. She just vanished from the museum in the middle of the afternoon. After the opening was cancelled, Bhagat and I went over to her house to see if we could find her. Her dog was locked out and she was not there."

"Violet was murdered," Phoebe announced excitedly.

"That's ridiculous," said Henry automatically.

"Well, I don't know why. She fools around with other women's men. She's just the sort of female who might get murdered."

"There's no evidence of that at all. The most likely thing is that she was involved with this fellow Tyrone and his gang. They are probably even now somewhere in West Virginia melting Chandra down and casting Washington Monuments."

"Why Washington Monuments?"

"Eiffel Towers have already been done."

"Oh. Why West Virginia?"

"That's where I'd go to do something like that. The other possibility is that she went somewhere and committed suicide. That's what she said yesterday she was going to do," Henry said, miserably. The more he thought about it, the more likely it seemed. "I just didn't believe her."

"Of course you didn't believe her. That kind never commits suicide. I could believe something like an accidental overdose, but not suicide."

"I don't see how you can say a thing like that."

"You said she left her dog outside. I wouldn't. That is, I wouldn't if I were going to go to West Virginia and I certainly wouldn't if I were going to commit suicide."

"That doesn't make any sense at all! In the first place you wouldn't have a dog. And the other thing is you wouldn't go to West Virginia. You aren't the type." Henry didn't know about Phoebe and suicide, but it seemed unlikely.

"That's it exactly! She isn't either."

Henry didn't understand Phoebe's reasoning, if that is what it was. But he felt she might be right. And if Violet was murdered, it might have something to do with $10 million worth of gold. Then, again, it might not. It was also possible, he supposed, that she had simply gone to a movie.

* * *

Friday the first of December was not one of Henry's better days. The Chandra exhibition should have opened today to the general public, and, of course, it didn't. The night before, Phoebe had kept him awake speculating about the theft and what she referred to as "the murder." She seemed to regard Violet only as an element in a puzzle, not as a recently departed person (physically or spiritually). Henry was trying to deal with it by not thinking about it. To that end, he had had several more drinks and now his head hurt. Not only did his head hurt but his ankle itched. He must have picked up one of Herbert's fleas at Violet's place. He always got terrible reactions to flea bites. Fleas knew it and lay in wait for him.

Unbeknownst to Henry, the *Post* and the *Star* were onto the theft before he got to his office and Dillyhay Plover had detailed one of his many flunkies to wait at the foot of the tower stairs for him to arrive. "Mr. Scruggs! Don't go up to your office! Mr. Plover has to see you first!"

Dillyhay was the director of the Smithsonian's Office of Public Affairs. Public Affairs is often called Public Information in other agencies, but Dillyhay's idea of public information was the kind of view you get trying to look over a stone wall twice as high as your head. He liked to paper that wall with propaganda thinly veiled as press releases.

"I don't have time to talk to him. I expect the press is waiting for me in my office."

"That's what Mr. Plover wants to talk to you about. He told me to tell you that you can't talk to them." The young journalism graduate intern was clearly uncomfortable. She regarded Henry with some uncertainty, but she was determined to stop him from going up the steps. That is what she had been sent to do. She grabbed him by the arm and tugged.

"I don't dance," said Henry as he pulled away. "Tell your boss he's being silly and that I'll decide what to say to the press."

"Please! Mr. Scruggs! You have to tell him that yourself. He won't take it from me!" The girl looked to be in great distress.

Henry's heart was not made of stone and besides, being yelled at by twenty-one-year-old girls hurt his head. "Well, all right, but it's not going to change anything." Henry followed her through the door on the second-floor landing.

Dillyhay's office was on a floor that had been erected years earlier in one of the Arts and Industries Building's galleries, making two floors where there had been one before. Personnel was below and had tall windows that now extended right to the ceiling. On the floor above, Public Affairs had only the arches from the original windows and the arches went clear to the floor. If you put your head right against the glass, in addition to getting your ear cold, you could look down through a narrow gap into the Personnel offices. There was something symbolic about this, but Henry had not worked out just what it was.

"Scruggs!" said Dillyhay when he entered, "I have spoken to Secretary Vernon."

Well, hooray for you, thought Henry.

"And she agrees that I should be the only one in the Institution to talk to the press about the theft of that thing."

"Do you know what 'that thing' is?"

"I don't particularly want to know. All I'm going to say is that the matter is under investigation."

"Well, that seems harmless enough."

"Exactly! We can get out a release when the investigation has been completed."

"Why don't you just tell the press you never heard of the Smithsonian and doubt such an institution exists? Then they can get back to covering City Council and things people really care about reading."

"You haven't changed your attitude, have you?"

"I suppose not," said Henry with a sigh.

"Well, you have your orders. You don't have to like them. And you better stay away from your office just in case the press tries to see you there."

* * *

Henry called Gerald from Dillyhay's outer office. Gerald told him he was supposed to go to Colonel McKeown's office and when and if he got finished there, he was to take administrative leave for the day, anything to keep out of the way. When Henry got off the phone, Dillyhay came out of his office to say that he had just spoken to the under secretary and he wanted to speak to Henry right away. The under secretary trumped the director of the Protection Department. Henry trudged downstairs and through the tunnel to the Castle. He climbed the stairs to the second floor with a growing feeling that the establishment was closing ranks,

Rossmore Owens, the under secretary, was a few months short of seventy and up against compulsory retirement. In the past, he had been the most reasonable of administrators, but now there were those who said that he didn't want any trouble, anything that would disturb his plans to retire in the spring to his house in Annapolis. Ordinarily, Henry didn't have much to do with him. It was only when there was big trouble that Ross dealt directly with those a few levels down in the hierarchy. In the crunch, Ross was a hands-on man.

Henry was kept waiting in Owen's outer office. After a quarter of an hour, Colonel McKeown arrived and breezed right past Henry. After a few more minutes, the under secretary came to his office door and summoned Henry.

"Can't say I'm glad to see you, Scruggs." Ross looked tired. He returned to his desk, walking as though his back hurt him and he couldn't quite straighten up.

"Sorry, sir. No offense, but it wasn't my idea."

"No, I don't imagine so. Mr. Plover seems to be the one who thinks I should talk to you. I wanted Colonel McKeown here as well. I gather you were supposed to see him anyway."

"Yes, sir." Henry remained standing. He hadn't been asked to sit down.

132

"Mr. Plover is right, you know. You had better let us handle this theft business."

"Yes, sir. I mean, yes I know what he thinks but I don't necessarily agree."

"I didn't think you would. But you have to remember that some people might regard you as a suspect."

"Me, sir?" Henry sat down without an invitation.

"That's right, Scruggs," said Colonel McKeown, "we can't entirely rule you out. Of course that doesn't mean that we, personally, suspect you."

"Thanks."

"You or that designer you have been working with, Miss—"

"Strauss, Violet Strauss."

"That's the one. You might pass the word to her as well."

"I can't. I don't know where she is."

"You better sure as hell hope you don't," McKeown said, cryptically.

"Colonel, perhaps you had better explain what you and Mr. Scruggs are talking about."

"Yes, sir! Well, it appears some caterers might have had something to do with the disappearance of the golden idol. It was where it was supposed to be and then the caterers came and then the caterers left all at once and the thing was gone." McKeown's prose wasn't elegant but he had about summed it up.

"You mean the statue was gone?"

"Yes, sir."

"What Colonel McKeown is trying to say," explained Henry helpfully, "is that the statue was last seen a little while before the caterers arrived, and later, when we found that the statue was missing, we looked for the caterers and couldn't find them either."

"That's what I just said, Scruggs." McKeown gave Henry a shut-up look. "Anyway, Scruggs here said in his statement last night that he knew the caterers and that they were people he had met through some broad he knew on Capitol Hill, only he only knew her first name. Apparently Scruggs is something of a swinger." Colonel McKeown made no attempt to hide his disapproval. "Is that right, Scruggs?"

"Exactly right, Colonel. I couldn't have explained it better myself."

"Well," continued McKeown, either missing Henry's sarcasm or choosing to overlook it, "we asked Scruggs whether Miss Strauss knew the caterers and he said we ought to ask her. Notice that he didn't say no."

"I didn't say yes, either."

McKeown ignored Henry. "The only reason we can think of that the Strauss woman might have disappeared was that she was somehow involved with the caterers and they cooked up the theft between them."

"Among them."

"Huh?" Colonel McKeown stared at Henry. "Between them. Between Strauss and the caterers."

"There was more than one caterer. Three, actually. Among Miss Strauss and the caterers."

"Cut it out, you two! I've got more to do than sit here while you quibble!"

"Sorry."

"Sorry, sir. Scruggs is a pain in the—"

"Get on with it!"

"Sir, the caterers had a cart that was big enough to hold the statue if you tipped it over."

"The statue, not the cart." Henry was determined to help out.

"The day-shift guard said that the caterers unloaded the cart from a truck at the loading dock in the basement. They took it upstairs on the elevator. A few minutes later they came back down and loaded the cart back on the truck. The guard said they were in a real big hurry. They told him that they had got the wrong museum, that they were supposed to be over at Natural History. Then they tore out of there and a few minutes later the guard went off shift at four o'clock. That's all he knows."

"Didn't the guard look inside the cart?" asked the under secretary incredulously.

"No, sir. Things like that happen all the time. He didn't think anything of it."

"Did you ask about Miss Strauss?"

"Yes, sir. The guard didn't see her. He knows her. He knows all the Exhibits people."

"What do you know about these caterers?"

"Only that it is the first time they have ever worked for the Smithsonian. Special Events says they got the low bid. And Scruggs has given us what he says are their first names. Oh, yes, and one of them is probably a Communist, sir!"

The under secretary covered his eyes. He didn't want even to think about this being a Communist plot.

"What about the exhibition?" asked Henry.

"What about it?" asked the under secretary. He was very weary and it wasn't even lunchtime yet.

"It hasn't been opened yet."

"Oh," said the under secretary. "Colonel, do you see any reason why we shouldn't open it now? Are your men through in the gallery?"

"Yes, sir, it can be opened to the public any time you want."

"I don't suppose there is any reason for any fanfare now that this gold statue is gone. Colonel, you may as well give the order to have the guards open the gallery."

* * *

As they were leaving the under secretary's office, McKeown told Henry to go over to see the Metropolitan Police. "They're looking for your caterer friends, Scruggs. It will help your case if you are very helpful."

"My case!?"

"Your case. You ain't off the hook, yet."

* * *

It was well after dark when Henry found a parking place on Capitol Hill. It wasn't very near his house, but for once he felt he didn't have to be fearful and hurry to the safety of his front door. Surely nothing else could happen to him now, and besides, he had plenty of protection, of a sort. It was a good thing, too, because he was dead tired. That afternoon with the police had been long and hard and you would have thought he was the prime suspect. It got particularly bad after they wormed it out of him that Tyrone and his helpers were really Violet's friends.

135

Somehow that made it look worse for Violet and also for Henry, who seemed to be covering for Violet.

After he finally got released by the police (with the injunction not to go far and the promise that he would be hearing from them again), Henry went over to Violet's house to see if she might have turned up. Somebody had, but it hadn't been Violet. If she had gone to a movie, it was more than a double feature.

Violet's place had been gone over again, possibly by the police. Herbert knocked Henry down and was about to eat him when Henry bargained for his life with two large cans of Alpo. It didn't seem possible to abandon Herbert again even if Herbert would have allowed it (Herbert was becoming neurotic on the subject), so Henry brought him along home.

So it was that he had nothing to fear from the muggers in the street. Not so, however, from behind the door of his house, where Phoebe was waiting. Henry unlocked the door and pushed it open. He pulled on the leash and Herbert shuffled into the room.

"What the hell is that? A Yeti?"

"Phoebe, say hello to Herbert."

"Are you out of your mind? You can't bring that dog in here!"

"Shush, Phoebe!" Henry whispered loudly, "Herbert doesn't know he's a dog and now's not the time to tell him."

"That's Violet's animal, isn't it?" Phoebe demanded, ignoring Herbert's sensitivities.

Henry hesitated. "It used to be."

"She gave it to you? I'm not going to have that thing in the house! How could you bring home something that belonged to that woman?" Phoebe was gathering her outrage.

"Phoebe, Violet's still missing. I couldn't leave Herbert in the house alone. He might starve."

"You could have turned him loose on the street."

"He wouldn't be able to take care of himself. He thinks food comes in a can."

"God!" That belied Phoebe feelings. She never invoked deities with any serious intent. "Couldn't he learn to eat rats like any other wild animal?"

Henry sighed. "I'm going to put Herbert in the backyard. It

isn't too cold tonight and he's pretty woolly. Maybe he will survive. Tomorrow we can figure out what to do with him." Henry pulled Herbert toward the back door. Herbert took a detour by Phoebe's chair and paused to shake off a few fleas. Phoebe hastily tucked her legs under her, out of the way, and wrinkled up her nose. Not surprising—Herbert had probably never been washed, and smelled decidedly doggy. Henry tugged and Herbert continued on his way, sniffing here and there as he went.

Henry returned to the room and sat down on a straight chair. He rolled down his socks to look for fleas. He found one, which he captured between his thumb and forefinger. Holding the flea tight, he went upstairs to the bathroom and drowned it in the toilet, flushing it away to the Blue Plains treatment plant. He made another check of his ankles. No more fleas. They were probably hiding in his trouser cuffs.

* * *

Saturday, he took the dog out walking and headed in the general direction of Hazel's house. It did not help that he could not remember Hazel's last name. Perhaps he had never known it, though the police had refused to believe that. It had been such a long time since that night in January (or was it February?) that he wasn't very clear about where Hazel lived. Ordinarily he could find his way back anywhere he had driven, but Violet had driven the car that night.

Herbert and Henry walked and walked and then they walked some more. There were dozens of places that looked like they might be Hazel's. And she might have moved on somewhere else or in with somebody. Henry looked around to see if a policeman was following him. They might have put a tail on him to find Hazel. On the other hand, he might try to follow a policeman in hopes that the copper might be first to find Hazel and he could march right up and hand over Herbert.

Either way, it was going to look bad if Henry managed to find Hazel in the presence of the police. Then they would be bound to believe he was in with the plot.

Henry tried to remember whether Hazel had a dog. Would she join the evening parade? What time did single girls walk

137

their dogs on Saturdays? Probably early, Henry thought. Early enough so there would be time to make dates and get ready for them if there was any getting ready to be done. But it was only the middle of the afternoon and there weren't any girl/dog teams out yet. He was getting cold and tired and Herbert took to sitting down. A hundred-and-forty-pound fuzzy immovable rock.

"Come on, Herbert, let's go home." Herbert yawned at Henry and got slowly to his feet, dragging his bottom for the first few steps. They went home by stages with frequent rest stops. Phoebe was out shopping and wasn't at home to complain, so Henry swiped a large box of fish sticks from the freezer and put them in the oven to thaw. Herbert went to sleep with his nose at the oven door waiting for his supper.

If Henry didn't find him a home immediately, he was going to have to go buy some dog food. Violet had always fed him canned dog food or, if she was out of it, which was more often the case, she just gave him some of whatever she was having. That was going to have to stop.

Herbert was going to have to come to grips with being a dog. He was going to have to learn to get along on those big eighty-pound sacks of dry dog food. Ugh! thought Henry as he felt a pang of sympathy for Herbert.

In the meantime Henry made himself a pot of oolong tea. While he waited for the tea to steep, he inspected his ankles for fleas. There weren't any. They had probably moved into the carpet for the winter.

After tea and Herbert's dinner, they set out again. It had gotten colder and would soon be dark so Henry loaded Herbert and a bottle of Scotch into the Corvair. It was a lot warmer and easier on the feet. The Scotch would warm the insides. Henry drove toward the downtown and then turned back toward Capitol Hill. He tried to remember that night. He was sure they had taken Massachusetts Avenue and then turned left. But where? Onto Eighth? No, it had to be Ninth. Henry went half a block North on Ninth and parked the car. They got out. In spite of the cold, Herbert was happy enough to be back on the sidewalk

138

again with its interesting smells (odors? stinks? Probably both).

"Okay, Herbert, you lead."

Herbert snuffled around for a while and then found a trail that appealed for him. He struck out at what was for him a brisk walk. At the next intersection he turned the corner and continued half a block where he tried several gates for odors. He raised his fuzzy leg on these and sprinkled them—leaving his calling card. Then without pausing even to sniff the next several gates, he trotted positively to an open iron gate and down a half dozen steps to the door of a basement apartment. Herbert knew where he was. He swatted the door with his paw and woofed. Henry helped out by pushing the door-bell button.

Hazel's pretty face appeared at the glass panel in the door. She looked at Henry without recognition. It was, after all, dark outside. Herbert struggled to his hind legs and stuck his nose against the glass. Hazel opened the door. "Vi! I've been trying to reach you! Come on in, Herbert!"

Henry followed Herbert into the apartment. Hazel looked surprised. "Hello. Where's Violet?"

"Hazel—don't you remember me?"

"No, I don't believe so. But come on in! Any friend of Herbert's—"

"I'm Henry." Hazel looked at him curiously and Henry realized he should have put on his three-piece suit. Corduroys, a leather jacket, and a beret didn't correspond to the image Violet had promoted.

"Where's Violet? Are you back with her?" She had placed him but looked him over critically.

"I wanted to talk to you about that. Violet's missing." Henry told Hazel about the theft and how Violet and her other friends were missing. "It seems possible that your friends Tyrone, Rosa, and Floyd might have stolen the statue."

Hazel looked very uncomfortable. Henry held up his bottle of Scotch and Hazel looked immediately happier. A Pavlovian response, Henry thought. Hazel hunted around for two more or less clean glasses. She had forgotten to fill the ice trays so Henry poured neat whiskey into the glasses. It would sterilize them

139

better anyway. He averted his eyes while Hazel topped up her glass with Coke.

It took Henry several hours to worm it out of Hazel that she had heard Tyrone and the others talking about stealing the statue. She had not been sure they really meant to do it, but Violet had at least suggested how it could be done. Hazel was sure that Violet wouldn't have been involved herself, but that she was very good at thinking up things.

Hazel was frightened by Henry's report that Violet had threatened suicide again. She knew that Violet probably wouldn't do it but it upset her all the same. Now Rosa was different. When Rosa threatened it, it was time to call the rescue wagon. In fact Rosa had just gotten out of the sanitarium again after her most recent attempt.

Where they were all living, Hazel didn't know. Perhaps all together. She had a telephone number for Tyrone. It took Henry another hour to get the number from her but part of the delay was because by then Hazel would have had trouble finding the door. (She seemed to have an instinct for the bed.)

Before Henry left, Hazel agreed to keep Herbert, but by then she would probably have agreed to about anything.

* * *

Monday morning Henry got into the office as late as he could manage and still be seen at his desk before it was time to go to lunch. Phoebe had gone in early, by comparison. Henry had stayed home to enjoy a leisurely breakfast and read through a book of toccatas by Carlos Seixas. The andante to the G-minor toccata still ran through his head as he climbed the sixty-two steps to the Foreign Affairs Office. Fifty-three, fifty-four, two steps on the landing, fifty-five, fifty-six, fifty-seven, fifty-eight, fifty-nine, sixty, sixty-one, sixty-two. Henry managed to time the end of the toccata for the top step. Some day, he thought, he would have to have an office with a piano in it.

There were a lot of yellow call slips on his desk, most of them left over from Friday and most of them from some Carl Harrison. That name was vaguely familiar, but Henry couldn't place it immediately. Well, there wasn't really time to get involved in telephoning anybody before lunch. He had better go now if he

140

were going to get a table in the Commons without having to wait forever in line. Phoebe was always late so there was no use counting on her to get one. He got to his feet headed for the stairs. Sixty-one, sixty, fifty-nine . . .

* * *

Mystery meat. That's what the Commons was serving today. It masqueraded as veal parmigiana but under all that cheese and tomato glop it was just plain mystery meat. The word had spread and Henry was lucky to get a table at all. He ordered a Czech beer and settled down to wait for Phoebe. It was just as well to wait because the line at the buffet was long and he could see from where he sat that the mystery meat was going to run out soon and then the line would stop moving until some more was brought up from the kitchen in the basement. Henry amused himself by counting the number of words in Milton's sonnet on his blindness. If he could remember it all. It had been a long time since he had thought about it.

"Are you saving this for me?"

Henry looked up. Taylor Maidstone was standing over him, his expression daring Henry to say no. "Not exactly; I was expecting Phoebe."

"She's not very large and maybe she won't come at all." Taylor sat down without being asked.

Henry looked down at the small round table and calculated three plates. If everybody held their drinks, then maybe. Or if they ate in shifts. "I thought you were in Bhutan." The moment he said it, he was sorry. As a matter of principle, he always pretended that Taylor's extended absences in exotic places were about as exciting as a day off at the dentist.

"It was Nepal and as you can see, I'm not."

"But you were?"

"Well, yes, but then I've been lots of places." Taylor enjoyed being exasperating.

"I know where you were; I saw your letter to Hamilton. How was your sex with the whoozits?"

"The Kaani-hod, you must mean, and your mother or your guardian will have to accompany you before I can tell you about it."

141

"I think I'd rather not know. But speaking of that part of the world, your help was much needed earlier this year. I had to curate an Indian exhibition. It opened on Friday."

"In the Smithsonian? Are you qualified?"

"In MHT. I—"

"Forget I asked that. Now that I think about it, most of the exhibitions in the Smithsonian are put together by unqualified persons."

"I don't know that that is a fair state— Oh, here's Phoebe, we'd better find her a chair."

Phoebe liked Taylor and was willing to put up with a certain amount of inconvenience for the amusement he provided. Taylor Maidstone was an irresponsible genius who posed as an anthropologist. He drove traditional anthropologists, ethnologists, and the like up the wall. They were not amused. Everybody else was, except for the administrative and budget people. People who didn't really count. Taylor ignored budgets and other things like that and insulted his managers if they complained.

The line was momentarily short while the first wave was feeding and the second wave was waiting for tables. Henry's party went after their food. Henry put his beer on the floor and everything else fit on the table.

"What is this Indian exhibition? It is hard for me to imagine what you might do."

"It is on Chandra."

"Chandra? Who is Chandra?"

"K. V. Chandra, of course. This is his sesquicentenary. I thought you were an expert on India."

"I am. Actually, nobody is, but I know as much about India as anybody else."

"And you never heard of Chandra?" It was hard to believe.

"Now that I think of it, there was some fellow in South India. A minor Indian separatist, if I remember correctly. But it seems odd for the Smithsonian to celebrate his anniversary, don't you think?"

"I don't know why you find it odd. Chandra was, in his own way, just about as important as Gandhi."

142

"I must say that is a quaint revisionist view. Did you come to the conclusion yourself, or did you have some help?"

"Well, you make it clear why the exhibition was needed. He is almost unknown in this country."

"Taylor," said Phoebe, "this is Henry's big exhibition. You shouldn't make fun of it."

"I wouldn't dream of dimming his luster, Phoebe, dear. I've heard of this Chandra, but it's only because I've spent the past fifteen years in that part of the world. He was a very minor figure. Not now, of course, since the Smithsonian has apparently immortalized him."

"You should go over and see the exhibition. I wrote a biography that tells how important he was."

"Did you get your information from somewhere or do you have a natural gift for fiction?"

"The Indian embassy provided all sorts of biographical material."

"I'd like to see it. I thought I'd read most of the literature."

"Well, the most useful stuff was unpublished material. Published references only mentioned him occasionally. I guess it must be hard to get anything published in India that competes with Gandhi for attention."

"Actually, it wouldn't be all that difficult. The Nehru faithful have never been all that fond of Gandhi. Who got you to do this exhibition?"

Henry explained about the approach by Bhagat and Adair Blake. Taylor listened intently.

"Bhagat Gupta—I know about him. He has a reputation for being shifty. Even in India where there are at least a hundred million shifty people. And Blake, I know him well. Too well, actually. He has interfered with my research in India for years."

"But the whole embassy has been involved. Both of them, actually—the Indians' here and ours in New Delhi—"

"That settles it," he announced when Henry had finished, "you've been had. Now it only remains to discover why you've been had. They might have done it just for the sport of it. I would have if I'd thought of it first."

"I think it has something to do with the murder!" Phoebe exclaimed.

"Murder? Has somebody been murdered? Why haven't I heard anything about this?"

"Don't you read the papers?" Phoebe was not above a little fantasy, herself. She had decided it must be murder because she had often thought of murdering Violet herself. And if there had been a murder, it must have been reported in the papers. Things like that always were.

"It wasn't in the papers because there hasn't been any murder," Henry corrected.

"Well, the theft was in the paper," Phoebe said, reluctantly abandoning the higher drama. "Surely you read about that."

"I read the *Hindustani Times* when I can get it. I don't recall any mention—"

"There was something in the *Washington Post.*"

"If it was in the funnies, I probably saw it, but I don't remember it."

Henry broke in. "We had a statue of Chandra in the exhibition and it was stolen."

"What kind of a statue?"

"A solid gold statue of Chandra as Vishnu. Set with rubies and riding on the back of a turtle. With four hands."

"Feet, you mean," said Phoebe. "Turtles don't have hands."

"Don't pay any attention to her. Vishnu has four hands, of course. And the face was of Chandra."

"Vishnu got up as Chandra? That seems highly unlikely." Taylor demanded a full accounting of all that had been going on.

Henry got so immersed in the story that he forgot to put in his order for chocolate truffle pie until it was all gone. After lunch he was left with the feeling that all was not right with the world and it wasn't just chocolate pie. He still hadn't told anybody what Hazel had told him about Violet being mixed up in the theft. It didn't make much sense. It made even less sense now that Taylor raised doubts about the statue. What was really going on?

Ten

It was about on step number forty-three of his climb to the Foreign Affairs Office that Henry decided he was going to have to do something about it. If he had indeed been had, he wanted to know for sure. He supposed that the only way to find out was to do some research. Research that he should have done in the very beginning.

But first he'd better return Harrison's call. Henry remembered him now. He was a *Washington Post* reporter who had once taken him and Phoebe to the Occidental to pump him for inside information on the Smithsonian.

The Occidental had come down in the world. Henry decided he would hold out for the Madison this time. The main dining room, not the little buffet in the lounge. The *Post* could afford it.

* * *

"Harrison."

"Mr. Harrison, this is Henry Scruggs. I believe you've been trying to get in touch with me."

"Scruggs? Just a minute. Oh, yeah, at the Smithsonian. Listen, Scruggs, we talked before. More than a year ago."

"I remember."

"I want to talk to you about that missing idol thing."

"It isn't an idol."

"Well, whatever."

"I don't know anything about it.

"But you just said—"

"I know. But I've been told to say I don't know anything."

"A gag order, huh? Look, maybe we can have lunch and you can explain what you aren't supposed to say."

"Sorry, I've already had lunch."

"I meant tomorrow."

"Well, I don't know—"

"What I had in mind was Harvey's. I seem to remember you like to eat. You know they serve all the hot rolls you can eat. They're really good. Go good with soft shell crab."

"They're out of season. They're not as good frozen."

"Okay, you can have something else. What about stuffed flounder?"

"That would be nice, but what I'd really like is to have lunch at the Madison."

Harrison was silent for a moment. "Well, I could probably manage that. It would save me taxi fare." The Madison was right across the street from the *Post*.

"Not the lounge. In the main dining room. With an appetizer and a premium Scotch. Maybe two."

"Jeez . . . I don't know, Scruggs. I'd have to get something awfully good for that. And exclusive. You can't give anything to the *Star* or the *Daily News*. And what do I do if you decide you can't tell me anything?"

"I already told you I can't. But if you invite Phoebe Casey to come along she can tell you anything she wants."

"Is that the dame who was with you last time?"

"She's not a dame, but yes, she's the one."

"But what if I have to ask you a question? She might not know the answer."

"You can ask Phoebe. Then I can tell her. I don't have any secrets from Phoebe. Of course anything I say to Phoebe has to be off the record."

146

"Well, I might could spring for the Madison. But I'll have to get back to you."

"Remember, Phoebe will want an appetizer too. And the drinks." Henry hung up before Harrison could object.

* * *

When the subject of the Chandra exhibition first came up a year before, Henry should have gone to the Library of Congress and done some research on Chandra. He had thought about it, but had decided not. There was bound to be too much material and Henry was a slow reader. If he had gotten bogged down in that kind of research, he would never have gotten everything else done. But now there was no help for it. He had to find out if Taylor Maidstone was right.

The first fifteen minutes in the Library of Congress were enlightening. It was a wonderfully organized place, out of keeping with the baroque splendor of its great entry hall. There were no references in the card files on Chandra. Visions of thick volumes of learned discourse in tiny print evaporated. They were replaced with a creepy feeling that something was very much wrong. There were other entries under the name Chandra, but none were listed as K. V. Chandra. Henry started looking under "India—Independence movement, British in India," and under the names of contemporary viceroys. Henry was reassured, but only a little. Here and there K. V. Chandra, or Chandra not otherwise identified, cropped up. A minor intellectual and separatist leader. A small thorn in the side of the British raj, but no more. Damn Bhagat! And Blake! And just about everybody! The most interesting thing that Henry discovered was a modern reference to recent efforts of a small group of Indians to gain recognition for Chandra. That source mentioned that Chandra's name had been added to Gandhi's in the Indian request to Vice President Humphrey for cultural exchange exhibitions. Nobody had cared enough to turn down the Chandra supporters.

Henry's first impulse was to go to Bhagat and demand an accounting. But Taylor's words nagged him: "You've been had. Now it only remains to discover why." He needed to find out a whole lot more before he spoke to Bhagat.

* * *

Tuesday morning there was a note from Harrison when Henry
got to his office. Lunch was a go for one o'clock. Henry alerted
Phoebe and settled down to do a couple of hours of work. It had
been so long since he had done anything useful that he hardly
knew where to start. In his In box he found a number of overdue
requests for exchange visitor certificates—research fellows coming to the Smithsonian midyear. He rolled a form DSP-66 into
his typewriter and started to fill out the most urgent. Nothing
happened. The typewriter didn't make any mark. Some bastard
had been using his typewriter and run out the ribbon. He looked
closely at it. There was no ribbon cassette. Some worse-than-a-
bastard had stolen it. Gerald? Dreamy!? Henry got to his feet and
went over to the temporary typist/receptionist.

"Have you got a spare ribbon for a Selectric II?"

"No, sir, there aren't any."

"Not any at all?"

"No. I looked. I used mine up last Thursday and couldn't find
one. I had to take one out of that typewriter over there. It wasn't
being used." She pointed toward Henry's office.

Henry tried to keep calm. "You mean in that office in the
corner?" She nodded. "All right, you're fired," Henry said with
even tones. Too even, perhaps.

"But I work for Temposec. You have to pay me to the end of
the day."

She knew exactly what to say. She must be used to it, Henry
thought. "I don't care. Just go back where you came from."

"What about the work Mr. Blackman gave me to do?"

"Just dump it in the wastebasket. Gerald ought to do his own
typing. Everybody else does." Henry opened up the receptionist's typewriter and retrieved his ribbon.

Henry finished his exchange visitor certificates and was off to
lunch before Gerald noticed he didn't have a typist anymore.

* * *

There is almost certainly no grand hotel in Washington that
looks less grand than the Madison. It is somewhat like a prosper-
ous insurance company or perhaps something to do with bank-
ing. Inside, however, it looks reasonably spiffy as long as you

148

don't worry too much about the size of the public spaces. If twenty people wanted to sit down at once, somebody would have to bring his own chair. Of course the Madison's usual clientele of princes and millionaires is not given to hanging around in the lobby.

There are some real antiques around and some gold leaf. A piano that they won't let you play. Henry wasn't too keen on that. It was said that the owner had burrowed underneath Fifteenth Street to build a vault for the rest of his antiques collection. If it were true, Henry thought it was a good place for the stuff.

But the main dining room was the place to be in Washington if you wanted to have excellent food, perfect service, and elegant surroundings. It was a place that made *Washington Post* reporters nervous because sometimes the publisher or the executive editor ate there. Harrison had asked for a table in the darkest corner away from the windows on the north. He looked around, furtively, as he entered.

Henry strode in as though he owned the place. After all, he had just fired a clerk (albeit without authority to do so) and the room was probably full of executives who fired people all the time.

They had Glenfiddich. Henry would have preferred something more exotic, but Grant's whiskeys were certainly good enough to drink. Phoebe ordered a margarita, a pleasant though poisonous drink in Henry's opinion. As he might have expected, Harrison ordered Canadian Club—high living for the undiscriminating palate. Henry and Phoebe ordered the gravlox appetizer and the fresh tuna with green peppercorn sauce. Harrison ordered a steak—high living for a gourmand.

"Try to keep the bill down, will you?"

"We're only having one dessert, Carl, dear," cooed Phoebe. She was already on her second margarita. "And we'll make it worth your while." She breathed heavily on Harrison and interposed her glass between them, peering at him across the small, salt-rimmed pond of tequila.

The spell was broken by the arrival of the gravlox. Harrison looked on while Henry and Phoebe devoured their appetizers.

He isn't having a good time, Phoebe thought; I'll fix that. "Just when did you realize that the theft of the statue and the murder were connected?" she asked.

"Murder? What murder?"

"Why, the murder of the designer of the exhibit, of course."

"How come the police haven't said anything about it?"

"Because, I suppose, we're the only ones who know about it. Except for the murderer, naturally. And possibly the murderee. But that is a spiritual question."

Harrison pumped them for details. It was something Henry was allowed to talk about. Nobody had said he couldn't. He explained how Violet was missing under ominous circumstances and how he and Bhagat had found her darling dog abandoned. "It has to be murder or suicide, unless she wandered away from home and simply got lost."

"It couldn't have been suicide. It had to be murder," said Phoebe with conviction. "Or she's lost. I can believe that."

"What makes you say that?"

"Because Miss Strauss was a loose woman," said Phoebe. "She had everything to live for." Henry hid a grin with his napkin. Harrison frowned while he tried to decide if his leg was being pulled.

"What Phoebe means is that we don't think Violet was the type to kill herself. She wouldn't go through with it even if she threatened to do it."

"Did she threaten it?" Harrison was getting cautious.

"Oh yes. The day before."

"Where's that waiter? I'm going to cancel the main course." Harrison had decided it was his leg being pulled.

"Don't panic, Carl. We're perfectly serious." Phoebe put down her glass and tried very hard to look perfectly serious, with indifferent success. She continued, "Don't you think it is just a little bit odd that she died the same day as the ten-million-dollar statue disappears? One that she discovered in India? And who would leave their beloved dog forever out in the cold?" Phoebe would, for one. Phoebe's argument might not have been convincing to most people, but Harrison, being a reporter, couldn't resist the idea of a mysterious death coupled with the disappear-

150

ance of a valuable art object, and involving a dog. He abandoned the idea of cancelling the rest of the lunch and got out his spiral notebook.

"We think there was an attempt on her life in India. She had already selected the statue and she was the only link we had with the owner. Except for the American and Indian embassies, of course." Henry paused to think about American and Indian. It would have been better to have said Indian and American to avoid confusion with Native Americans, as some call them.

He went on, "There is some reason to suspect an official conspiracy. She almost died in a hotel in Trivandrum. We think that after that attempt failed, they decided it would be better to do it in the United States so that the Indian connection wouldn't be so obvious." Henry's mind raced along, about three words ahead of his tongue, though it occasionally lagged behind.

Better and better! Harrison was scribbling away in his notebook. "Who is 'they'?" he asked without looking up.

"Are," said Phoebe.

Harrison looked up this time. "R? What do you mean R?"

"Are—*they* takes *are,* not *is,*" Phoebe said pedantically.

"You can't say 'they takes are,'" corrected Henry. "It ought to be 'They take are.'"

"Come off it!" Harrison fairly yelled. People at nearby tables looked around, people who included the executive editor of the *Post.*

"Well, we have to be careful what we say if it's going to be used in the paper." Phoebe put on her proper look.

"Jeezus! It was my question, not yours!"

"Things are always getting misattributed."

"What is this about an official conspiracy?"

"I don't know anything about that, I'll have to ask Henry."

"The Indians, Phoebe, a whole bunch of their agencies were involved. And our embassy in New Delhi. They all had a hand in getting the statue here."

"But what sort of a conspiracy?" Harrison was poised to write. Reporters love conspiracies. If they should ask, he was now prepared to spring for two desserts.

151

"We don't know yet. When we do, we'll know who the murderer is."

"And the thief, too, Henry. Don't forget the thief."

The tuna arrived as did the steak. The latter was bloody. Henry put on his sunglasses. Proper grammar was shelved while salt and pepper made the rounds and everybody began to eat.

"What are you going to do about it?" Harrison had obviously been thinking while he chewed his rare beef. "Are you going to catch the murderer?"

"I suppose we have to. Anyway we have to get the statue back. The exhibit doesn't look right without it." That had worried Henry from the first. People were going through his exhibition and thinking, Well, is this all there is to it? It needs something. It surely does.

The luncheon plates were taken away and dessert ordered. Phoebe quite sensibly ordered sherbet, but Henry chose a rich chocolate layer cake. It almost made up for the chocolate truffle pie he missed getting yesterday. Their host ordered apple pie with ice cream. The sort of thing you would expect from a journalist.

"Is there anything else you haven't told me?" Harrison asked over coffee. (Henry had tea, of course.)

"No, I don't think so."

"Henry, tell Carl about Chandra."

"We don't know anything for sure. Maybe we ought to save that for another time. After we do some more checking."

"S-C-R-U-G-G-S? Is that how you spell your name? I want to get it right when I credit you for all you've told me," said Harrison.

"Yes, I get your point. My real name is Reliable Source. I'm sure you can spell that. Well the thing about Chandra is that he apparently never existed. At least not as the important figure described in our exhibition."

"Christ!"

"That of course depends upon your point of view," said Phoebe. "There are indeed those who say that Christ was only a minor historical figure. But I think most people would argue with your comparing him to Chandra."

152

* * *

What to do about this whole affair was very much on Henry's mind as he climbed the steps to his office. Almost without being aware of it, he counted the steps: fifty-one, fifty-two, fifty-three, fifty-four, two for the landing, fifty-five, fifty-six, fifty-seven, fifty-eight, fifty-nine— There was someone standing at the top of the steps blocking Henry's way. Without looking up, Henry knew it was Gerald. Nobody else would wear checked trousers like those. He suspected they were sold only by government agency recreation associations. Henry stood on the fourth step from the top, number fifty-nine. "Yes, Gerald?"

"Where the hell is my secretary?"

"You don't have one, Gerald. Don't you remember? We couldn't get permission to hire one."

"You know damn well who I mean! Miss Tipton! The temporary!"

"*Whom*, Gerald. You mean *whom.*" Henry looked up at Gerald. Gerald was turning rather pink. "If you mean the person who was sitting at the front desk, she was a receptionist. And perhaps a typist, but certainly not a secretary."

"Temposec called and said you fired Miss Tipton. Why did you do that? You can't do that!"

"She was a thief. I didn't think you would want her around if she were dishonest."

"You had no authority!"

"I did it for your own good, Gerald. You should do your own typing. Your hands are getting pudgy."

Gerald backed off (in disbelief) and let Henry climb up the rest of the steps. Henry explained about the typewriter ribbon, but Gerald didn't think it was a good excuse. He made Henry call Temposec and invite Miss Tipton back. "Tell her to bring her own ribbon," Henry told Temposec before Gerald snatched the phone out of his hand and hung it up.

There was one good side to the Temposec affair. It made Gerald so mad he forgot to ask why Henry was just getting back from lunch at 3:36.

* * *

153

Wednesday's *Washington Post* put the Chandra affair on the front page under a headline that said SMITHSONIAN MURDER? The subhead was more explicit: 'Murder and International Conspiracy Linked to Theft of Statue from the Smithsonian—Why Was the Beloved Dog Abandoned in the Cold?.' Henry was summoned to the under secretary's office. Dillyhay Plover was already there. Dillyhay accused Henry of talking to the press.

"Not guilty, Mr. Owens," Henry said, ignoring Dillyhay. "Someone else must have told the *Post* that Violet's murder is tied to the theft. It is a reasonable conclusion, however. I don't think you need to demand a retraction."

The meeting didn't accomplish anything. Dillyhay wanted Henry summarily fired, which was difficult to do since Henry still worked for the State Department. But the under secretary was more interested in the substance of a criminal conspiracy, if there was one and it involved the Smithsonian. Since Violet was still missing, he was prepared to believe there was a connection with the theft even if murder was not necessarily involved.

Over Dillyhay's protests the under secretary told Henry to look into the matter if he could do so discreetly. Dillyhay appalled the under secretary and lost whatever influence he might have had by saying Henry couldn't even take a shit discreetly. Henry left the under secretary's office with the feeling that he had gotten better than he deserved.

Miss Tipton was back at the FAO front desk and she looked at Henry with mixed feelings of hostility and triumph. She had, after all, gotten yesterday afternoon off with pay. And, she was back in spite of Henry. Henry noted, however, that she brought her own typewriter ribbon. Doubtless the Smithsonian would be billed for it at three times its normal cost.

During the afternoon, Taylor called. He wanted to meet with Henry and wanted to bring Hamilton Sealyham along. Sealyham was allied with Taylor in opposition to the anthropology establishment in the Museum of Natural History. They shared a common jaundiced view of the Smithsonian, the anthropology profession, and indeed the world at large.

Henry looked outside his window. The weather was turning nasty. He decided it would be best if they gathered at his and

154

Phoebe's house. He would make pizza and Taylor could bring the beer. To be on the safe side, he gave Taylor careful instructions on the kind of beer he should bring. India Pale Ale should be about right. Lots of it in case it snowed and nobody could get home tonight.

* * *

The pizza dough was rising in a bowl floating in a dishpan of hot water when the guests arrived. Taylor deposited all but four bottles of ale on the kitchen door stoop to keep cold. The party settled down by the fire for a council of war.

Hamilton led off, "We are convened as a quorum of sanity in our beloved Institution and come together, also as a company of friends, to discuss grand larceny and foul play concerning this lady—Violet? Is that her name? She, the Godiva of the Pachyderm, and sadly the casualty of matters reported in this morning's *Washington Post.*"

"Not at all," countered Taylor, "we are here to discuss whether Henry has been had and if so, why? And inevitably, I suppose, by whom. I am not at all concerned with someone relieving us of a probably bogus Indian relic, and while I can sympathize with Henry for losing one of his string of girlfriends, there are doubtless plenty of replacements available. I can give Henry a few pointers on filling the job if he needs help. Oh, yes, we are also here for Henry's pizza."

Phoebe was looking irritated and Henry thought it was time to get down to business. "I was called in to see the under secretary this morning."

"I must say, Mr. Ambassador, I'm not surprised. Your excellency has been very naughty." Sealyham shook his head at Henry in gentle disapproval and took a deep draught from his glass of ale. He reached for a handful of salted almonds.

"You'll be job hunting, I presume. I can give you a recommendation if you want one. It is only fair to warn you it will probably do you more harm than good." That was a typical Taylor comment and was likely true.

"Oh, I'm not fired yet. Partly because I don't work for the Smithsonian, of course."

"I forgot about that. I forgot you are a screwer, Henry, not a screwee."

"Taylor, dear boy, I really don't think there is actually such a word as *screwee*," said Sealyham. "In all other respects, of course, I agree with you."

"Order in the court!" Phoebe knocked her glass against the coffee table, spilling some of her ale. "If we are going to save Henry's hide, we have to find the criminals. We can't let Henry hang!" Phoebe said this last without ringing conviction.

"Well, of course, children, let us get down to cases." Sealyham looked unbelievingly into his glass. It had become almost empty.

"Who stands to profit?" asked Phoebe over her shoulder as she went after more ale.

"Whoever got the statue, of course," said Taylor. "It can be melted down to make crowns. We should be looking for a dentist. And an ornithologist. The rubies might induce robins to lay eggs."

"Robins' eggs are blue, not red."

"Oh."

"And anyway, the owner will be indemnified to the tune of ten million dollars," Henry observed.

"That is a lot in rupees," observed Taylor.

"No, it has to be paid in dollars." Henry explained about the government indemnification provision and how the owner had insisted on it being paid in dollars.

"Then the motive is clear. The owner planned to lose the statue. Nobody who doesn't expect to lose something would care in what currency compensation was made." Taylor was not always practical in money matters.

Sealyham started on his new bottle of ale. "Taylor, dear boy, that simply doesn't make sense. There would be no call for insurance at all if it were not for the possibility of theft. That doesn't mean that the owners of all insured objects plan to have them stolen. If the owner just wanted the money, the statue simply could have been sold without going to all this bother."

"Unless the owner stole it himself!"

"How like a woman, Phoebe. You assume is was a man that

156

stole the statue. And Hamilton is quite wrong. I never insure anything and I certainly don't want anything stolen."

"I could have said 'him or herself,' Taylor, but men commit most crimes so it hardly seemed worth the trouble."

"Children, children. Let's keep to the subject." Sealyham had once been a teacher and was used to keeping order. "For the moment we will entertain the hypothesis that the owner had a hand in the theft. Is that all right?"

"I have to go make the pizza," said Henry as he got to his feet. The rest followed him to the kitchen. He divided the dough into separate portions for three large pizzas. He oiled the pans and started working the dough into crusts while Phoebe fed him ale.

"It seems obvious to me that the first thing that has to be done is to find out who the owner of the statue is." Taylor hunted around for some paper and wrote down his thought before he lost track of it. "Once we know who the owner is, we can find out whether he could have stolen it." Taylor made no apology for having adopted Phoebe's presumption that it was a man.

"If we all take turns, see how nicely we proceed?" observed Hamilton. "Now may I suggest the next question: Who had the opportunity? There must have been lots of people who had the opportunity. I, of course, did not."

"Well, if we are satisfied that only Indians have the motive to steal the statue, then we only need to worry about eight hundred million suspects. Of course there were probably only two of that number who had an opportunity to steal it." Henry was artfully placing slices of mushroom, onion, and green pepper on the pizzas. The crusts were already covered with tomato sauce containing gobs of garlic, onion, jalapeños, cilantro, and other herbs. He had to be restrained from adding more cumin. Pepperoni and cheese were yet to come.

"Bhagat Gupta and who else?" asked Taylor.

"His little nephew, of course. What's his name?"

"Somnath."

"What about Tyrone?" asked Henry. "He is the one who probably stole it, after all." He was ready enough to abandon the Indian angle because he knew something the others didn't.

"No, he's not an Indian. He probably stole something else,"

157

said Taylor. "Has anybody checked to see what else is missing?"

The pizzas were too big to cook all three at once. The first two went into the oven and the party returned to the living room to wait.

"I have something to tell you about Tyrone. But first I must swear you all to secrecy."

Everybody swore readily. Too readily, actually, for Henry to have any confidence that the secret would be kept, but he went on. "I heard from a good source that Violet discussed with Tyrone and his friends a plan to steal the Chandra. My source said she didn't believe that Violet really intended to participate in the theft herself, but that she planted the suggestion."

"That's worse," said Phoebe. "The worst thing you can do is to get somebody else to do your dirty work."

"That's another possibility. Maybe Phoebe murdered Violet for not stealing the statue personally. A case of justifiable homicide if I ever heard of one."

"Shut up, Taylor," said Phoebe without replying to the charge.

Hamilton shushed everybody again. "I think we should refine our earlier hypothesis to the effect that whoever actually stole the statue, they did it for the Indians or the Indians did it themselves. Do you agree with that, Mr. Foreign Secretary?"

"I resigned that post and am now a short-order cook. It was a promotion I couldn't turn down. But I don't think Somnath could pick up a half-ton hunk of gold, and besides he was less than an hour out of my sight. As far as I know, Bhagat didn't come to the museum at all on the day of the theft, at least not before the theft was discovered. That makes Tyrone the most likely suspect, along with Red Rosa, Ugly Boy Floyd, and possibly Violet. Still, I have my doubts. Tyrone wasn't but a moment in the gallery and he sure got out of there in a hurry for someone pushing a cart loaded down with half a ton. According to the guards, the caterers weren't in the building more than ten minutes, if that."

"Then the theft is simply not possible," said Taylor. "Go look again, Henry, the statue must still be there. Assuming, of course, it was ever there in the first place."

158

"Children, I think you are going about it the wrong way. You have two unknowns; you need two equations."

"Huh?"

"What Hamilton means," explained Phoebe, "is that you have to consider the murder at the same time as you consider the theft."

"All we know for sure is that Violet disappeared," said Henry. "There might be other reasons besides murder."

"But you told the *Washington Post* that—"

"We were just paying for our lunch. It was a big lunch; there had to be a big scoop." Henry served up the pizza. It would be less messy after it cooled a bit but nobody wanted to wait. The third pizza went into the oven to cook. More ale had to be brought in. Flakes of snow blew in when the kitchen door was opened. Henry had been right about the weather.

"The first thing to determine is why this young woman—Violet—has disappeared on the day of the theft."

"One might equally ask, Hamilton, why should the theft have occurred on the day she disappeared?"

"Well, I just thought, Taylor—"

"I can answer the second question," said Henry. "It was the only day when the gallery would be certain to be empty during public hours. Before the opening day, the gallery was full of Exhibits people. After it opened, there was always a possibility of visitors. Nobody could steal it after hours because people have to sign in and out and the guards notice anybody wandering about."

"Tell them the other thing about your girlfriend, Henry, about the threat."

"She isn't my girlfriend, Phoebe." It wasn't like Phoebe to harp on things like that. "It is just that Violet said on Wednesday, the day before the theft, that she was going to kill herself. She didn't mean it."

"Well, if I were going to kill anybody, I couldn't choose a better time to do it. Who heard her say that besides you, Henry?"

"Well, nobody—"

"Then it figures that you killed her," Taylor didn't sound at all judgmental. "You made it look like suicide, but you ne-

159

glected to put the body where somebody could find it. That was very careless, Henry."

"No, wait a minute, Somnath was with us."

"Aha! Behold your murderer."

"I am reasonably sure he was at the museum all day."

"There you are! The *thag* could have killed her! He had plenty of time to do it!"

"You mean *thug,*" corrected Henry.

"Wrong. When have you ever heard me say something I didn't mean, Henry?"

"Quite often, as a matter of fact."

"Children! Children! *Thag* is Hindi for thief. It shares a common Sanscrit root with *thug,* so Taylor is right, oddly enough. But let us get back to the business at hand. I believe the *Post* said something about an attempt to kill her in India. Where was this Somnath person then?" asked Hamilton.

"In India, I believe. Certainly not here."

"I think," announced Phoebe, "that little Violet was killed to cover up the link with the owner of the statue. She dealt with the arrangements in India."

"That makes perfect sense to me, Henry. Also, I believe your other pizza is burning." That was not reassuring. Things that made perfect sense to Taylor were often nonsense.

Henry knocked over his chair getting up. The pizza was not burnt, but it would have been in another couple of minutes.

Hamilton Sealyham delivered the majority statement at the end of the evening: "There is simply no help for it. Someone is going to have to go back to India, Mr. Ambassador, and find out more about the statue. You could ask the Indian cultural counselor—what's his name? Gupta? But that might not be a good idea since he may be involved with whatever's going on."

"You might also watch out for this Somnath person," advised Taylor.

"His job with the exhibition is finished. I thought I might assign him to University Programs."

Sealyham looked horrified. He comforted himself with another slice of pizza.

Eleven

"Where have you been?"

"Where do you think?" Dreamy dropped an armload of packages on the conference table in the middle of the room.

"Oh. I guess you've been out Christmas shopping."

"My, you are the clever one, Henry! Did you miss me that much?"

"I need some travel money, Dreamy."

"Don't we all! This weather is getting me down, too. Where should we go?"

"India. I've got to get to India right away."

"Christmas in India? Why not the Caribbean? It's cheaper. We could go to Aruba."

"Not us, me. I've got to go to India and check on this statue business."

Dreamy hung up her coat and picked up her packages. She turned her back on Henry and sashayed toward her office. "Put in a proposal," she called over her shoulder. "We won't grant it, but you can apply if you want to."

Henry hurried after her. "Why not?"

"I can't send you to India on another research development for the same project, Henry. Dear," she added a bit sarcastically

161

to let him know she didn't like having supplicants trade on friendship. "Besides, the Indians on the Subcommission would never approve it and they don't even meet until April. By then it will be getting too hot to go to India."

"What if I tell you that I think there may have been irregularities on the last trip. Did Violet ever file her travel voucher?"

"Now that you mention it, no. But she wasn't supposed to file it. You were. You are the principal investigator."

"Oh. Well, I can't file it now because Violet never gave me the information and now she's disappeared. Maybe even dead."

"That's okay. Not okay if she's dead or only missing, but okay you can pay all the money back."

"Be serious, Dreamy!"

"I am serious. But I suppose if you think money was misspent we could use administrative funds to pay for an accountant to go over and see."

"An accountant!" Henry had his own opinion of accountants, which he doubted Dreamy shared. "But, Dreamy, I think that a fraud has been perpetrated in connection with the exhibition. It might be a criminal matter. And if we don't find out the truth, the U.S. Government is going to be out ten million dollars. In real money, not rupees. Think how good it would look to Congress if you could go to the next budget hearing and tell them how you spent a few *rupees* to save all those real dollars!"

"Hmm. All right. I'll pay for you to send a lawyer."

"Actually, I had one in mind."

"That's what I figured. Okay, we can send your live-in lawyer. Two weeks."

"She needs per diem for four."

"Three, then and not a kopeck more."

"Paisa. Kopecks go with rubles."

* * *

"Now Phoebe," said Taylor firmly, "stay away from the American embassy. If they find out you are in India, they will do everything possible to obstruct you."

"I don't see why."

"They obstruct everybody. They conceive it as their purpose."

"Taylor's right," said Henry. "Sort of. If Blake is involved in

162

anything improper, he will certainly try to obstruct you. Or worse. But embassy people ordinarily are very helpful. I certainly was."

"When were you last promoted?"

Henry calculated. It had been longer than he thought. "Almost five years ago," he said grudgingly.

"I rest my case."

"How do I get my per diem money?" Phoebe had her air ticket in hand but the rupees for per diem and local travel in India could only be disbursed after she arrived.

"Try to get the Embassy Science Office to authorize it. Then you can pick up the cash from the disbursing office and run like hell. If you make it outside, you can meld into the crowd. There are so many people in India that nobody will be able to find you unless you want to be found. You might also want to put on a sari. If you prefer, you can always wear a dhoti, of course," Taylor added.

"Violet had a sari. I can get it for you," Henry offered.

"Ugh!"

"That's all right, Phoebe, I have one you can take," said Taylor.

Phoebe giggled. "I wouldn't want to take yours, Taylor."

"You are welcome to it, I've got several."

"She would look better in the dhoti," Henry decided. "But don't worry about going to the embassy. I asked Dreamy how to avoid Blake's office, and she says that the U.S. Foundation for Indian Research can disburse the money. You won't have to go near the embassy."

"Then it's just conceivable you might succeed with your mission, Phoebe. What you should do is go first to Banaras Hindu University and see Professor Anjana Thairani. She is a political scientist." Taylor pulled a letter out of a pocket and handed it to Phoebe. "I wrote this letter to Dr. Thairani in Sanskrit to keep nosy persons from reading it. Officials will pry into your baggage, but don't worry, they won't be able to read this.

"I don't ordinarily recommend political scientists for anything, but she is an exception. If she can't tell you all about Chandra, she can refer you to someone who can. But she may not know anything about the graven image. To my mind, that is the most peculiar thing about this whole scam. I hope Thairani can help you because most of the other people I know don't speak anything but obscure languages and very probably wouldn't talk to a woman at all—particularly a skinny Western one."

"I am not skinny!" Phoebe started to take off her sweater. Miss Tipton, the Temposec lady, looked curiously through the glass partition into Henry's office.

"Take it from me, Taylor," Henry said hurriedly, "Phoebe is not skinny. She's just small-boned."

"I was speaking from the Indian point of view. Many Indians equate Western pulchritude with famine in the land. Well, to get on with it, you should try to keep us informed of any progress you make with your investigations. That way, if you disappear and are never heard from again, we won't be left completely in the dark."

Phoebe shuddered. "I can't very well send messages through the embassy, and letters probably take forever. I'd be back before the letters arrive."

"Presuming you come back at all," said Taylor comfortingly. "No, I certainly wouldn't suggest you send cables through our embassy. Just write us a nice letter and go into the local Pan American office and use your wiles."

"My wiles?"

"Certainly. Just get a returning American to post it for you when he arrives in the States. Your wiles should work fine on an American. If you feel that's too unreliable, make a copy or two and use your wiles more than once."

"I'll be sure to pack lots of wiles."

"And American postage stamps. All this cleverness could be defeated by the lack of proper postage."

* * *

Henry drove Phoebe to Dulles to catch the Pan American flight. He was increasingly reluctant to have her go. "I should have found a way to send Taylor. He would have been perfect for it."

"Don't you think I can do it?"

"Of course I think you can do it. It's only that I wouldn't mind

164

seeing him go. I don't like having you away. Anything can happen when you travel. Especially in India." Henry had a profound mistrust of airplanes and with very little effort he could also conjure up visions of horrible train wrecks and other disasters. "If I don't come back, you can always find another Violet. Maybe she will turn up, or the police might find Red Rosa."

"You know I don't want another Violet." It was something they had not talked about, except by occasional inference. "She just swiped my soul for a while. I got it back."

"I wanted to drive a stake through her heart, but I couldn't find it."

Henry turned into the short-term parking lot and then they were involved with a checklist of passport, immunization certificates, tickets, travel orders, traveler's checks, baggage, camera. At the last moment, Phoebe pulled off her heavy coat and stuffed it in Henry's hands.

"If you miss your flight out of London, you'll freeze!"

"I won't. And I'm not going to carry that blanket around India. I have a raincoat in my bag."

"It isn't supposed to rain this time of year."

Waiting in the concourse for Phoebe's flight to be called, they held hands. Henry tried to think of something to say, but he couldn't find any words. He settled for looking at her face and trying to memorize it. He knew that a minute after she was gone the sharpness of memory would fade and he would be left with that curious mixture of geography and the personality that seems to constitute long-term memory. Why the face and not the hand? Henry didn't know. He shifted his gaze to Phoebe's hand and tried to memorize it. It was a nice hand. Not big enough to be a pianist, of course, but fine for about anything else. He kissed it.

* * *

The Monday following Phoebe's departure, Henry dragged himself into the Smithsonian shortly after ten. The latest contribution from Temposec was sitting at the reception desk. She was a lady of sixty or so. She wore an apologetic expression. "Pardon me," she said, "are you Mr. Scruggs? There is a gentleman waiting in your office. I fixed him tea. I hope you don't mind."

She seemed anxious to please. Henry supposed she had been out of the job market for quite a number of years. He looked through the glass into his office and saw it was Bhagat and not an insurance salesman. "No, no, you did just the right thing, Miss—?"

"Oh, pardon me," she said again, "Marriage. Mrs. Marriage."

Henry gave her his warm, welcoming smile (the one that had once made Violet ask him whether he wore dentures) and he went on into his office.

"Good morning, Bhagat."

Bhagat looked at his watch before he responded. "Good morning, Henry." His manner managed at once to censure Henry for being tardy and to forgive him, magnanimously.

"I hope I haven't kept you waiting long."

"Nooo," he said drawing it out doubtfully. "I just wanted to inquire whether there has been any progress in finding my statue."

"Your statue?"

"Well, yes. I speak of course as a representative of the Indian Government."

"You've been in touch with the police?"

"Certainly. They have found nothing. But my Government assumes that the Smithsonian is doing something about it as well. You have quite a large museum police force, I believe?"

"Our Protection Department, you mean? It does our investigations, but something like this is far beyond us. Everyone around here believes that if the statue is to be found, it will be when it is sold. That means the police will probably find it. It certainly won't be sold to the Smithsonian."

"No, of course not. Well, I suppose we ought to consider filing a claim for the insurance—indemnity, I believe you call it? You can let me have the necessary forms and we will get things started."

"I will have to look into it. As far as I know, nobody has ever filed a claim before under the arts indemnity program. They may have to create the forms."

Bhagat looked uncomfortable. "There's not going to be any problem getting payment, is there?"

166

"No, of course not. Though I hope we will recover the statue before it comes to that."

"Yes, well, we all hope so," Bhagat said doubtfully. He got to his feet and started putting on his coat. "Henry—"

"Yes?"

"Have you heard anything from Violet?"

"Not a thing."

"I confess, it makes me rather uneasy. What about her dog? Do you suppose anyone is taking care of it?"

"I took Herbert to one of Violet's friends."

"I'm relieved about that. Oh, one more thing, Somnath is rather at loose ends now that the exhibition is open. Tell me, should he go back to India or is there something he could do at the Smithsonian?"

"I've been meaning to have him go see Hamilton Sealyham. You know Hamilton?"

"Yes, of course. That is an excellent idea. I'm sure he can find something to do with conferences. Perhaps we can have one on international art theft."

* * *

Henry called the under secretary's office and made an appointment. Mr. Owens was tied up all day in a meeting of the Executive Committee of the Board of Regents, but his secretary was able to schedule something for Tuesday morning at 9:00, a time which, needless to say, did not please Henry. Henry suggested that Owens's secretary invite General Counsel Hayward Bodde and Colonel McKeown. Henry would have invited them himself, except that they would have turned him down. Nobody turned down the under secretary, except maybe Secretary Vernon or the Regents themselves.

It took a lot of strong tea to get Henry going the next morning. He felt his nerves jangle as he climbed the stairs to the second floor of the Smithsonian Castle. Sort of like sleigh bells. Everybody else was already in the under secretary's office, acting as though it were the most normal thing in the world to be at work by 9:00.

"The Indians want to file their claim for the gold statue. I had a visit from their cultural counselor yesterday morning."

"Is there any reason why they shouldn't?" Owens's question was directed at the others as much as it was to Henry.

"Protection is keeping in constant touch with the police," answered Colonel McKeown. "There have been absolutely no leads to the whereabouts of this fellow Tyrone and his gang. Or of the Strauss woman."

"From a legal point of view, the Smithsonian is not involved. Foreign indemnity claims are a matter for the Department of Justice and perhaps the State Department. The Smithsonian's official position would have to be that the Indians can do what they like." That was what Bodde was best at—finding reasons why things didn't concern the Smithsonian.

"It was my understanding when we got involved in this exhibition business," said Owens, "that there were program considerations that made it necessary. Has something changed that I don't know about?"

"No, sir," said Henry. "Our activities in India still might be affected by this. It all depends upon whether the Indian Government takes an interest in the statue or whether they regard it as a personal casualty loss of an individual."

"How likely is it to be the latter?"

"Not very. My impression is that Mr. Gupta, the counselor, regards the loss as an Indian Government matter."

"Well, is there anything we can do to recover the statue?"

"No sir, nothing that I know of," replied Colonel McKeown.

"Then there's nothing to be done but let the Indians pursue their claim. Do you agree?" The under secretary looked around the room.

"Yes, sir."

"Yes, sir."

"No, sir." Everyone looked at Henry curiously. "There is something fishy about this whole business. As Mr. Bodde knows, I asked Miss Casey to go to India to look into the history of the statue and while she is there, to find out if there is something funny about the Indian request to do the Chandra exhibition."

"I did not approve her travel. She has gone to India on her own time. It seems to me that Mr. Scruggs is asking her to find out things he should have investigated before the exhibition

168

ever took place." Bodde did not like Henry and was only too happy to stick it to him when the opportunity presented itself. "In any case, none of this can have anything to do with the fact of the theft. I am satisfied that the Smithsonian has not been negligent since the statue came into our custody, however remiss we might have been in planning the exhibition."

"Certainly not," agreed Colonel McKeown. The guards, after all, belonged to him.

"Just what do you think is, as you say, fishy, Mr. Scruggs?" The under secretary was not one to get sidetracked.

"It is just that the conditions of the loan established by the lender suggest that the statue was expected to be stolen. Somebody wanted payment in dollars for something they couldn't have gotten permission to export from India."

"Who is the owner?"

"That's another thing. All the arrangements were made through Mr. Gupta and through Mr. Blake, our cultural counselor in New Delhi. The only other person who might have known about the ownership was Miss Violet Strauss and now she is missing. As I told you before, I am not entirely convinced that she has not met with foul play." Henry wondered about "foul play." Everybody always said it, but it seemed like a silly expression.

"But you have no proof of any of this," Bodde said in his best courtroom manner. That was deceptive, of course, because he had never tried a case in court.

"I don't have it yet. But I have high hopes for Phoebe."

"Humpf," said Bodde.

"When does Miss Casey get back?" asked Under Secretary Owens.

"In a little over two weeks."

"All right, we can stall the Indians that long."

* * *

Henry got back to his regular duties. Ella Alle, the personnel specialist for The National Collection of Fine Arts (NCFA) called to say that Dr. Lumley Ricketts had just been appointed the new Director of NCFA and would Henry please do whatever was necessary to keep him from being deported. Ricketts? The

169

name was vaguely familiar. "Ricketts? Why do I know the name?"

"He is from England. He has been a visiting senior scholar at NCFA."

"Oh God! That's right. He's an exchange visitor. How can an Englishman be made director of a museum that specializes in American art?"

"I wouldn't know about that. I just process the papers."

"Well, this Ricketts is not a U.S. resident. You can't hire him. As soon as his exchange visit is over, he has to go back to England."

"It's too late for that; we've already processed his appointment. Now the Immigration Service says he has to leave the country."

Henry groaned. "I'm not surprised. When does he have to depart?"

"Oh, he has a little time. He has until the end of December."

Henry counted. "Eleven days! That doesn't give me time to do anything!"

"Well, you have to do something."

Henry pulled his copy of Ricketts's exchange certificate and checked the dates on it. "His status has already expired! He was supposed to have left almost a year ago!"

"That's what I'm talking about. He has something from Immigration"—Miss Alle poked through her file—"a deportation order."

It was just the sort of thing to get Henry's mind off of the Chandra affair. He spent the afternoon with the director of Personnel, Mr. Sawyer, explaining how he had done wrong. Since the Smithsonian's exchange program was a government program, subject to more than the usual number of restrictions, there were so many transgressions that Henry hardly knew where to start: (a) Dr. Ricketts would have to leave the country for at least two years at the end of his exchange visitor appointment; (b) as an exchange visitor, he couldn't be given a regular staff appointment: (c) he couldn't be given permanent employment until he got immigrant status; (d) he couldn't convert to immigrant status without leaving the United States; (e) even if Dr.

170

Ricketts went abroad, he couldn't get an immigrant visa until he got labor certification; (f) he still couldn't get an immigrant visa until getting preference status; and (g) even if you got everything else sorted out, Ricketts would still be under a writ of deportation, which made everything else immaterial and required that he apply to the attorney general for permission to apply for the immigrant visa.

"The first step is to delay the deportation somehow. I'll work on that. The second is for you to advertise the job of director. You can't fill a job with an alien unless you can show you aren't able to find a candidate who's a citizen or permanent resident. That is what a labor certification is."

"Oh, we did that."

"You did? Miss Alle didn't tell me."

"Yes. We got permission from the Civil Service Commission. You have to do that for a federal appointment."

Henry sighed and began to try to explain to Mr. Sawyer why that wasn't the same thing.

"Well, I certainly am not going to advertise a job that's already been filled! That would cause all kinds of trouble!"

Henry argued with Sawyer until quitting time. Then he went home and fixed a large drink. There were now only ten days left to save Ricketts, and three days had to be taken out for the Christmas weekend. Not even nearly enough time.

And there should have been a letter from Phoebe if she found anyone in New Delhi to take it, but the mailbox was empty except for junk mail and a letter from his father. His father had seen an account in the *Chattanooga Times* about the theft at the Smithsonian. The story read like somebody had really been negligent or worse. He said he had told everybody around home that Henry couldn't be involved. "That's right, isn't it son?"

* * *

Thursday morning was spent dialing the main phone number for the Immigration Service's Washington District Office. Henry got through twice to a real person but both times he was put on hold and eventually cut off. At noon, he walked up to Vermont Avenue and had lunch at the Empress. Chicken with walnuts and hoisin sauce. Then he crossed the street to the INS District

Office. By showing his State Department I.D. card, he got past the guard to the upper floors and then he roamed around the corridors until he found someone willing to talk to him. It helped that most of the obstructionist clerks were out doing their last-minute Christmas shopping.

Henry found out that no writ of deportation had yet been issued in Ricketts's case and that he was under an administrative, not judicial, order to leave. An INS officer who wanted to leave the office early finally gave in to Henry's entreaties and agreed to give Ricketts a delayed voluntary departure that amounted to a six-month extension. Now something might be possible. And who knows, in the next six months the State Department might send Henry to Kabul or they might fire him and send him back to Tennessee.

He was sufficiently distracted by the Ricketts case that when he returned to his office in the late afternoon he neglected to count the steps. That boded ill. Mrs. Marriage, who had now been with the office uncommonly long for a Temposec, met Henry at the top of the stairs and handed him a note:

3:15 P.M.

Mr. Scruggs—

A Mr. McKeown called to say that Miss Strauss has been found. You are to go down to the city morgue and identify the body.

M.M.

Nobody in the office had any idea where the morgue was, it not being the sort of thing you'd ordinarily know. Henry looked it up in the phone book and headed off in his car to southeast Massachusetts Avenue.

It was beginning to rain and it was the shortest day of the year so it was already getting dark. He strained to see the street ahead and crossed Nineteenth Street before he expected and almost found himself in the emergency entrance of D.C. General. He had to ask for directions to the morgue.

What bothered Henry most about the morgue was that nobody seemed much concerned about Violet. She was just another body in a city that saw too many bodies even of young women. The water in the Potomac River had been cold so you could still recognize her. Henry had seen bodies before. That goes with being a consular officer. But this was the first one he had known and who had not been through the hands of a mortician who fixed things up so the deceased looked better than in life.

It was a little anticlimactic, seeing Violet that way. Henry had decided days ago that she was dead. All the same, Henry was numb. He did what he was told. If they hadn't told him to do anything, he would have just stood there, maybe forever. But they led him to a room where papers were put in front of him to be signed. They asked him about her relatives. Henry tried to remember whether Violet had ever mentioned any. He decided it was just something they had never discussed. But there must be some. Henry said he'd ask Smithsonian Personnel to check its records.

Henry was told that Violet had been found washed ashore at Blue Plains. Any farther and it would have been a matter for Prince Georges County, and the District of Columbia Morgue wouldn't have minded that a bit.

Henry drove home by way of God knows where. It took him half the night.

* * *

On Friday, almost nobody did anything. The long Christmas weekend had already started for most of the people in Washington. Henry didn't have anybody he had to give gifts to, but he left work early to shop for Christmas. Groceries. He was determined to lose himself in his kitchen over the holiday weekend. Two fine filleted and boned trout for Saturday—broiled with lime juice and cracked black pepper. A light dusting of paprika, of course. Good with grits and a small salad. For Sunday, Christmas Day, there had to be brisling sardines and crackers for breakfast and a small bird for a midday dinner. Henry chose a duck. That was another thing Phoebe didn't particularly like. She was convinced that you couldn't get all the fat cooked out.

173

Of course you couldn't if you hurried it, but Henry had nothing but time.

He would play Clementi sonatas on his piano and between each one he would take the duck out of the oven and prick holes in the skin to let the fat drain out. He would start with *Opus 13 Number 6*. If it was good, he would call it duck Clementi. That sounded better than calling it duck Scruggs. Most anything did. With the duck he would fix brown rice. Not wild rice, which is hardly worth the trouble. No way to ruin brown rice unless you forget to look at your watch. Time it at forty-five minutes and be careful not to put in too much water. He picked up a jar of caviar and thin-sliced Roggenbrot for a late Christmas Eve supper. With Phoebe gone, he could have all the cold vodka he wanted and nobody could criticize.

On the Monday holiday he would make his main meal with *fettuccine pesto alla genovese*. To be good it ought to have mushrooms. To go with that, he would have to make his own salsa: two diced spanish onions, two cans of Hunt's canned Italian tomatoes, nine chopped, pickled jalapeños, half a bunch of fresh cilantro, lots of garlic, cracked black pepper, and a little vinegar. That was a salsa to eat from a bowl with a spoon, not to pour on anything because you couldn't taste whatever was under it. (Though it was fine over rice and better over rice and beans, come to think of it.) There was not going to be time to do justice to fixing dessert. Henry decided just to pick up a half gallon of rocky road ice cream from Howard Johnson's.

He wouldn't think about Phoebe. He wouldn't remember Violet.

There was no letter from Phoebe in the Saturday mail. Who is Phoebe? There were a few Christmas cards from people Henry didn't know well enough to send cards. And there was a letter from Aunt Martha. Aunt Martha wrote once a year to say that she couldn't understand why she hadn't heard from Henry. Henry couldn't understand it either. He made a vow to write to her. Soon but not today. Today was trout day. And Handel, he thought. Some of the suites for piano would be nice.

* * *

174

Phoebe's letter came on the day after the Christmas Monday holiday. The duck had been good, but not so good you'd want to give it any special name. Next Christmas he'd have to try Haydn sonatas while it cooked. Duck Haydn would do for a name but perhaps duck Eisenstadt? No, duck Esterhazy, unless the name had already been used.

Phoebe's letter bore a Chicago postmark and showed Friday's date. That was pretty good time from Chicago during the Christmas rush.

Varanasi, December 18

Dear Henry,

No problems in New Delhi. Got my rupees from the Foundation and stayed overnight. Never saw so many people in my life. Retreated to hotel (Ashoka).

Your friend Blake tried to pick me up in the hotel bar. I told him I worked for a law firm and was on vacation. Used the name Sadie Scruggs. Figured he wouldn't think anybody in their right mind would have made up either one. Could have used Phoebe just as well now that I think about it.

Blake asked if I were related to you. Told him not that I knew of. Almost told him I was your first wife but decided that might sail too close to wind. Is that correct metaphor? I never know.

Caught Varanasi plane next morning. Nobody told me it was a milk run. Might as well have taken train. Stopped Agra. You can see Taj Mahal from the air. Probably best way to see it if Agra streets anything like New Delhi.

Our other stop was little place called Khajuraho. The plane took an unscheduled 24 hour layover (one does not need Blake in this country to mess things up) and I was able to see the local attraction which is an inordinate number of odd temples. They are mostly devoted to sex, apparently. Walls all covered with carvings showing men and women copulating and doing other things I couldn't quite identify having led sheltered life until I met you. Judging by Indian standards you don't know as much as I thought you did.

All very interesting from sociological point of view. Since locals have nothing else to do but look at these carvings, Khajuraho ought to be biggest city in world assuming pornography really makes people do it.

On to Varanasi. Found Taylor's professor friend. Tell Taylor that Professor Thairani says his Sanskrit is the next thing to illiterate. She thinks Taylor is a nut but he obviously has very old soul and may be bit senile. Childish is the word she used but senile is what she meant.

However, she is very interested in Chandra, being descended from family that married one of his descendents. She calculates there must be thirty million people in India with that sort of Chandra connection. However, the actual number living descendents might be as many as fifteen thousand. Generations are closely spaced (child marriage), and Indians have big families except for Chandra himself who had only one child, Devi, born 1861. Chandra's descendents also had high infant survival rate, which Thairani thinks due to their having been moderately well off.

Whatever the reasons, there are apparently a lot of descendents in Varanasi area where it seems Devi settled and had 15 children of whom maybe a dozen lived to produce more. The consequence is a modest movement (by Indian standards) to promote Chandra reputation but Thairani thinks Chandra had minimal impact on development Indian independence movement.

To compare Chandra effect on India to that of Gandhi ludicrous, she says, but admits that he may have been one of several who had some impact on young Gandhi prior his education in England.

Chandra may have had more influence on Rabindranath Tagore whose lost, unpublished early novel, variously entitled *Other Homes, Other Worlds*, or *Long*

Journey to Kerala, was said to be based loosely on Chandra's life.

Thairani introduced me to genealogist Sushital Subrahmanian who has made a study Chandra descendents. I give you the interesting limb of family tree: (1) Chandra (2) Daughter Devi Chandra (3) Grandson Vijay Subrahmanian (4) Great grandson Mahinder Subrahmanian (5) Great great granddaughter Raksha (6) Great great great grandson *Bhagat Gupta.* What do you think of that?

Bhagat has a younger brother whose son is Somnath, a great great great great grandson of Chandra (if I counted the greats right).

Thairani has heard of Bhagat Gupta and thinks he is a bit of a sharp character but that he has apparently done well in the Ministry of Culture, a job which he got through family connections. She was not aware he was involved in effort to revise Chandra's historical record.

There! Isn't all that food for thought?

Am leaving for Trivandrum day after tomorrow to try to find out about the statue. Thairani never heard of it but says anything possible especially in India and most especially among Chandra descendents. She has given me several names of people in Trivandrum who should know if it exists. (But we know it does, don't we?)

Varanasi is quite beautiful and seems less obsessed with sex though there are an awful lot more people. Do you suppose that isn't where babies come from?

Carnally yours,
Phoebe

There was also a note from the Coroner's Office. Violet's inquest was scheduled for December 27.

Twelve

It was as quiet as death. Taylor and Henry sat at one of the big tables for four and the Commons was almost empty. The manager had tried to cheer things up by serving a better than average buffet but it didn't help much. It was the first workday after Christmas. Almost nobody was around since there were only four work days before New Year's and lots of people were using up their extra annual leave. You could only carry over a certain amount of annual leave beyond the end of the leave year and anything above that amount would be lost.

Taylor stared at Henry. For the first time ever, possibly, Taylor didn't have anything to say. Henry had told about how he had seen Violet's body and how it had been found in the river. She obviously had committed suicide just as she said she would. Taylor looking mournful was something to behold—doom shadowing his normally impish features. Saturn eclipsing Mercury.

Henry had held back his feelings with food and music, but now they had descended upon him. He was terrible company. Why had he suggested lunch with Taylor? Probably because he hoped Taylor could cheer him up. And the letter. Phoebe's letter! Henry had almost forgotten about it! He pulled it out of his inside jacket pocket and handed it without a word to Taylor.

Taylor read it twice with a smile growing across his face, his eyebrows climbing into peaks. "What do you make of this, Henry?" he asked when he finished reading.

"You were perfectly right, Taylor. Bhagat put one over on us, damn him!"

"On you, Henry. He put one over on you. And of course I'm right. I always am," Taylor said with a touch of sadness. He folded up Phoebe's letter and handed it back to Henry.

"What do you suppose she will find at Trivandrum?"

"Nothing. There is nothing to find."

"I mean information. There is surely some information she can find out."

"No and maybe yes."

"I don't understand, Taylor."

"I mean there is probably nothing there to find out. But if I'm proved right, which I always am, that will tell us something."

* * *

Henry was working during Christmas week because his leave balance was below the maximum and, besides, it was a way not to think about Violet. Or Phoebe, for that matter. Anyway, Christmas week was the most peaceful time of the year to be in the office. None of the scientists in the Museum of Natural History were traveling at that time of year, so they couldn't get into trouble abroad. That meant that Henry was not having to devise ways to extract them from foreign jails or hospitals, or get them into countries that didn't want them, or track down their lost equipment, or get some foreign government to release fossil echinoderms so they could be studied at the Smithsonian.

No new museum interns were arriving and Henry had already sent exchange visitor documents abroad for midyear pre- and post-doctoral fellows. The agencies that programmed foreign visitors for the State Department were leaving Henry alone this week. Teatime could stretch from lunch to an early quitting time during which there could be much good conversation, provided you could find anyone around to invite to tea.

Henry got bored. He never expected it to happen, but it did. Even Dreamy was away, Dreamy who was always good for getting

179

you waked up on a sleepy afternoon. Ronald Hipster was in the office, but that was like having another file cabinet around except that it wouldn't stay put.

He wondered how the investigation was going. He called Colonel McKeown to find out. The phone rang a long time, but eventually somebody answered it. Colonel McKeown wasn't in. When would he be back? In January, the voice said as though that were a damn fool question. Henry tried to dredge up another name. Apple. "Is Inspector Apple in?"

"Just a minute." In a distance Henry heard somebody yell, "Hey Grannie! Phone."

"Inspector Apple."

"Inspector? This is Henry Scruggs. I'm calling about the golden statue. You know, the one that was stolen at the end of November. I was the curator of the exhibition."

"Yeah, I know. What about it?"

"I just wanted to know whether there have been any developments."

"It's still missing, if that's what you mean."

Henry told Apple that he had somebody in India investigating the statue. Apple didn't seem particularly impressed. Henry said he thought he'd just go over to the exhibition hall and take another look around. "Want to come?"

"Why the hell not?" replied Apple. That was the measure of how boring things were this week in the Protection Department.

* * *

The Inspector and Henry got a sleepy guard out of the guard station in MHT and took him into the Chandra exhibition gallery. Henry hadn't been there for some days. It had gotten so it was painful for him to look at the exhibition. There seemed to be a great big empty place on the porch of the little ashram where the golden statue had so briefly stood. Cyril Rochester, one of the other Exhibits designers, had tried to fill the void with some bolts of Indian fabric and a few clay pottery pieces borrowed from the Natural History Museum. It just made things worse—it cluttered up what had been a simple evocation of Chandra and made it look like a museum-shop display.

Phoebe's letter made Henry feel better about the exhibit now.

180

After all, it was a sham, so what did it matter what it looked like? There were two visitors in the room, both reading Henry's Chandra biography. They seemed impressed, but what did they know?

Henry paced slowly around the perimeter of the room. He couldn't see anything unusual. He joined Apple and the guard in the middle of the room. "Your men examined every inch of the room?"

"Yessir. There isn't anywhere they didn't look. And that idol was pretty big, I guess."

"More than eleven hundred pounds. It would be like moving a Steinway grand piano."

Apple thought a moment. "Difficult but possible, I guess."

"And hard to get hold of. I mean there weren't any handles on it. We had a hard time getting it into place after we unpacked it." The Indian music that had been playing since they entered the room was suddenly interrupted by the staccato sound of Henry's little double-headed drum that bridged the transition to another piece of the music. A peculiarly Indian sound, Henry always thought when he heard it. He walked over to the wall panel covering the tape recorder and opened it up. The continuous-loop tape was moving quite happily along despite the earlier forebodings of the audiovisual technician. Henry closed the panel and rejoined the others.

"Inspector, it doesn't look as though you can install that audio equipment from this side of that panel. Is there another access?"

The guard spoke up. "There's a whole room back there. It's got lots of equipment."

"How do you get into it? From the next room?"

"Right back here. One of the wall panels opens up. You don't notice it because the room's painted so dark."

"Was it checked after the theft?"

"Yessuh! We went over everything. We even looked in all the ceiling panels. Every one of the ceiling tiles removes—for ventilation, wiring, and things like that."

"He's right, Scruggs. All these wall panels and ceiling panels are removable. Only the columns are permanent. But that still doesn't explain where your idol went. We checked all the possibilities."

"Could I see the utility room?"

"Well, we've been over every inch of it, but I suppose you can see it if you want to."

The panel swung out heavily but easily. It was just about behind the ashram, and the area was so dark you wouldn't have found it if you didn't know what you were looking for. The guard felt in the dark and switched on a light. It wasn't enough light to do serious work by, but you could see the room was empty except for odds and ends like some rolled-up electrical cable, a few boxes of what looked like hardware for the wall-panel system, and then of course there was the back side of the audio equipment panel and there was a large circuit breaker panel. As Henry's eyes grew more accustomed to the dim light, he made out other things—a piece or two of angle iron, some rope, things that looked like pulley blocks, some cans of touch-up paint, and a toolbox much too small for the Chandra statue. Otherwise, the room was as clean as a whistle. You could sit on the floor with white duck pants and not get them dirty.

* * *

Henry stopped in at the coroner's office on Wednesday. There had been an inquest the day before and now nobody particularly wanted to talk to him. The paper he had signed at the morgue was enough. They said there was nothing unusual about Violet's death, that it had been by drowning.

There was one thing, something that wasn't considered particularly out of the ordinary in Washington. She had enough heroin in her to have overdosed her if she hadn't drowned. That wasn't seen as any reason the body shouldn't be turned over to her relatives for burial, and it had already been sent to Chillicothe, Ohio, to her mother. Her mother! Henry couldn't imagine what Violet's mother would be like.

* * *

On the way to the Eastern Market for bagels on New Year's Eve afternoon, Henry encountered Hazel walking Herbert, or vice versa. Henry had decided to walk rather than drive because the weather had turned rather nice and, anyway, he had to fill up the

182

long weekend somehow. Herbert knocked him down. He probably didn't mean to, but Herbert knocked lots of things down just by leaning on them. So if Henry had wanted to avoid Hazel, he didn't have a chance. Try explaining that to Phoebe.

Hazel helped him up. Pretty Hazel. Henry wondered if she were pregnant again. She invited him over to celebrate the arrival of the new year. If it showed up at Hazel's place. It might not, considering the kind of parties she and her friends gave.

His first impulse was to go and try to get in bed with Hazel. That lasted about seven milliseconds. His second impulse was to run and hide. He didn't want to wake up again in an emergency ward oxygen tent, though he could think of a worse alternative—waking up as a member of the cast in *Outward Bound.* This lasted a full minute while he dusted himself off and patted Herbert to show there were no hard feelings.

Henry's third and final impulse was to accept Hazel's invitation. Perhaps he could find a clue to Violet's murder if that was really what it was. Before he went he could get a long-acting penicillin shot, could cover himself with 612, could take a Tedral, and could swallow a small bottle of olive oil to ward off the effects of alcohol. Oh yes, and a hard hat and safety shoes, and now that he thought about it, some condoms, though that crowd probably thought they were square. Perhaps some rubber gloves, and don't forget your Swiss army knife. Maybe a wet suit would be a good idea.

Well, anyway, he went home and Cloroxed his blue jeans so they wouldn't look so new and he found a sweater that had been found somewhat earlier by a moth. He didn't shave his normally nude lower lip. No, he changed his mind. If worse came to worst, he didn't want to be rejected by Hazel because of a scratchy smooch. Now, if he had one of those faces than turns blue twenty minutes after you shave, he would have shaved off all his scraggly whiskers. That kind of blue beard would put a woman in her place, wherever that was. Henry didn't exactly know.

Henry took along two cases of Samuel Smith Nut Brown Ale. That meant he had to drive over to Hazel's, but he could always leave the car parked there and walk back. To make sure he didn't change his mind, he locked the ignition key in the car after he had unloaded the ale. Now he would have to go home and get his other set of keys before he could drive again.

The ale was safer than whiskey. Henry knew exactly how much ale he could drink and still survive. Also, all that fluid would help in case somehow a pill got mixed up with it. Heaven forfend!

* * *

Herbert and the sound of loud rock music met Henry at the door. In the ensuing struggle, Henry dropped the case of beer he was carrying. None of the bottles broke because the case landed on his toes and the steel caps in his safety shoes absorbed the impact. Henry smiled to himself. He was prepared for anything.

"Hi!" Too late he remembered that was the wrong thing to say. Violet's friends had always just grunted when they arrived. The apartment was already smoky but you could still make people out. Burt was there with his blond Afro hair making him look a bit like a pom-pom.

Henry's eyes were adjusting to the gloom. Good God! Henry moved closer to see if it were his imagination. There was Tyrone, dressed in black leather. He looked Ba-ad. He was sort of tangled up on the sofa with Hazel. And that other boy (they were all twenty years younger than Henry) was there, Floyd, the one with the ponytail and the first stages of male pattern baldness. Sitting in Hazel's one easy chair was an emaciated young man wearing mud-encrusted cowboy boots that looked like they were customarily worn at a construction site. Henry hadn't seen him before. Over on the bed was a lump facing the wall. It appeared to be a small person of some sort.

Henry got out a bottle of ale and sat down on the end of the sofa with Tyrone and Hazel. It was crowded. "Happy New Year," he said. Tyrone belched. Hazel sort of smiled at him, which for Hazel was positively loquacious. Henry started to say something else, but either nobody could hear anything over the noise of the rock music or nobody wanted to talk or both.

Henry worked on his first bottle of ale while Tyrone appeared to be giving Hazel a whole body massage. She was smoking marijuana and sipping something compounded with Coca-Cola. She seemed to be in some sort of rapture. Her heavy, knit sweat suit had parted in the middle and the division was steadily becoming wider. It was running out of Hazel's waist and was rapidly getting into dangerous territory. Henry watched, fascinated, almost hypnotized, as more and more of Hazel was exposed in the dim, smoky light.

Henry was saved from having to choose between finding another place to sit, or witnessing altogether too much, by new arrivals, a boy and a girl who looked like middle-class suburbia. The girl couldn't have been more than nineteen, and the boy a bit older, but not much. They got introduced to Henry because the girl asked. She was Curtis, she said, and the boy with her was Bud. Herbert growled at Bud. Thought he was too middle class, probably.

The party was evidently being largely bankrolled by Curtis and Bud, who had brought a large box of assorted liquors and things like potato chips and cheese. And a number of small plastic bags of white powder and larger plastic bags of what looked like marijuana.

If they were having to rely on the kindness of suburban juveniles, Tyrone must not be working now, which wasn't surprising. Hazel got up and pulled up her pants and down her top, to help stow away the provisions. Tyrone struggled with the zipper of his tight leather pants, but it appeared he decided it wasn't worth the effort. Hazel returned with a large hookah with four tubes, and set about firing it up.

The eight track had run through its repertoire, so there was a moment when conversation was a viable option to noise, sex, and drugs.

"How goes it, Tyrone?

"Can't complain, man."

"I guess you saw Violet's obituary in the paper."

"Somebody told me about it."

"I guess you guys are all broken up about it."

"That's right, hurt us real bad." Tyrone looked as though somebody had told him Violet got a parking ticket. He got up and got one of Henry's ales. "Where you get this shit?" he asked after he sat back down.

"Good, isn't it?"

Tyrone made a face at him and relit his reefer.

"You didn't stay around to cater our museum opening. How come you left so fast?"

Tyrone jerked his head around to face Henry. He looked at him hard. "Wasn't nobody there. We thought we musta come to the wrong place or the wrong night or something."

"I heard the fuzz is looking for you."

"Who's that?"

"The fuzz—the police. A gold statue disappeared from the museum about the same time you did."

"Hey, man! The police don't want me. I didn't have nothing to do with that statue."

"I'm glad of that. I wouldn't want you to get in any trouble."

"Besides, it was gone when we got there."

"It was what?!"

"Gone, man. We couldn't take anything that was already gone." Tyrone evidently decided he had exhausted the subject. He went to get himself a decent drink—a malt liquor—and turned his attention to Hazel, who had to be awakened before she could cooperate. Conversation was impossible anyway because somebody had remembered the eight track and had put on some more hard rock.

Curtis, the girl from the suburbs, sat down on the arm of the sofa. Bud couldn't find room, so he sat on the floor on one of Henry's feet. He appeared not to notice. "You a teacher?" Curtis asked. She had a high, piercing voice that could be heard over the hard rock. She had sat on the arm at Henry's end of the sofa and her bottom was sliding slowly toward Henry's lap.

"No, are you a student?" Henry yelled as loud as he could.

"Yes. I go to Sweet Briar. How do you know Hazel?"

"I was a friend of Violet's."

"Oh." Curtis was silent for a moment. Bud handed her one of the hoses from the hookah and she sucked in a lungful of smoke. She held it for a moment, her eyes bulging a bit, and then she put her lips against Henry's mouth and blew in the smoke.

Henry was caught by surprise. He felt his lungs constrict and go into an immediate asthmatic attack. Curtis appeared not to notice. She sucked in some more smoke.

186

Henry fumbled in his jeans pocket for his bottle of ephedrine. Curtis evidently thought he was just being familiar with her bottom and she slid the rest of the way into his lap. It became distinctly hard to breathe. Henry got the cap open and fished out a 25 mg capsule. He swallowed it with some ale.

"Oh! I want one!" Curtis took two ephedrines and popped them into her mouth. "Here, have some of Henry's pills!" She offered them to Bud, who passed them around. Everybody had some, including the lump on the bed who had rolled over at the mention of pills and who turned out to be Rosa. She had been joined on the bed by the cowboy boots and the ponytail. Bud now had the other chair.

Tyrone was busy again with Hazel's exercise suit and Henry's attention was distracted between Hazel's emerging body (it struck him that it was a bit like a caterpillar emerging from a cocoon) and Curtis. Curtis was winning because Henry found that there was nowhere that he could put his hands that did not get into what civilized people consider a girl's forbidden territory, particularly if she is young enough to be your daughter. Maybe too young. The fleeting thought raced by that she must be somebody's daughter. More marijuana smoke came flooding in from her rose-tasting lips. Henry found, oddly, that the acute stage of his asthma was receding. Perhaps his bronchial tubes were being destroyed and were offering no more resistance. Perhaps he had died.

"I heard about Violet," Curtis said, "I didn't know her, but it was so sad." Curtis looked unimaginably sad. "Were you her middle-aged lover? Will you go back to your wife, now?"

"What wife?" Henry was confused.

"Of course you have a wife. I can tell. All older men are married."

Henry thought for a moment—a short moment—of Phoebe. "Yes, I suppose so, unless you would—"

Henry was saved from getting himself more involved with Curtis by Rosa, who had gotten up off of the bed and announced it was time to party, by which it immediately became apparent that everybody was to inhale some cocaine.

"I don't think it would be such a good idea after taking

187

ephedrine," Henry yelled over the sound of the hi-fi. Nobody paid him any attention.

After the cocaine, which Henry firmly believes he did not ingest, Henry remembers the party as getting pretty weird. Large blocks of time passed without there being a sense of time. Henry had a fragmentary recollection of being on the bed with Rosa, who was arguing Marxian dialectics with him and telling him that his (Henry's) kind was historically obsolete and must be destroyed. Or was it converted? He couldn't exactly remember. There was also something about Rosa being out on a weekend pass from the mental institution.

* * *

It was better than last time. For one thing, he recognized immediately that he was in an oxygen tent, so there hadn't been that awful disorientation. And for another, he had some fragmentary memory of the previous evening (even if it was a couple of days ago as he later learned from the nurse).

The clearest recollection he had was of the explosion. Reconstructing it later, he decided that must have been when the police burst through the door with a battering ram. There had been something about body searches and Rosa screaming about pigs. Then there was a jolting and bitterly cold ride somewhere during which Henry went into acute asthma. Or maybe he had a heart attack, as Violet would have presumed.

Because of Henry's asthma attack (that's all it was) and the fact that nobody really thought he was going to live, the police sent him off to the hospital and neglected to charge him with anything. All the others were accused of narcotics possession, and various lewd and unlawful acts, not to mention aiding the flight of fugitives. The fugitives themselves were booked for grand larceny as well.

So Henry simply went home after he was released from the hospital, well rested and having had time to think things over without distractions. Of one thing he was convinced and that was that Tyrone was telling the truth when he said the statue was already gone. Tyrone and his friends had panicked because they had gone to the museum to steal it and they had neglected to put any food in the cart in case they had to go through with the catering act. They couldn't brazen it out, so they ran. That was something to remember, Henry thought, if you ever plan to steal something you should be prepared to pull out undercover at any point.

Then there was New Year's Eve. What a bunch of people! It seemed that Rosa stood alone (or sprawled alone, was more like it) in the group for having any intellectual interests, however peculiar, though it might have been that Henry just couldn't remember what the others said, if anything. A thought occurred to him and he checked his blue jean pockets. His condoms were gone. They probably fell out of his pocket, he told himself, when he took out his ephedrine.

*   *   *

The rest of the week improved steadily. On Thursday he remembered where he had left his car. By Friday he felt as good as the weather was bad. A steady northeast wind off the Atlantic brought in a cold misty rain that missed being snow by about three degrees.

Nothing exciting had happened at the Smithsonian except that Dr. Ricketts had decided to make a quick trip to England to see his aged mother remarry for the sixth time. His departure from the United States was of course construed by INS as the voluntary departure arranged by Henry, and therefore the six months he was allowed to stay at the Smithsonian were now gone.

Everybody wanted Henry to issue another exchange visitor certificate which would get Ricketts back immediately but which, of course, Henry could not legally do. The only possibility was to file a temporary worker petition (H-1) and try to get the two-year foreign residence requirement waived and get INS to look the other way about hiring a temporary worker to fill a permanent position. Henry would try, but once again it was sailing close to the wind and it was likely that Dr. Ricketts would still be in England to attend his aged mother's next divorce.

The Ricketts affair came at a critical juncture in Henry's time at the Smithsonian. It was being decided whether the Smithsonian would pick up his salary so that he could resign from the State Department. If the Smithsonian was not to exercise its option, as it seems to be called in sporting circles, Henry would have to go back to an uncertain future in the Fudge Factory, from which he had been away too long to expect to be promoted in this lifetime.

The Smithsonian was more or less evenly divided on the subject of Henry. There were those who were mad at him for not finding a solution to the Ricketts affair and then there were those who felt only Henry could solve it if anybody could. He had other enemies and partisans as well, but for the moment it was the Ricketts bridge that had to be crossed.

On Friday evening Henry played his piano nonstop until the Chinese laundry proprietor next door started pounding on the party wall and shouting something in muffled Cantonese. Henry went next door and told the laundryman that he was only trying to drive out the rats. The laundryman said something that sounded very much like "Ah, soo—" and Henry went back to his piano, but more softly now and with the top closed. Eventually his back hurt so much and the ends of his fingers were so raw that he stopped and had a Scotch—the first drink he had had since the previous weekend. Then he had another. He sat there drinking and wasting the evening. But it wasn't entirely wasted; it came to him, what to do about Ricketts.

To celebrate or maybe it was to drown his lonesomeness, Henry didn't stop drinking when he should have. Sunday arrived before he expected it. Where was Saturday? Well, Henry supposed it didn't matter. He was okay as long as he didn't move his head suddenly, in which case his brain caromed off the inside of his skull. Also his stomach felt like it belonged to somebody else. It felt better after he fed it tomatoes and cottage cheese.

He spent much of Sunday in a darkened room trying to reconstruct Saturday. If he had been out at all, he had definitely come back home because he had awoken this morning in his own bed and alone. Well, he supposed it would come back to him eventually. A thought struck him and he looked at his wrists. If he had been in a hospital, there should be one of those body tags on a wrist. No sign of one. He looked at his big toes. Nothing there either, but toe tags were only for corpses, he supposed.

Monday night, the ninth, there was another letter from Phoebe. The rain had stopped and the temperature had dropped into the low twenties with a brisk northwest wind. Henry had walked home from work and his hands were numb in his gloves. When he pulled Phoebe's letter from the mailbox, a particularly strong gust of wind took the letter into the next yard and into a leafless but not thornless pyracantha bush. Henry extracted it with care, while almost losing his gas bill, which he managed to step on. Holding everything tightly, he extracted carefully his door key from his pocket and was pushed by the wind into his house. The next time he would remember to open the door before he tried to get his mail.

Trivandrum, January 4

Dear Henry,

The trip to Trivandrum unbelievable. Took train, don't know why. I suppose I wanted see THE REAL India. Did. After Gaya (a town), I upgraded ticket to first class. Of course I had to lay over to do it.

Gaya remarkable. Beautiful, too, if you like that sort of thing. Met this handsome Indian. Sorry about that—I was lonely. Gurdip showed me the Vishnu-pad Temple built, he said, over footprints of Lord Vishnu. Gaya seems to have as much to do with death as that other place with birth. You would think India would have reached equilibrium.

Gurdip offered to marry me which was nice of him even though he probably just wanted to immigrate to the States. Told him no, my husband wouldn't permit it. Offered me huge ruby if I would divorce you. Probably glass. If real maybe it would be worth it. Of course we're not married but that is only a detail. Actually make it easier. Did you know Indian men are not circumcised? You probably do. Not that I think you make study of Indian men but you do know all sorts odd things.

Missed my train. Don't know how I let the time slip

191

by. Stayed over second night and saw more temples out of town and also some old caves. Remarkable ancient masonry inside.

Finally arrived Trivandrum. Exhausted. Slept eighteen hours.

Tracked down Dr. Kaul, the friend of Professor Thairani who is somehow connected with Chandra interests and lives on the site of Trivandrum ashram which is now destroyed. Dr. Kaul laughed at idea of a gold Chandra. Had there been one descendents would have melted it down long ago. Asked him about Bhagat. He does not personally know Bhagat but has heard of him.

He said that Bhagat's branch of the Gupta family lives in the Varanasi area. Branch has had more than its share charlatans. Guptas were kings in ancient times. Dr. Kaul suspects there is no connection with modern family except if you go back far enough everybody is related to everybody else.

Dr. Kaul said personally he thinks K. V. Chandra is underrated but that India has got more than its share of gods already and doesn't need another.

Staying couple more days here to use up per diem. Have some other names to follow up. Sending this letter now hoping it beats me home.

About uncircumcised Indian men. I just heard it from somebody, that's all.

If I can make connections New Delhi I should be home on PanAm January twelfth. Have I got a thing or two to show you!

Love, Phoebe

It was time Phoebe was coming home, Henry thought. He felt as though he were about to self-destruct, and from Phoebe's letter, she sounded just as bad. Gurdip! What a name! Obviously he was a bounder who preyed on unescorted women. Henry ought to stay in the State Department and see that Gurdip never, ever, got a visa.

* * *

On Wednesday, Henry arranged for Secretary Vernon to hold an intimate luncheon party in the secretary's parlor, at the east end of the second floor of the Smithsonian Castle. It was just about the most exclusive place you could dine in Washington, except maybe the second floor at the White House.

Besides Secretary Vernon, there were six guests—the assistant secretary of state for Educational and Cultural Affairs, the director of the Washington field office of the Immigration and Naturalization Service, the general counsel of the Department of Labor, Smithsonian General Counsel Bodde, and Henry. Oh yes, and the chief justice of the Supreme Court who was also, *ex-officio*, the chancellor of the Smithsonian. The food was prepared by B & B Caterers and because nobody paid any attention to cholesterol in those days, there were braised sweetbreads preceded by a cold baked fresh salmon with a dill sauce. Henry insisted on a chocolate icebox cake made from the recipe in the old *Boston Cooking School Cookbook*. Nobody could resist that.

Nobody did. After everybody was well fed, Henry brought up the fact that 20 U.S. Code gave the Smithsonian the authority to make its own determination when it was necessary to hire a foreigner.

For years, nobody had paid much attention to that bit of the Smithsonian's authority, and other agencies had effectively negated it by imposing on the Smithsonian their own general authority to regulate the employment of aliens. What the Smithsonian wanted was for State, Labor, and INS to agree to cooperate in letting the Smithsonian hire Dr. Ricketts immediately, as an "alien of world renown in the arts and sciences." It could be done if everybody agreed.

There was a trade-off, however. Henry had to get Bodde and Secretary Vernon to agree that if State, Labor, and INS stepped back on the Ricketts case, it wouldn't open the floodgates for the Smithsonian hiring all sorts of aliens just because they agreed to work cheap or it liked their looks or whatever.

Anyway, at the cost of about $100 per plate (which included an open bar, of course) for seven people, the Ricketts case was solved. A good immigration lawyer would have cost $1,000 at

193

least and still might not have gotten the desired results. Henry just hoped that Ricketts was worth it. Personally, he doubted it.

For the moment, Henry was riding high and he seemed assured of being hired by the Smithsonian. And Phoebe was coming home tomorrow. And though it was too early to be absolutely sure, it seemed unlikely that he had picked up VD at Hazel's party, though he had found two fleas in his socks. You would have thought that the fleas would have wandered off to suck somebody's blood while he was in the hospital. There was plenty of it around. But Henry guessed that even fleas didn't want to stay in a hospital any longer than they had to.

⬤ Thirteen

Henry got the second traffic ticket of his life for a moving violation trying not to be late for Phoebe's return at Dulles Airport. There shouldn't have been a police car on the limited-access road. Only a crazy person would be speeding in the cold driving rain mixed with sleet and what cop wants to deal with a crazy person? As it was, even after the cop held him up for half an hour, he was almost an hour early. He wished he still smoked. He was nervous and impatient and needed something to do with his hands. Of course if he still smoked he would probably be dead by now in which case he wouldn't be nervous and impatient at all. So there you are. Henry counted the chairs in the waiting area and when he was finished, he started on the panes of glass in the terminal. He couldn't count the waiting passengers because they kept moving about. Stand still, dammit!

Phoebe was first off the people carrier. Violet had been last. Maybe that told him something about how they felt about his meeting them. Maybe not.

"Hi."

"Hi."

"Did you have a good flight?"

"Umm."

"I don't like airplanes."

"Umm."

Henry took Phoebe's carry-on (carry-off?) bag. Phoebe walked beside him toward the escalator that led to the downstairs baggage pickup. She didn't touch him. Even on the narrow escalator there was a space between them. This was silly, he thought. He counted the seconds it took for the escalator to take them to the floor below.

"Phoebe! Hold up a moment. You forgot something."

Phoebe looked around. There was her pocketbook and Henry had her carry-on. "What?"

"Me." Henry dropped her bag. Something breakable inside broke. He held out his arms.

"I thought you'd never ask."

* * *

"They found Violet," he said as they drove toward Washington. The rain wasn't as hard now, but it was getting dark and the temperature was dropping. The north slopes of hills looked suspiciously like they might be freezing. Henry slowed down and concentrated on his driving while he conversed with Phoebe abstractedly.

"Dead?"

"Yes. Drowned. In the Potomac."

"I was sure of it. A woman like that doesn't go away of her own accord."

"Of course you never liked her."

"Why should I? She wasn't very nice. Not even to you. I couldn't forgive her for that. Some people spoil everything they touch."

"Do you think I was spoiled?"

"It was a near thing. Somebody must have thrown her in. She wouldn't do it herself."

"I don't know. They say she had enough heroin in her to kill her if she hadn't drowned. I don't think she used heroin. We need to look for the connection between her death and the theft."

"Have they found your catering friends?"

"They are in jail. I talked to Tyrone and he says the statue was

196

gone when he arrived at the museum. Somehow I believe him."

Henry carefully avoided mentioning the circumstances of his meeting with Tyrone.

"Henry, dear, you tend to believe the best of everybody."

"No I don't. I don't expect much of people, so I'm never disappointed by them. I'm certain Tyrone intended to steal the Chandra. I think he just never got the chance. That's not the same as believing the best of him."

* * *

Phoebe gave her report to the Chandra Scam Working Group, which met at Henry's house on the evening of her return.

"I think we have to come to the reluctant conclusion that the Chandra statue never existed," said Hamilton Sealyham. Hamilton was used to running meetings. That is what he did for a living and it was only natural that he took the lead in stating the problem. "I, for one, resist the idea that our foreign secretary has been hallucinating throughout this whole tragic affair, and choose to think that there is some other answer. Perhaps we have been worshiping a false god?"

"I told you that a long time ago," said Taylor Maidstone. Taylor never ran meetings. As a matter of fact, he generally broke them up.

"Indeed you did, Taylor, but at the time there was no reason why anyone should have taken you seriously. Now we have some evidence. Evidence of consensus if not the senses."

"I stand corrected, Hamilton. All I had was inductive reasoning based on my life-long experience dealing with Indians. Now we have the word of a totally unknown Indian who may be completely insane, for all we know. That is quite a different matter."

"But Taylor, you have known Professor Thairani for years and she is the one who recommended Dr. Kaul. I don't see how that makes him a totally unknown Indian. Who might be insane," Phoebe added. She was suffering from jet lag and in no mood to humor Taylor.

Henry was tired, too. He had just driven out to Dulles Airport and back, seventy miles under poor driving conditions. His nerves were raw. "I'll accept that the statue might not be what it was purported to be, but there was something there. What do you suppose it was?"

"Personally, I can't say, my dears, because I never saw it, not that I think you didn't, I hasten to add. I think I may speak for all of our little group in assuring you that we believe you when you say you think you saw it." Sensing the mood of the others, Hamilton was obviously retreating from his earlier confidence in Henry.

"Nor did I; I never saw it either," said Phoebe.

"I wasn't even in town," said Taylor. "That makes you the only one who saw it. What does that tell you, Henry?"

"Well, it certainly doesn't tell me I imagined it. We had to get a crew of laborers to unload the packing case. Even the customs people saw it and waived customs duties. Bhagat saw it, too."

"Well, if Bhagat says he saw it, we can be sure it wasn't there. But if it will make you feel better, we can stipulate that you think you saw it. Even Hamilton agrees, which weakens the case, of course, but does give a certain appearance of unanimity." Taylor poured himself another drink of Scotch and appeared to be settling in for a long night's baiting of Henry, not to mention the others.

"Children," said Hamilton soothingly, "perhaps we should accept that our Ambassador Henry saw something that was got up to look like a statue of Chandra. Since it must have been a lot of bother to perpetrate such a hoax, we might be well to consider what could be gained thereby."

"Something glittery to stick in the corner of the exhibit hall. Indians might go to some amount of trouble for that. They sew mirrors onto their tents." Taylor was still being fatuous. The longer he could prolong the evening, the more of Henry's Scotch he could drink.

"Insurance," said Phoebe.

"Insurance," everybody agreed. Insurance fraud was something everyone could understand.

"If the purpose is to collect on the insurance, then there are several possibilities." Henry turned them over in his mind.

Hamilton looked dubious. "There's only one if the statue doesn't exis—"

"There are three." Henry had it straight now. "Perhaps only two, if the statue really is gold all set about with rubies. Bhagat might steal the statue and then claim the money. Then he would have both. Or, if Bhagat wanted dollars and he couldn't get his government's permission to sell the statue abroad, he might just expose it to theft and collect the insurance. That would be just the same as selling it, as far as Bhagat is concerned."

"You can rule that out," Taylor snapped, "Bhagat would never settle for a fair price if there were a chance to double it."

"But the statue isn't real. I thought everybody was agreed on that."

"We think it isn't real, sweet Phoebe, but we don't know for certain. If it is a false god, then the theft doesn't accomplish anything but to get the graven image out of the way. Nobody would want it; it would be much too incriminating. Unless, of course, someone were trying to incriminate someone else." Hamilton was, as usual, trying to approach the problem logically, with only modest success because he had a penchant to complicate things.

"We also only have Henry's word that his friend Tyrone didn't steal it." Phoebe wasn't entirely convinced, particularly since Tyrone was a friend of Violet's.

"Even if through some unbelievable mischance Ambassador Henry is wrong, Tyrone may have stolen it for somebody else, some art collector with the delusion that the idol is real. I believe I am correct that most art theft is done on order and I doubt that this Tyrone fellow is an art collector, whatever his delusions may be. On the other hand if it is really gold, Tyrone might be acting out of simple greed." Hamilton was pleased with this bit of logic.

"There are other possibilities. You could use it for a hat rack or possibly a doorstop." Henry thought it would be a nice garden ornament, too, but he didn't have a proper garden. Ideally, you would place it in a garden pool so the turtle would be partly submerged with Chandra (or Vishnu, as the case may be) riding on its back.

"You wouldn't murder someone for a doorstop, Henry."

"Not for a doorstop. A hat rack, maybe." Henry had taken to

wearing hats because his thinning hair no longer provided much protection. Lots of places, he had noticed, didn't have hat racks.

"Ambassador Henry has a point. We should enlarge our vision in this affair. I submit, for example, that this fellow Tyrone, far from suffering from accidie, may actually be an acolyte of some mysterious priesthood that worships this Chandra. Do you think that is possible, Taylor?"

"It is not only possible but likely. In this case they must be worshipers of Vishnu who believe Chandra was the second coming."

"More like the eleven thousandth coming, if I remember my Indian mythology. But it is that sort of thing we should be thinking about. And to be more mundane, we ought also to consider how whoever it was got the statue, if there actually was one, out of the museum." Having framed the discussion question, Hamilton sat back and waited for the group to provide an answer.

Henry thought about it for a minute or two while the rest of the group suggested completely implausible answers. He then held up his hand.

"Yes, Henry, it's up the steps on the right," said Taylor in his usual smart-ass way.

"No, I mean I want the floor."

"Go ahead, Mr. Ambassador, don't pay any attention to Taylor."

"I think the statue never left the gallery. At least not in the normal sort of way."

"I should have thought of that," said Taylor, "somebody painted the statue to look like a guard or maybe a janitor and it has been there all the time."

"I never considered that, but that's an idea." Henry frowned as he thought about how you might do it.

"An idiotic one," said Phoebe.

"Yes," continued Henry, "an idiotic one but an idea all the same. The police haven't come up with anything even that good. Actually, that reminds me of something I saw. Or didn't see, to be more precise."

200

"Mr. Foreign Secretary, one hesitates to criticize someone in your exalted position, but your excellency is not making any sense."

"I know. But I think I know where our golden Chandra went."

"Does it explain Lady Violet's final, tragic journey as well?" asked Hamilton.

Henry thought about that one for a moment. The more he thought about it, the more plausible it seemed. "I think so. I think it very well might."

"Well, for goodness sake, tell us so Taylor and I can go home and sweet Phoebe can get to bed. She looks all in, aren't you, Phoebe dear? Phoebe? Are you there, Phoebe?" Hamilton waved a hand in front of Phoebe's eyes. Her only response was to begin snoring softly. Air travel always gave her a stuffy nose.

"I will show you if you will meet me tomorrow morning. It will be simpler than trying to explain it to you."

"If you wish, Mr. Foreign Secretary. Shall Taylor and I meet you at the gallery at, say, nine A.M.?"

"Are you out of your mind, Hamilton? This only involves mayhem and grand larceny. Henry wouldn't even get to the Judgment Day before ten."

* * *

"You see, the statue is still here, in a manner of speaking," said Henry the next morning as he led his three friends into the gallery. A lone tourist was looking at the exhibition happily but uncomprehendingly, and the room was otherwise empty.

"Where? I don't see it?" asked Phoebe.

"We should have known, Phoebe. The statue was made of rubber and someone simply stuck a pin in it and deflated it. All that remains to be discovered is whether it went pop or s-siss. If it was pop, somebody probably heard it."

"Don't be silly, Taylor. Henry had to get the laborers to unload it. It couldn't have been a balloon."

"Perhaps it was full of yogurt," Hamilton suggested. "No, I suspect that would have left a mess. The answer is just plain water. It could have leaked away or perhaps evaporated."

Phoebe sighed. Ten hours of sleep had done wonders for her. She had come to the museum light on her feet and with her eyes sparkling. But her energy was a thin veneer and the boys were making her tired again. She was also a bit put out with Henry for having refused to talk about the case at breakfast this morning. She had retaliated by refusing to allow him to read the funny papers, which were in the back of the sports section. She never read the sports section except when she needed to buy new automobile tires, which, for reasons only known to tire dealers, are only advertised in the sports section. "Show us the statue, Henry," she demanded.

"Okay, come with me." Henry led them around behind the exhibition's ashram where he took out a flashlight and hunted for the recessed handle on the wall. He turned it and pushed. The panel swung back to reveal a dark space. Henry felt for the light switch and after touching a number of odd-feeling things in the dark, found the switch and flicked it on. The room filled with light, albeit dim. "Do come in."

The room was quite empty. Empty, that is, until the four of them crowded in. Everybody looked around. "It's not here; it's empty," said Hamilton. He sounded very disappointed.

"Except for those things." Phoebe pointed to the neat little pile of paint cans, the coiled extension cords, rope, the bits of angle iron, and the like. "How big was it? Would it fit in a paint can?"

"Of course not."

Taylor walked over and kicked one of the cans. It tipped over and the top came loose, releasing a flood of dark blue paint that matched that on the gallery walls.

"You made a mess, Taylor. The floor was clean and you messed it up," Phoebe criticized.

"That's the whole point," said Henry. "The floor was clean. Look at it!"

Hamilton bent over. It was not easy for him to do, since even his kinder friends would have called him portly. He rubbed the floor with his finger. "Clean," he announced, and straightened up with a slight, soft grunt.

"You're too late, Henry. It's gone, if it was ever here. If it even existed." Taylor seemed unaccountably pleased.

202

"Hamilton is right. It's too clean. That's why I brought you all here."

"The janitors cleaned it up. They must occasionally do some work around here if only to relieve the boredom. And maybe nobody goes in here to get it dirty."

"You don't have to go into a room to get it dirty, Taylor; there's dirt in the air, everywhere. It is called dust." Phoebe rubbed the toe of her shoe on the floor. She frowned. It made three furrows in her forehead—one vertical, two converging from either side. The angle of the overhead light emphasized the lines and made her look sort of gargoylish. "The janitors didn't clean this. It isn't gummy."

"Exactly! When museum janitors clean the floor they automatically spread gunk on it and buff it down. If they buff it, it's shiny. If they don't, it stays gummy. This was cleaned by an amateur!"

"The Exhibits people. Dr. Fat Dog came in and said: 'Hey you fellows, let's police up this place.' That's your answer if anybody really cares."

"Ah, Taylor, dear friend," Hamilton proceeded cautiously because an argument with Taylor could escalate before you knew it, "I don't believe so."

"What Hamilton means is Exhibits people would quit first. They have a strong sense of what's in their contract. No, somebody cleaned up the place and I think I know the reason why. They didn't want to leave any tracks in here."

"You mean that when everybody thought the statue was stolen it was just hidden behind this partition? Your thief took quite a chance, Henry."

"No, it was gone, Hamilton. It just passed through here." Henry was walking slowly around the room, bent over and looking at the floor through the bottom of his bifocals. Suddenly he dropped to his knees and tugged on a ring in the floor. With considerable effort he got a section of the floor to come up. He slid it onto the adjacent floor. "The Tiber!" he announced.

"The Tiber! Of course!" Hamilton hurried over and peered into the hole. A damp odor and gurgling sound emanated from the opening.

"What is the Tiber? Is that a cute name for a sewer, or is Washington really Rome, as its architecture might lead us to believe?"

"My dear Taylor, you are indeed a newcomer."

"Well, I've been here for years and I don't know what it is."

"Phoebe, you are evidently not a student of Washington history. The Tiber has some aspects of a sewer, perhaps, but it is far more than that. More than a century ago the Tiber was a respectable stream which flowed along the north side of the Mall. When freight was brought from inland to Washington via the Chesapeake and Ohio Canal, barges came right into town on Tiber Creek. It was said of the Tiber that it was 'first a stream of pure water, fed by many tributaries, then a canal, then an open sewer of dreadful memory, then a paved street.' The name was come by honestly, I believe. One of the seventeenth-century land grants that was eventually included in the City of Washington was Rome Plantation.

"The Tiber drained the swamp that used to cover much of Washington south of Pennsylvania Avenue, and still does, I suppose, though a hundred years ago it was confined to tunnels and paved over to form Constitution Avenue. It is still a rather large stream. It, or a part of it, is right down there." Hamilton pointed down into the hole. He picked up the paint bucket Taylor had kicked over and tossed it in. There was a faint splash some twenty feet below. "I think Henry is right. Somebody dumped our Mr. Chandra into the Tiber."

Taylor looked thoughtful. "Less fitting than the Ganges, but still a decidedly Indian way to go. I think that it suggests that the statue is a fake. But we can't prove it unless somebody is prepared to go down into there to recover it. If it is real, then someone may have retrieved it from outside the museum."

"As far as I know, you would have to take the statue through the tunnel all the way to Buzzard Point, Taylor. I think that is where the Tiber flows into the Anacostia River. It must be two miles. Imagine all the rats between here and there."

"It's hard to believe that somebody carried the statue through the utility room. That would take four men, perhaps?" Hamilton looked doubtful.

204

"Carried it or more likely rolled it."

"Rolled it? Was it round?"

"On a dolly or something like that, Phoebe."

"But where is the dolly, then?"

"I imagine it went with the statue." Henry stared down into the hole. It was too dark to see anything and, besides, the dolly would likely have floated away.

"That explains Violet, Henry," said Phoebe, softly.

"Yes, I know. I've been thinking about that."

* * *

"Scruggs, I don't follow you, why would anybody dump all that gold into a sewer?" Colonel McKeown shown his flashlight down into the hole.

"To get rid of it before somebody found out it wasn't really gold."

"I saw it when it came in. It was gold all right. And there were all those rubies, too."

"Those are called paste in the fake jewelry trade. And somebody did a good job of applying some gilt."

"You can tell if things are gilded, can't you?"

"I imagine they used the mercury gilt process. Then you almost couldn't tell. They probably poisoned some poor bastard to get the thing faked. Mercury gilt is very toxic. They have to boil off the mercury. The vapors destroy your central nervous system. Hatters used to clean felt with mercury. That's where the expression 'mad as a hatter' came from." Henry was showing off, as usual.

"I don't know," said Phoebe, "there's another way they could have gilded it."

"How?" asked Henry.

"By association," replied Phoebe with a smirk. Taylor grinned at her and patted her on her behind. She jumped.

"I think that somebody, probably Bhagat Gupta, had the thing made and gilded. Then he had it insured for as much as he could. I don't know what it would cost to have it done in India, but I bet he could turn a pretty nice profit."

"Well, that is a motive I can understand. I suppose we better go in and look for it. If we find it, who do you suppose put it there?"

"It has to be Somnath Gupta. He can't have not known what his uncle was up to and he is the only one who would profit by it and who had the opportunity."

"And Violet. Wasn't she disposed of the same way?" Phoebe shuddered as she suggested it.

"I think so. It might have taken several weeks for her to wash down into the Anacostia River and on into the Potomac.

"Jeezus!" said Colonel McKeown. "How the hell can you prove it?"

"We can look for the statue. If it is there and is a fake, then it would be pretty good circumstantial evidence that the Guptas are involved."

"What about those weirdos they got in jail now? Does this mean they're not involved?"

"No, but the police might want to hold onto them until we are sure about the Guptas. There should be enough reason to hold them on other charges." Henry didn't mention how, by that logic, he should have been in jail with them.

"Ambassador Henry thinks they intended to steal it, but didn't get here quick enough," explained Hamilton. "They thought it was gold like everybody else."

"What Hamilton means is that they, like everybody else, thought it was gold, not that they thought everybody is gold."

"Shut up, Taylor," chorused just about everybody.

* * *

Nobody was able to get the Smithsonian labor crew to go down into the Tiber. Henry didn't blame them. If the Tiber had been the only means of escape, he would have chosen life imprisonment. However, there were people working for the city who did things like this all the time, apparently. It took several days to arrange it, of course. In the meantime, Henry asked McKeown to check on the prisoners. There was no way that he was going to show up at the jail to see them in person. He could just imagine one of them pointing at him and yelling, 'Hey, why isn't he in jail too?'

He, personally, arranged bail for Hazel and was prepared to

let the others rot. He might have gone bail for Red Rosa too, but it seemed that she was probably as well off in jail as she would have been in the psychiatric hospital. The two suburban kids, as you might expect, were bailed out by their respective parents.

The Chandra statue was found about a hundred and thirty yards downstream from the museum. The water had pushed it along until it caught on other debris. It was lifted out through a manhole on Constitution Avenue just beyond Twelfth Street. Traffic was stopped for hours. Henry had alerted Carl Harrison (hoping for more hospitality, possibly at Harvey's this time, since another trip to the Madison seemed unlikely) but somehow Channel 5 TV heard about it too, so Carl didn't get an exclusive. So much for Harvey's.

It was lead. And indeed it had a fine, heavy plating of gold. The tumbling in the Tiber had knocked out a few of the rubies but those that were left were nicely made from red glass. The statue must have cost Bhagat a lot to make.

*   *   *

"Hello, Bhagat?"

"I am sorry, sir. The minister has had to return to India. Who is this speaking?"

"This is Henry Scruggs at the Smithsonian. Dr. Gupta's departure, it was rather sudden, wasn't it?"

"Yes, sir. A family emergency, I'm told."

"And his nephew, Somnath?"

"I believe he had to return with the minister."

"Well, I'm sorry to hear it. We'll miss them both. Will they be returning?"

"I can't say about that."

"No, I suppose not."

*   *   *

"I think what happened, Phoebe, is that Bhagat watches Channel 5 news. He must have packed his bags right away and gone."

"Back to India? There must be a lot of unhappy relatives there."

"Exactly. He must still be here, somewhere. I suspect he went to ground, as they say about foxes. Since they wanted all those dollars, he and Somnath must have had in mind settling in the United States. Now they'll have to do it without their dowry."

"I'm sure they'll get by. Why do you think they did in Violet? They must have, you know."

"I can only assume that she was trying to shake them down. Violet was smart enough to have figured all this out and just foolhardy enough to think she could pull it off."

"Or maybe she didn't care. Her way of killing herself when we least expected it."

 **fourteen**

The Metropolitan Police took a little longer in finding out that the Guptas had taken a powder. For one thing, the investigating officers had to go upstairs in the police hierarchy before anybody could approach the Indian Embassy. Nevertheless, they eventually made the same call Henry had a day earlier, only theirs was to the Indian ambassador. He, of course, referred them to the first secretary and head of chancery, as any right-thinking ambassador would. The first secretary, being a proper professional, referred them to the State Department's Office of Protocol.

Now, the police department already had its own liaison officer with the Office of Protocol, and that officer went to work on the problem. However, somebody else in the police department simply looked up Bhagat Gupta's address in the Diplomatic List and went and asked the neighbors. Gupta had left, they said, without even stopping the newspapers or leaving cards with the post office. Indeed, mail and newspapers seemed to be accumulating at the front door.

From the police call to Protocol, it snowballed slowly, gathering interested offices as it went and so it was that on Wednesday, the fifteenth of February, there was a meeting in the State Department in one of the first-floor conference rooms on the west side of the lobby near the auditorium where press briefings are held. Henry Scruggs secured the following draft minutes of that meeting. In its final form, the document was reclassified "personnel-confidential" and is unavailable for publication.

CONFIDENTIAL

MEMORANDUM OF CONVERSATION

Subject: Meeting held by the Deputy Chief of Protocol regarding the activities of the Indian Minister Counselor for Cultural Affairs

ATTENDING:
 For the State Department:
  George Trebble, Deputy Chief of Protocol
  Giancarlo Longo, Assistant Legal Advisor
  Minor Majors, Director, Indian Country Affairs, NEA
  Florence Tillinghast, Deputy Assistant Secretary for
   Education and Cultural Affairs
  Albert Butts, Assistant Director, Office of Security,
   SCA
 For the Smithsonian Institution:
  Col. Vance McKeown, Director, Protection
   Department
  Henry Scruggs, Foreign Affairs Liaison Officer (Note
   that Mr. Scruggs is on nonreimbursable detail from
   the State Department, Foreign Service.)
 For the Metropolitan Police:
  E. Charles Fain, Assistant Chief for External Affairs
  Lt. Hobart Jones, Bunco Squad

<u>Trebble:</u> Gentlemen—and, um, Miss Tillinghast—Protocol has called this meeting because it seems that there has been an attempt to swindle the United States Government out of some—

<u>Longo:</u> Ten million.

210

<u>Trebble:</u> Yes, ten million dollars. An accredited Indian diplomat, Mr. Gupta, may be involved in that and possibly in a homicide. We have done some investigating ourselves, but before Mr. Bert Butts goes into that, I would like to have the Metropolitan Police bring us up to date on the progress of the investigation. I should say that I do not feel that State has been kept adequately informed in this matter and in view of its extreme sensitivity—

<u>Fain:</u> It's hardly the fault of the police. The Smithsonian has been doing its own investigation—~~going off half cocked, if I may say so~~

<u>McKeown:</u> Sir! There is no point in going on with this if the Assistant Chief is going to make unfounded accusations. I move we strike his remark from the record.

<u>Trebble:</u> I agree. Miss Sappington, strike that about going off etcetera. However, the police's point is well taken. Perhaps the Smithsonian should do the summary.

<u>McKeown:</u> Well, I would first like to say that the Smithsonian is in no position to develop the proof required for an indictment. We have no police powers other than very limited ones in Smithsonian facilities.

We have, however, done what we could and have put together a hypothesis which, I'm afraid, is quite complex, but is supported by, or at least consistent with, the known facts.

When the case first arose, I assigned Mr. Henry Scruggs to conduct our investigation.[*] I should point out that his position is unique in that he is a State Department officer assigned to the Smithsonian and already serving as curator of the Indian exhibition, as well as having worked closely with the murder victim and with Mr. Gupta. It will save some time if I turn our presentation over to Mr. Scruggs.

* [Editor's note: Our copy of this memorandum bears a marginal note in Col. McKeown's introductory presentation, to wit, "bullshit," believed to be in Mr. Scruggs handwriting.]

211

Scruggs: First I should explain how this exhibition came about—

Trebble: We know all about that.

Fain: That doesn't concern us, I believe.

Scruggs: Oh. Okay, what I will tell you then is how I believe the crimes were conceived and executed.

I think that Bhagat Gupta conceived the plan to swindle the Americans out of as many dollars as he could. He was aware of, and perhaps even involved in, the effort by descendents of Chandra to get the U.S. to hold a sesquicentennial exhibition. Of course the commitment was made by then Vice President Humphrey and when he wasn't elected, the exhibition was forgotten. When Gupta was assigned to Washington, he had his chance to pressure the Smithsonian into honoring the Humphrey commitment. It had worked, of course, some years ago with the commitment for a Gandhi exhibition.

Trebble: I thought you were going to skip the background.

Scruggs: A little bit of it is essential.

Tillinghast: Let him go on with it. I for one would like to hear it.

Scruggs: Thank you, ma'am. Well, Gupta needed to enlist some State Department pressure as well. He hardly knew where to start in the Department in Washington, so he got Adair Blake, his counterpart at our embassy in New Delhi, to light a fire under the Smithsonian. He certainly knew Blake when he was with the Indian Ministry of Culture in New Delhi. I can only suppose Gupta offered to deal Blake in or that he had some handle on Blake that would make him subject to blackmail. From Blake's enthusiasm about the exhibition, I am convinced he expected to make money.

Tillinghast: Did we know about Blake?

Butts: This is the first I've heard of it. I'll have the regional security officer get right on it.

<u>Scruggs:</u> Gupta must have raised the necessary capital, likely from other family members, and then set about to produce a cast lead statue and to gild it so it could be passed off for solid gold. I think he added the fake rubies so he could get the insured price up to ten million. Then the Smithsonian played into his hands—as he probably knew it would—when we insisted on sending someone to India to coordinate the preparation of the exhibition. He certainly knew that there was insufficient money available for the exhibition to pay for the services of an experienced curator so it would certainly be me or, if someone else, Gupta was prepared to suggest Miss Violet Strauss.

<u>Trebble:</u> Miss Strauss?

<u>Scruggs:</u> The Smithsonian exhibition designer who was murdered. The Smithsonian did not want to send me because they regard me as a museum amateur, so they were only too happy to send Miss Strauss. The end result, of course, was her death. Poor Violet. Gupta had already made her acquaintance. Gupta wanted someone he could lead into "discovering" the Chandra statue. But he also had to have somebody who would be defeated by trying to deal with the bureaucracy of the Indian Ministry of Culture and would strike out on her own to pull together an exhibition. This was another place where Blake's assistance was needed.

Gupta went back to India ostensibly to help Violet but actually to guide her into finding the statue. Violet was a dangerous choice in that she was smarter than she sometimes seemed and could be quite reckless. I can only suppose that she caught on that there was a scam being worked or that Gupta or his associates thought she had.

It is even possible that she might have demanded a piece of the action, as I believe it's called. Violet could do some rather surprising things. At any rate, there seems to have been a hasty and ill-conceived attempt to murder her with a drug overdose while she was staying at a hotel in Trivandrum. It failed and no further attempt was made in India, probably because of the danger that the whole scheme would be blown.

Still, Violet was an overdose waiting to happen and she had often threatened suicide. It must have appeared that getting rid of her in Washington would present no particular problem.

The next piece of the plot was the money. It had to come from the insurance because this was basically an insurance fraud scheme. Gupta wanted the Smithsonian to purchase the insurance. It would not only save Gupta a lot of money, but in case of loss of the statue while it was in Smithsonian hands, we would have to make the claim on his behalf. But we couldn't find the money for commercial insurance so we had to arrange a U.S. Government indemnity. ~~That was even better, of course, because what insurance company would be more inept at investigating a claim than the U.S. Government?~~

Tillinghast: You better have your secretary strike that last bit. We have enough trouble with Congress on the indemnity program as it is.

Trebble: Mark it out, Suzy.

Scruggs: Now, Gupta needed to get somebody he could trust close to the exhibition project. For that he imported his nephew, Somnath Gupta. For all we know, Somnath was involved with the part of the plan that took place in India. He attached Somnath to me as a museum intern, financially supported entirely by him. That should have alerted me, but I needed all the help I could get and I suppose I didn't want to know if there was a catch.

As soon as the statue was received in the United States and was in the hands of the Smithsonian, it had to be stolen, or appear to be, as soon as possible. That was a problem Somnath was in a position to work out. At this point, it seems that two plans were hatched. The primary one, the one of the two Guptas, was the one that actually succeeded. I will deal

214

with that one second because there was another plan that did not work.

This second plan was Violet's own, I think. She threw temptation in the way of the person we know as Tyrone—

<u>Lieutenant Jones:</u> His real name is Prester Hobbit. He has a prior record of burglary and shoplifting, nothing major.

<u>Scruggs:</u> I'll call him Tyrone, if you don't mind. Violet knew him by that name. Well, she told Tyrone about the statue and explained how easy it would be to steal it. This was, of course, very foolish because Tyrone was bound either to get caught or to abandon the statue when he tried to melt it down and found it was only lead and glass. But Violet was probably high on something when she came up with the idea and, anyway, as I have explained, she could be very reckless.

Tyrone and a couple of friends occasionally worked for caterers, so they set up as a catering company. He was sufficiently familiar with the business to approach the Smithsonian with a bid low enough to guarantee acceptance. He borrowed a steam cart big enough to hold the statue. I saw the thing and it was the type you use to keep food hot until it's ready to be served. He also had to rent a truck to deliver the cart and take it away again. I say he rented them, but of course it's possible, even likely, that he stole one or both of them.

Tyrone didn't expect to see anybody he knew during the few minutes he planned to be in the museum. As it was, he encountered me outside the gallery and I recognized him and his two accomplices. They brazened it out and again I should have known something was very wrong. I suppose I'm just not naturally suspicious.

I went down to the basement to try to find Violet, and Tyrone entered the gallery. When he saw the statue was gone, it was too much for him. He panicked and practically ran out of the museum pushing his empty cart. I suppose he felt that when the cart was found to be without a load of refreshments, he would be blamed for the theft. Not very logical, but Tyrone doesn't seem to be the thoughtful type.

215

Tyrone and one of his associates, a creep named Floyd, lay low for most of December. The other one, a weird girl named Rosa was, as usual, in a mental hospital much of the time. They thought it was safe to go to a party on New Year's Eve, and the police picked them up.

Tyrone insists the statue was gone when they arrived at the museum on the thirtieth of November. He has never denied that they had planned to steal it.

Now for the other plan. It was much simpler. Somnath just got Violet to go with him into the utility room adjacent to the gallery. Somehow he injected her with a lethal dose of heroin and dropped her down through the access hole into the Tiber.

Trebble: What the hell is the Tiber?

Fain: The Tiber's an underground stream. Boss Shepherd covered it over a hundred years ago. It's been used for criminal activity before, but not recently.

Scruggs: Somnath planned on Violet drowning. The narcotic was just in case—to keep her from walking out the other end at Buzzard Point. I suppose he thought the body might not ever be found. Lots of young women disappear and particularly ones with a history of psychiatric problems.

Fain: You bet your life—

Scruggs: Then Somnath slid the statue on wooden dowels onto a dolly. We found a few splinters on the statue's platform. He must have rolled the dolly into the utility room and down the hole. The dowels and the dolly followed. They probably will never be found. We know that Bhagat Gupta was aware of the Tiber and its being under the north end of the museum, because in my first meeting with him and Adair Blake we discussed it. He was able to assign Somnath the job of figuring out how to dump the statue into it.

After a suitable time of hand-wringing, Bhagat Gupta asked for his ten million. However, one of the Smithsonian's anthropologists, a South Asian specialist, returned to

216

Washington after being away for most of the year and he expressed doubts that there ever was a gold statue of Chandra. We sent our assistant general counsel, Miss Casey, to India to talk to people who might know the truth. Without having Bhagat Gupta to misdirect her, she was able to find out that there was no such antique gold statue known to exist and that Bhagat Gupta was one of the descendants of Chandra.

Upon Miss Casey's return to Washington, we decided that probably nobody really wanted the statue as long as it could simply be hidden, and appear to be stolen. The Tiber was the only answer we could think of. We got the city to look and there it was. Channel 5 carried a report on the ten o'clock news of its recovery from the creek. One or both of the Guptas must have seen it on the news and they seem to have skipped town.

Trebble: Thank you, Mr. Scruggs. Now I suppose we have to decide what to do about it. Don't we have an extradition treaty with India?

Longo: We do, and it covers murder, but India might stand on Gupta's extraterritoriality. It could affect the nephew's case, too, if he is considered a member of his uncle's household.

Scruggs: Somnath entered the United States with an F-1 student visa, not an A visa, so he should not have had diplomatic status.

Longo: In that case, we could get the nephew. The one problem I can see is that the case against him is largely circumstantial and the Indians might resist on that account.

Butts: I don't think you ought to count on extradition. If my information is correct, they never returned to India. In fact, INS says there is no record of them leaving the United States.

Trebble: Well!

Fain: I guess that means we ought to put out an APB on them. Might be hard to find them, though, because there are lots of Indians in this country. Of course, I don't suppose that Mr. Gupta, being a diplomat, has any ties with anybody except those here in Washington. But I doubt he and his nephew will show up here.

Trebble: Under the circumstances, I suppose we ought to consider this matter closed as far as the State Department is concerned. It will remain so unless the Indian embassy raises it again. I don't think that will happen, do you, Mr. Majors?

Majors: Not if I may brief them informally on the case against the Guptas.

Trebble: I think you may be permitted to do that. Now, unless any of you have anything else to add, I think we can wind this up. Thank you all for coming, gentlemen. And Miss Tillinghast, of course.

* * *

Henry was walking out of the State Department building with Fain, Jones, and McKeown. "I guess you're pretty proud of yourself, Scruggs?" asked Fain.

"I owe it all to Colonel McKeown's direction," lied Henry.

"Uh, huh." Fain knew oil when he saw it. "I just think you ought to know that we didn't exactly forget you were at that New Year's party."

Henry's heart paused for a moment. A long one. "You surely don't think I had a hand in the Chandra affair or Miss Strauss's murder?"

"No. Not at the moment. But there was dope at that party. I just wanted to put a word to the wise that if you were involved with anything like that, you better clean up your act."

Henry blanched. "I was only there as part of the Smithsonian's investigation. Nothing more."

"I bet. If it was nothing more than *poon-tang* you better get it somewhere else. The hospital did a thorough workup on you and unless they messed up the lab work, all you had was asthma and about the amount of marijuana you would expect from

218

being in a room full of pot-heads. We decided to give you the benefit of the doubt. Once."

"Yes, sir." Henry couldn't think of anything else to say.

* * *

The Chandra affair was very much in the news but Henry had little more to do with it. An obscure group of American Hindus came to see him and asked for the rather battered Chandra statue. They called it the Chandra avatar of Vishnu, so they evidently had their mythology straight. Henry explained that it was somewhat the worse for wear from its tumble in the Tiber. They said they didn't care, that they would fix it up and give it the honor it deserved, in their temple in Bethesda. Henry referred them to the police who were holding the statue for evidence in case the Guptas were ever brought to trial.

Somnath was actually apprehended in Chicago a few weeks later. He had somehow gotten hold of a bogus Social Security card and had applied for a job in a bank, to what purpose it was never discovered. Henry privately suspected it was embezzlement that he had in mind. The bank applied to have Somnath bonded and the existence of an outstanding arrest warrant was discovered.

For some time, Somnath denied his identity, but when he realized he, alone, was going to be blamed for everything he began talking and could not be stopped, even by the public defender. He admitted everything, more or less. He claimed he had been under the influence of his uncle Bhagat, who, he said, had kept him dependent upon drugs and in a state of diminished capacity.

* * *

The following extract is taken from Somnath's confession and was read into the record of the trial:

Q: Did you in fact murder Miss Violet Strauss?
A: I don't think so, sir.
Q: What do you mean, you don't think so?
A: I just pushed her into the hole.
Q: You mean into the Tiber? The underground river?

219

A: I don't actually know. It was just the hole in the floor of the museum where my uncle instructed me to put her.

Q: Didn't you hear the water when you opened the trap-door?

A: It might have been a well.

Q: With rushing water?

A: Perhaps. I don't know very much about wells. You see, in India it is the common people, village people, who have to do with wells and things like that.

Q: Miss Strauss had taken an overdose of heroin. Did you give it to her?

A: Oh, yes! I gave it to her. She asked me to.

Q: You injected her with heroin? Is that what you mean?

A: Oh, yes! We took it together. We shot up, I think you call it.

Q: That's what we call it. And didn't you know it would kill her?

A: Oh, no! I knew she would drown first.

Q: Then you intended to drown her?

A: Certainly not! It was my uncle's intention. I would never murder anybody.

Q: But if she had not drowned, she would certainly have died from the overdose. Do you still maintain you didn't intend to kill her?

A: No, sir, she was not murdered. She committed suicide.

Q: How do you get that? She didn't take the dope herself or jump into the Tiber!

A: You do not understand, sir. On the day before, I believe it was, Miss Violet announced that she intended to kill herself. You may ask Mr. Scruggs. He was there at the time. He will tell you that I speak the truth. So we all were simply helping her to do what she wished. I gave her some extra heroin to keep her from suffering. It is no different from suttee in India. There, also, a friend might give a grieving widow a little something to deaden the pain when she burns on her husband's pyre.

Q: But she didn't ask to be thrown into the river, did she?

A: Not at all. That was odd, you know. She didn't seem to

220

want to go but then it is common in suttee for the woman to change her mind when she is on the threshold of nirvana. It is the responsibility of her friends in such cases to help her along the way. Otherwise, it would bring shame upon her and her family.

[The interrogator went off the record for 5 minutes.]

Q: Now, Mr. Somnath, you have earlier stated that you committed the acts for which you are charged because you were under the influence of your uncle, Mr. Bhagat Gupta.

A: Doctor.

Q: Huh?

A: My uncle is a doctor. Not the medical kind, of course, but he has a doctorate in art history from London University. You may also call him Minister-Counselor. That was his diplomatic title, though that may now be in question, I suppose.

Q: Well, whatever. Why were you under his influence?

A: He was my uncle! Respect was required! I might also say that it came naturally! And my uncle provided me with something.

Q: Heroin?

A: Yes.

Q: Were you the one who got Miss Strauss hooked on heroin?

A: Oh, no! That was my uncle. He had plenty. He got it through diplomatic channels.

Q: Do you mean the diplomatic pouch?

A: I don't know, sir. I suppose so.

Q: How have you been getting heroin since you and your uncle split up?

A: What do you mean by "split up"?

Q: Separated.

A: Oh! Well, you seem to be able to buy it almost anywhere in this country. Provided you have the money. It can be very expensive in the United States.

Q: How did you get the money?

221

A: I stole things.
Q: Can you give me a list of places you stole things?
A: No, I don't think so. There were too many.
Q: Where is your uncle now?
A: I do not know. We traveled separately and it was the plan that we should meet in Chicago. But he has not arrived. Do you suppose something has happened to him?

As Henry read news accounts of the trial, he doubted that Bhagat had introduced Violet to heroin. It seemed unlikely that Violet would have been innocent of anything that could be swallowed, smoked, or injected. In any case, it seemed plausible enough that Somnath could have gotten Violet to accept a lethal injection.

The police were content to have found Somnath and after that, they did not try very hard to locate Bhagat since it appeared that the problem of diplomatic immunity might preclude prosecution and might even compromise the case against Somnath were they to be brought to trial together.

Henry got back to his work, to the little everyday duties that gave him so much satisfaction. It was good to be back to being an ordinary bureaucrat and savor the simple pleasures of morning and afternoon tea and leisurely lunches with friends. Henry gave the teapot a shake to hurry up the steeping process.

The distinguished-looking gentleman in the Nehru jacket looked down at Henry and made a small noise to attract his attention. Henry looked up and in a moment scrambled to his feet. "Yes, sir! What can I do for you?" If there was anything Henry didn't need at the moment it was another Indian gentleman. He had had his fill. Nevertheless, a certain politeness was ingrained in him. It was his upbringing, and Henry let it flow.

"Mr. Scruggs? I have come all the way from India to see you." It was obvious from his manner that this was his first time in America, so Henry gave him his broad and welcoming smile. The one that made Violet ask about his teeth.

"Please, sit down." Unsaid was "You have come a long way and must be tired."

222

"Thank you. My name is Kaul. I come from Trivandrum."

"Yes indeed, Miss Casey told me she met you. You were very helpful. We very much appreciate it."

"It was nothing." Dr. Kaul did something with his hands that showed how nothing it was. "Your young lady, sir. She asked me about a golden figure. A statue of Chandra. Of course I didn't believe there could possibly be one. Not at the time. But I got to thinking about it and quite naturally I investigated it.

"Can you imagine my surprise! I spoke to a number of the old families. In India, our families are everything, you know. Or used to be at any rate. And still are to some extent. Well, as I was saying, I spoke to some of the families who were involved with Chandra a hundred years ago.

"A hundred years in India—that is nothing, absolutely nothing at all." He did the thing again with his hands. "Well the present-day members—they have all heard the old stories—and they told me that there was, indeed, a golden Chandra. Not what you would have imagined, but a Swiss lady, whose name I have not yet been able to discover, she came to India and stayed quite some time in Trivandrum. She was by training a sculptress. Not a great one, of course, not well known at all, in fact. But there were enough followers—and some rather well off; Chandra appealed most strongly to the intellectual class—that they gathered quite a lot of gold together and from a clay image made by the Swiss lady, a gold Chandra was cast. Nothing like the Vishnu figure your Miss Casey described, but a more contemporary sculpture. Of good size and quite valuable.

"It was reported to me that Chandra was very much disturbed when the statue was presented to him on his seventieth birthday. Just before the turn of the century, that would have been. Well, he was quite appalled in fact and ordered his followers to take it from his sight.

"It was never discussed again, at least not in his lifetime and so naturally none of the official accounts from that time mentioned it. However, the statue remained and what is most surprising, it remains unto this day.

"I have spoken to the present owners of the statue and they were quite pleased to learn of your exhibition at the great Smithsonian Institution. You know, the Smithsonian Institution is very well known in India and held in the greatest of regard. But forgive me, I am straying from my subject—an old man's failing, I fear.

"What it comes down to—boils down to, I believe you say—is that the owners of the statue would be pleased to lend it to you if you could extend your exhibition long enough for it to be shipped, and could arrange the necessary insurance, payable in U.S. dollars, of course—"

 **Epilogue**

In the early summer of the next year, Henry Scruggs was driving south on Route 411. He was alone and had been driving for hours. Atlanta was still miles away. He could tell he was going to fall asleep and if he didn't want to sleep forever he had better find a motel and put up for the night. It was the tourist season and the major chains and the nicer looking motels all had out their NO VACANCY signs. But he spied a vacancy a little way outside of Chatsworth. The motel didn't look like much but it looked better than trying to stay awake all the way to Marietta.

Henry pulled in. Close up, the motel looked clean enough. At least it didn't call itself TOURIST CAMP or CABINS, so there was probably indoor plumbing and sheets changed at least once a week if not between occupants.

The man at the desk was a bearded Indian with a turban. The turban was pinned with a single large ruby. He looked quite dashing, as sikhs often do. He looked up from the book he was reading, a distinctive blue copy of *Foreign Affairs Quarterly,* as soon as Henry entered the motel office. He had piercing eyes that he fixed unblinking upon Henry.

Henry would not have known Bhagat, not just to look at him. It was when he spoke that his impeccable University of London

225

accent gave him away. It shaved off his beard and moustache, and unwound his turban.

"Don't I know you?" Henry couldn't help saying.

"I do not believe so, sir. Perhaps you have stayed in my motel before?" He spoke now with a broader Anglo-Indian accent, dropping down several class levels.

"I must be mistaken." Henry forced his face to become blank. He paid for a night's lodging up front, as the small neatly lettered sign requested, and took the key to his room.

Inside, the room was nice enough. Better, in fact, than the outside of the motel might lead you to expect. Bhagat must have some sort of a thing going, God knows what.

Henry went into the bathroom and locked the door. He turned on the water in the basin and eased open the bathroom window. With difficulty, he wiggled out. He couldn't have done it a year ago, but Phoebe had made him buy a bicycle and use it to whittle away his middle.

He bent low to keep below the light from the other motel windows and moved quietly around the far end of the row of cabins. Then he worked his way from car to car toward the Corvair, finally reaching it and opening the passenger side door as silently as possible. Henry thanked his lucky stars that he had held on to the Corvair. It was getting elderly and things were beginning to go wrong. One of them, thank God, was the switch for the interior dome light.

Henry slid behind the wheel and put in his ignition key. He opened the driver-side door and used his left foot to give the car a shove. There was enough of a slope so that the car moved off slowly, with the slightest of scraping noises from one of the brake drums. He was halfway down the drive before he felt it was safe to start the engine and onto the highway before he turned on his lights.

There was no danger now of dozing off at the wheel. It was doubtful that Henry would go to sleep for a week. He thought about the Guptas. And Blake. Was Adair Blake running a motel somewhere in India on the high road to Poona?

His tires drummed on the tar joints between the sections of old concrete. They said to Henry:

226

They sikh him here
They sikh him there
They sikh him everywhere
Be he redeemed
Or has he sinned again
That dimmed elusive Indian

Sink me, thought Henry, as he sped along, an eye on his mirror. He didn't slow down for Marietta but continued on to Atlanta. If he could find an open gas station, he might keep on going until Jacksonville or perhaps Miami.